MW00997468

PRAISE
for
MARTIN
OLSON'S
GODAWFUL
WRITING

"The number of great books being produced is painfully small, but this is indeed one of them. When your dear ol' gran clutches her pearls and cries, 'Jaysus, the divil's in that book,' find a hallowed corner to wedge yourself in, and prepare yourself for the horror and goodness of this unholy treasure." —Michelle Franklin, author, *I Hate Everyone*

•

"A tour de force of Darkness. Olson's savage wit and precise command of the language provide the firepower for a literary feat unequaled since Mark Twain passed. Cherish *Encyclopaedia of Hell II*, the Good Book of the new millennium." —Barry Crimmins, political satirist, *Never Shake Hands with a War Criminal*

•

"Olson's poetic soul combined with his razor-sharp wit make for a mesmerizing read." —Claire Elizabeth Terry, author, *Thirty Minutes*

•

"Combine S.J. Perelman with Bierce's *Devil's Dictionary* and H.G. Wells' *War of the Worlds*, add a blood-curdling scream and the result is *Encyclopaedia of Hell*, a heady mixture of erudite wit, lyrical blasphemy and madcap gore." —Robert Sheckley, author, *Dimension of Miracles*

•

"A brilliant and disturbing look at human existence through the eyes of Satan. In my opinion, the best religious fiction since the Bible, even funnier than The Book of Mormon and Scientology." —Ron Miller, author, *Silk and Steel*

•

"I rarely laugh out loud while reading, but *Encyclopaedia of Hell* is the exception. On every page, that old gnostic *Deus Absconditus* cackles somewhere in his cosmic madhouse." —Marc Ian Barasch, author, *The Healing Path*

•

"This prodigious work, with supernal design and illustrations, is over-the-top Victorian, with touches of the divine Dante Alighieri, if the man had been as mad as our madcap Marty Olson." —Rudy Rucker, author, *The Ware Tetralogy*, and inventor of cyberpunk

•

"In *The Conquest of Heaven*, Olson's wicked and poetic wit is downright otherworldly. In this mythic satire, his twist on 'what fools these mortals be' is evocative and hilarious." —Diane Drake, screenwriter, *Only You* and *What Women Want*

•

"The strangest and funniest fantasy series ever, in which Demons conquer Heaven and Earth and devour their inhabitants. Before he publishes Book 3, let's hope Olson's insane asylum keeps him away from anything sharp, except his monstrous wit." —Ronald Shusett, screenwriter, *Alien, Total Recall, Minority Report*

THE CONQUEST OF HEAVEN:
A DEMONIC HISTORY OF THE FUTURE
CONCERNING THE CELESTIAL REALM
AND THE ANGELIC RACE WHICH INFESTS IT

© 2021 by Martin Olson

All rights reserved.

www.facebook.com/encyclopaediaofhell/

ISBN: 9781627311113

Feral House

1240 W. Sims Way, Suite 124

Port Townsend, WA 98368

www.FeralHouse.com

Design by Sean Tejaratchi

10 9 8 7 6 5 4 3 2 1

THE CONQUEST
OF HEAVEN
ENCYCLOPÆDIA OF HELL II

— ◆ —

A Demonic History of the Future
Concerning the Celestial Plane
and the
Angelic Race Which Infests It

— ◆ —

TRANSLATED
from the
DEMONIC *and* ANGELIC
by
MARTIN OLSON

— ◆ —

Illustrated by
Tony Millionaire
and
Mahendra Singh

Dedicated To:

Tom
The best brother any man can have.

Kay
The real angel in my life.

Jessica Parfrey
For taking the torch and leading the way.

———◆●◆———

Chief Story Editor:
Brian Lubocki

Book Design / Writing Consultant:
Sean Tejaratchi

———◆●◆———

Additional Illustration:
Albert Che • Tomas Hijo • Celeste Moreno
Antoine Gilbaud • Kaz • Joe Alaskey
Thanks to Oakland, CA band Hallucinator
for *Abyss* by Albert Che

———◆●◆———

Key Writing Advice from the following Heavenly Influences:
Andrew Lazar • Annette Van Duren
Casey Olson • Amit Itelman • Ken Daly • Mary Jo Pritchard
Kevin Rooney • Barry Crimmins • Michelle Franklin
Bill Kopp • Dan Povenmire • Swampy Marsh
Rob Bottin • Robert Sheckley

———◆●◆———

Special Thanks for Satan's Backstory:
Olivia Olson

———◆●◆———

In memory of
my friend and mentor,
Adam Parfrey

THE SIGIL OF LORD SATAN,
THE EVIL GLYPH WHICH STABS THE MIND
WITH SATAN'S POISON PEN

Lord Satan dreams the Hell Cosmos.

THE CONQUEST OF HEAVEN

ENCYCLOPÆDIA OF HELL II

BEHOLD!

A DELUXE COMMEMORATIVE EDITION

INCLUDING ARCANE HISTORICAL DOCUMENTS CULLED FROM SECRET DOSSIERS OF IMPERIAL HELL AND WRETCHED HEAVEN. CURATED FROM ANCIENT MIND-SENSITIVE SCROLLS IN HELL UNIVERSITY'S MUSEUM OF HATE

666TH PRINTING

EDITOR-IN-CHIEF
ARCH-DEMON MORTIMER PÖNCÉ

WITH ANNOTATIONS BY
DEMON EDITORS
AT
MIND CONTROL PRESS

May the personified Creator Reawaken By turning Its Power Switches on and off, Resetting any Random Programming Glitches in thy Personal Perceptual Timeline Due to the Uncanny and Inexplicable Algorithm of our Lord's Sacred Insanity

XTSSJY TK JANQ JATHFYNTS

Gjmtqi ymnx anqj atqzrj, ymnx Ittw yt Ijuwfanyd.
Xmfwujs dtzw Hqfbx fsi Yjjym ts nyx ufljx,
Fgxtwg Nyx Mnxytwnjx Bnym Gjrzxnsl Lwfanyd
Fx bj xtnq ymj xtzqx tk tzw Janqjxy Xfljx.

Xmziijw fsi xbjfw fx dtz xqtl ymwtzlm ymjxj Ajwxjx,
Ijrjfsnsl Ijrtspnsi bnym Wmdrjx tk Wjazqxnts,
Ktw stymnsl nsxunwjx ymj gqfhpjxy tk hzwxjx
Qnpj ymj knqym mjwjns ymtz rfd stb nsizqlj ns.

Bwjyhm! Wjanqj ymjxj wfsitr fhyx tk zspnsisjxx,
Ujwhmfshj hmtpnsl ymj hmtfy tk f Mjfajsqd Uwnshj,
Tw ymj xtwjx tk Mjqq'x Bmtwjx hfzxnsl Gqnsisjxx,
Ymjnw uzijsifx jskqfrji fx tzw Xytwd gjlnsx.

Xny gfhp ymjs fsi xsjjw fy Uzwj Mjfajs'x Htwwzuynts,
Jsyjwyfnsji gd tzw Mnxytwd'x Anqj Ijhtsxywzhynts.

THE STORY OF
MEATSPACE
JOE

The mystics were mistaken.

The point wasn't that the universe was made of mind stuff. The point was that it was shaped, somewhat sloppily, like a tube. The first inkling of sentience was at one end, and the end was at the other. In between were densities that broke through to each other like flats in a creaking Hollywood set.

When you come right down to it, it was a mess that barely held together. Whatever poor schlub thought up Creation apparently didn't really think it all the way through. It was all a bit on the impulsive side, if you look at the crazy fireworks of the so-called Big Bang.

After eons of self-regurgitations, all intelligent life-forms evolved from dense life-forms into evanescent light-forms. At the end of their evolution, they became balls of light, settling into a default astral body, appearing roughly eighteen years of age, at the height of physical health. Light-beings shared a meta-temporal view of things with their creator, in that the entire span of evolution seemed to take place in an instant, like time-lapse photography.

Reincarnation was a bizarre reality due to the immortality of the electron elementals comprising the life-field. An entity's incarnations were all completely different, and lacked a meta-memory circuitry to connect them. (Occasionally, life-forms did remember a past or future life, but it could be a drawback, rather than a boon; for who wants to remember being someone else?)

Ultimate Evolution was rather satisfying. Game over. Sit back, have a cocktail and relax. On a practical level, it meant that your evolved light-body now existed in many parallel universes simultaneously. When you looked at an object, like a pencil, for example, you saw its past, present and future—a seed becoming a tree, graphite crystal growing in rock, the tree cut, the graphite mined, the pencil manufactured and utilized, and finally, all of it decomposing into molecular rubble. So too was your view of every object, including yourself.

Ultimate Evolution also meant that the layers of gore and blood were stripped away and slowly replaced by sinews of light. So too were layers of scriptures and myths stripped from the mind, until the truth was clear, that everything and everyone was the same Being. And thus, no one was in charge, and therefore, everyone was in charge.

Joe was a light-being who had evolved after eons from mankind's meatspace. After a while, however, the constant information overload attached to each object became overwhelming and annoying to Joe. He yearned for a simpler time in his physical body, when he perceived things one at a time and enjoyed seeing the surface of things, rather than multidimensional views of everything. To Joe, unlike his other evolved brothers, the secrets of the universe didn't live up to all the eons of hype. He was bored at knowing everything and preferred the simpler, heavier dimension of Earth, where every instant wasn't drenched with profound meaning, where simplicity and playful ignorance were the comfort blankets of daily life.

Joe could only exist in the material world if the vibration of his light-body matched the vibration of Earth, which it didn't anymore. The only way he could return to a simpler time would be to somehow de-evolve back to a less sophisticated, more primitive state of vibration, making his light-body denser. If his body was in effect "heavier," it would tend to sink down through dimensions until it reached the parallel Earth matching his present level of vibration.

Now Joe had a mission. He began searching his cosmic environs for "things" he could absorb from outside himself that would make his light-body denser, heavier.

But first he wanted to make sure that this new obsession of his wasn't a terrible idea. He went online and made an appointment with a psychologist with a good Yelp rating named Dr. Debbie Pöncé. Dr. Pöncé was an expert in helping those who were dissatisfied with their lives. She said boredom with perfection was a common problem of balls of light. After hearing of Joe's mission, Dr. Pöncé explained that his level on the evolutionary chart was a function of the rate at which his light-body vibrated. She said that absorbing material and adding weight made sense, but that there were more direct ways to lower his vibratory rate. Lowering your intellect required serious meditation exercises designed to help you de-evolve, and depended on practicing to think more materialistic thoughts. Joe's glowing light-body was a representation of his high vibratory rate. So he knew that his thoughts would have to dumb down a lot by using intensive stupidity exercises.

While following Dr. Pöncé's dumbing-down procedure, Joe happened upon a gym on the outskirts of Nirvana frequented by disgruntled light-beings who, like Joe, were bored with the perfection of ultimate evolution. In the gym, these outsiders practiced group meditation exercises to become less intelligent. Similar to the methods suggested by Dr. Pöncé, they'd discovered that they could gain density by practicing thinking narrow, linear, pipe-line thoughts. They'd found that, by weaning themselves from metaphor and analogy entirely, the thought-streams in their heads would congeal into a "mental body," the reverse beginnings of a physical brain. Even better, they maintained, continued exercise of thinking only small, narrow thoughts also created a wall of thought-muscle in the manifesting brain. These muscles separated the higher evolutionary thoughts on the right side from the lower ones on the left side. By actively developing the illusion that you were separate from the oneness of the universe, could light-beings lower their vibrations, form a physical brain, and begin to experience things slowly and luxuriously, one thing after the other, as in the material world.

Joe joined the club and started exercising with his outsider friends. But while performing these Stupidity Exercises, he asked on the down-low if the gym happened to sell any dumbing-down protein to beef up his thought sinews faster while he worked out.

It turned out that one of the trainers dealt in the shadier black market stuff Joe was looking for. He gave Joe a pack of so-called "stereo-electrons," sort of like steroids. They were particles which interlocked with cells in the nervous system of the developing brain matter, lowered the vibratory rate of the brain and formed a wall of meat between the higher and lower parts of Joe's thought matrix. Just don't use too much of it.

But Joe wanted to de-evolve faster, figured he could handle it and started taking double doses of the mixture. Soon he became addicted to the stuff, as his brain sinews developed and thickened at an astonishing speed.

In addition to taking Stupidity Steroids, Joe was doing his Stupidity Meditation exercises three times a day, concentrating on separatist concepts and divisive and racist ideologies, meditating on them until he actually believed them.

It worked. Soon the wall in his mind solidified and he found that he was literally of two minds. Thrilled, he looked forward to savoring things one after the other. He could hardly wait to attain the human perception and see only the surface of things!

But soon, he noticed something horrible happening in his newly reconfigured thoughts. Not only had his thought-streams become swollen, contorted and disfigured, but the two halves of mind were now at odds with each other. The left brain, feeling a separation from the universe, could not stand interacting with the right brain, which felt oneness with the universe.

Trying to cool out his thoughts, Joe went downtown to see a thought movie. It was Christmas and, when he was human, this had been his favorite holiday. While floating in line at the theater, awash with the Christmas lights glistening and blinking in the streets and on the tree in the theater lobby, he could hear his brain lobes arguing. It reached a peak, and a fight began inside himself. Joe lost control and began thrashing wildly around on the floor. And with his newly beefed-up thought sinews, he was abnormally powerful. Nobody could stop what was about to happen as he had a mental breakdown. Joe knocked over the Christmas tree and trashed the snack bar. The light-being police showed up, tasered him and dragged him away.

Joe in effect went mad and was committed to an insane asylum. There he discovered that Dr. Poncé, whom he had thought was his ally, was really his enemy. As the head of a psychiatry board, she committed Joe to the most dangerous insane asylum in the cosmos. Even worse for Joe, the conflict in his mind had slowed down his de-evolution. To his shame, he was still occasionally thinking intelligent thoughts.

In the cosmic insane asylum, Joe soon found that he was the most violent mental patient there. Even worse, Dr. Odin, the warden of the asylum, wasn't really interested in curing him. Treating Joe would be a lot of trouble. Extra therapy meant extra man-power, which Dr. Odin did not have. Not to mention the long hours filing tedious thought-reports on Joe's progress. So Dr. Odin pow-wowed secretly with two light-body male nurses, a conversation witnessed by Dr. Odin's secretary Ramona. The nurses agreed to strap Joe to an illegal Unexistinator, a particle beam attached to a random number generator, and scramble Joe's particles. This would cause his particles to lose their spin, and Joe would dissipate into nothingness. In Dr. Odin's mind, Joe was a trouble-maker, and killing him would be more effective than years of treatment, never mind the reams of complex paper work.

However, Ramona felt bad about killing Joe, and sneaked to his cell to warn him.

Faced with the threat of unexistence, Joe rose to the occasion. He meditated vigorously until he was able to force the two warring sides of his mind to work together. Now he was able to create a clever plan and, with the help of Ramona, managed to escape from Odin's asylum.

Straight from prison, Joe stormed to Dr. Pöncé's office and confronted her about committing him to such a dangerous asylum. She revealed truthfully that she had had a secret agenda in doing so. Committing Joe would assist him in his de-evolution. Only the threat of personal extinction could motivate Joe to strengthened his two minds so that they could work together to significantly lower the vibrations of his astral body.

And, in fact, Dr. Pöncé thought that Joe might now be ready. She put her pencil in front of Joe's face and asked him what he saw...

Joe stared at the pencil... and for the first time, he didn't see the past, present and future of the thought-form pencil, he just saw its surface! Dr. Pöncé was right. The two parts of his mind had strengthen to follow his will, having learned how to work together to avoid death. Now Joe could savor things one after the other. Now he could finally experience the wonder of shallow, linear thoughts.

Tears streamed from Joe's eyes. What a joy to have a simple, mundane mind again! However, Dr. Pöncé clucked, there was the little matter of the negative side effects of growing denser, de-evolving and developing a physical brain. Namely, starting now, Joe might experience his descent through densities a bit too rapidly. As he ripped through thicker and thicker onion skins of parallel universes, he might, without realizing it, crash into the basest, bargain-basement dimension of the material universe.

Hmm. Joe wasn't exactly thrilled. He didn't want the change to happen quite that quickly. He had assumed that his de-evolution would be a gradual process, gently drifting into lower and lower levels until he stabilized back in the solid physical world. After all, it took him eons to evolve going the other direction, from a human to a light-being.

He wanted to stay where he was for a bit, so he could go to that new ephemeral Thai restaurant on the corner, perhaps have a thought-smoke and just cool out.

But it was too late. Dr. Pöncé gave Joe a touching farewell as Joe's light-body, having grown heavier each minute, finally fissured, shattered and dematerialized, sinking through the cracks in dimensions into the next-heavier density.

Joe cringed as he sniffed an unpleasant side effect of the transition, the smell of burning sneakers. The odor signaled his materialization into a density called The Transparent World, where he had, at least for now, reached equilibrium. This was the world of ghosts, a virtual density of murky emotions and shadowy creatures which could interpenetrate each other, a heavier astral vibration halfway between the mental and material worlds.

While waiting to transition past the Transparent World, he experienced a few universal, mundane activities, having a toothache and going to a ghost dentist, trying to find a decent ghost latte, or desiring a sexy ghost lover in the realm of shadows.

But as Dr. Pöncé had warned him, Joe's light-body was now on a rapid descent. Like a child trying to steer a toboggan down a hill, it was a process out of his control and one that could not be reversed. Joe found that his habitual linear thinking was making his particles heavier and heavier. Something had to give and it finally did. Joe dematerialized from the ghost density and partially materialized in Earth's normal physical world, at night, on Halloween. Not yet completely physical, he was amused as he realized that he appeared to human trick-or-treaters as a ghost.

Joe was frustrated. After working out so long and hard, he yearned to have the low IQ of a human. With renewed vigor, he resumed his dumbing-down exercises. One day, in the middle of his workout, Joe's dense particles finally and dramatically congealed into a bona fide physical body.

Joe had at last become one with meat.

Now fully entrained in the physical world, he found himself at a Halloween party in a city with machines, smog, rain, pain, lovers, apartments and parking tickets. No more flying around, now he was locked to the Earth, as if there were magnets on the soles of his feet. It was satisfying to be back here again, this time with the knowledge that the whole universe was just an immersive game and, as long as you were careful, that there was nothing per se to be afraid of.

His brain hungry for stupidity, more and more delicious, mundane, judgmental, racist, sexist, xenophobic, divisive thoughts filled his head. Even his ridiculous physical body was a novel pleasure with its bizarre thirsts, hungers and drives. It was not long before Joe found a lover, and found joy, peace and satisfaction in not examining his lover too closely. He had discovered the real secret of the universe, that real peace was bobbing on the surface of things, and not dipping into the quagmire of unnecessary thinking. At last, he had found his home and was determined to maintain his stupidity for as long as his physical body could sustain itself. He was determined never to evolve ever again.

But both he and Dr. Pöncé had made a deadly miscalculation.

The negative side effect of de-evolving didn't stop at the material level. Because of the power of his unorthodox, reverse-evolutionary momentum, and the drugs he was taking, he couldn't stop his thoughts from becoming narrower and more linear, making his body particles denser and heavier. The air around him became thicker, darker. He felt a pain in his chest. What was happening to him? The electrons of his physical body began vibrating at a lower level, making his existence on Earth incompatible! He screamed as he slowly dematerialized from the human world and slipped down the rungs of evolution into an even denser dimension, hardening into something akin to liquid plastic or thick molasses, which then solidified into something akin to transparent, wet cement. His essence, in essence, was trapped like a bug in amber—as his vibrations continued lowering.

Finally, Joe sank deeper still, toward the very densest dimension at the lowest end of the evolutionary spectrum. As he traveled downwards, he felt himself hardening in a tight black world so incredibly compact, even light could not penetrate it, so dense it seemed devoid of the possibility of change. Herein was an end to motion itself, and therefore an end to time.

Cold, frozen, timeless blackness.

And then, as the blackness, which was nothingness itself, wrapped around him like a crypt, he realized that his desire to become human again only made him a victim of his own desires. Now at The Bottom End of Creation, the Dead End of the Universe, he was trapped in an infinitely dense clot of pure, compacted nothingness from which there was no possible escape. This, in fact, was Meatspace Joe's final thought in the last, slowly flickering blip of his consciousness... as the last thought particle in his mind slowed, stopped and blinked out.

There was nothing.

Nothing.

Then, something rather unexpected happened.

The bottom suddenly fell out beneath him.

Unable to withstand its own incredible density, the bottom burst and Joe fell through it, still locked in the block of black nothingness. And as he tumbled chaotically, the thick black shell around him fissured, cracked and crumbled.

Meatspace Joe hatched from his egg of nothingness as he fell.

And from the egg, he emerged like the self-born Phoenix, a glowing light-being, roughly age eighteen, exactly as he had started. Ironically, the densest blackest dead end was in fact a secret short cut to the other end of creation.

The mystics were mistaken.

The point wasn't that the universe was made of mind stuff. The point was that it was a tube, connecting the highest and lowest densities that broke through to each other like flats in a creaking Hollywood set.

Once again in his light-body, back where he started at the highest plateau of the evolutionary scale, Joe stabilized and looked around. He certainly recognized the place, but he couldn't quite remember what just happened. And a fortunate thing it is to forget, or despair would surely follow. And who needs despair if you're a light-being?

This simple but awesome faculty of forgetfulness, usually thought of as a liability, was a created being's friend, a secret, self-protective function that kicked in once a being had explored the path of Reverse Evolution, and had thereby experienced all of the nooks and crannies of existence.

Forgetfulness was the only advantage that created beings had over their sad-sack creator. The creator could not forget the bad parts. But his creations had the ability to forget everything and start over with a clean slate. They could forget that boredom and death will eventually return. Having forgotten, they could experience things fresh, like a child, the way life was meant to be lived, with joy, like a strange and constantly surprising dream, and where the ending will always be a mystery.

TABLE
OF
CONTENTS

<figure>❖</figure>

<figure>❖</figure>

SPLENETIC THE FIRST
Phase One of the Invasion
89

SPLENETIC THE SECOND
The Invasion Pamphlet
89

◆

SPLENETIC THE THIRD
Events Concerning the Invasion of Heaven by Hell, Leading to the Detonation of the Time-Twister Bomb
97

—◆—

THE FINAL SPLENETIC
A Bonus Addendum to the Evil Reader

—◆—

Afterword, by Mortimer Pöncé

HORACE BIRDFIRE
ANGEL

Chief of Psychology, Hospice of Heaven, Celestia

To Whom It May Concern:

THIS IS, SHALL WE SAY, a feeler of sorts addressed to thee, Beloved Beings of Light on other planets and in other dimensions, to see if someone could please come to our aid and, if any of you have time, alert others to this urgent message? I mean no disrespect in asking you to act immediately and, if it works for you, to forward this message to every male, female and non-binary being on thine email list, if permissible within the protocols of thy browser attachments.

I, Horace Catallus Birdfire, the first and last angel inhabiting the sweet climes of Heaven, seek assistance. Some would crudely say that our beloved realm's greatness has of late been odiously defiled, its sweetness sucked away through the cracks between dimensions, like an innocent peneplain of hyacinths engulfed in a sulphurous chasm of hellfire. But hear not the unhappy descriptors of those uncouth few, for while 'tis true a sickness has overcome the city, leave us discuss that untoward calamity at a later time. Harken now to this cry for help on this, Heaven's unthinkable day of disaster. Here are the facts, dear friends:

At dawn, my angelic assistant Brother Bebo alerted me to an unexpected event, for the silhouette of a vast legion of Demon Warriors appeared on the horizon, marching in formation toward our glorious fortress. While Readers of a negative disposition might see this as bad news, open thine eyes to other wondrous possibilities borne by our loving universe. Perhaps the demons are curious about our magnificent realm, and have organized a native tour of our realm.☺ Or have brought gifts, their eyes wet with love and brotherhood! At the very least, we may think of this happenstance as bringing welcome *novelty* to our otherwise perfect lives! Thus, let us do our best to interpret this apparent invasion with cheery positivity. ☺

Since we are dealing in fact, I acknowledge that as I write I hear their distant tom-toms beating in time to the march of cloven hooves, pounding an inexorable rhythm, the disharmonious Hammers of Hell. But since our beloved Personified Creator *assured us* that our protection would *always* be his highest priority, we are skeptical that the demons will actually *kill* us. I mean, normally, our Personified Creator, with a snap of his, her or its fingers, depending on what gender it preferred on that particular day, would simply bewitch the demon interlopers, and thereby make attack impossible, making the invasion, in truth, an absurd amusement to our minds.

However, I should mention, there's been a *slight glitch* in our heavenly lifestyle over the past few eons, for it's a bit of an unfortunate coincidence that this little invasion happens to occur now, when our Magnificent Creator has, well, shall we say, been under the weather?

Since we of course have total faith in our Creator, it is comforting to imagine that this incident will conclude like the satisfying taste of a bowl of sweet mulberries and milk for breakfast in the freshness of a Spring morning. But perhaps I should emphasize a bit more, without upsetting my sweet Reader, that due to the demons' annoying marching and drumming, that this does appear to be *an actual invasion in progress.*

Still, I implore ye not to fret, O Light Bearers to whom this missive is addressed, for my loyal assistant Bebo and I have a plan: we intend to simulate a show of force by propping up weapons in the turrets over the city gates and aiming them below, for we no longer have angelic forces defending our city, for unfortunate reasons to be explained at a later date.

Thus, to get to the point, on the chance something *does* go awry, perhaps it wouldn't hurt if we had a little help? ☺ Thus, my little request, Beneficent Beings across the Infinite Bejeweled Tapestry of Intelligent Infinity, to cc your brethren the following message:

O YE AGENTS OF GOODNESS,
I HUMBLY REQUEST THINE ASSISTANCE,
TO CEASE THIS INVASION OF HEAVEN BY HELL,
IF IT'S NOT TOO MUCH TROUBLE.

So! If you have the time, dear reader, as I mentioned earlier, perhaps you could forward this *Invasion Manual* to every male, female and non-binary on thine own mailing list, for that would be *enormously appreciated*, when convenient, and, if at all possible within the context of your busy schedule, perhaps you yourself could actually *traverse Time* and physically pop in on our Heavenly coordinates, ASAP, meaning, perhaps, *right now?*

In that way, Heaven might perhaps be *saved* from Death and Ruin. No pressure, of course, O Light-beings, but I do hope to partake of thy dear visages soon! ☺

They are breaking down the Gates! I must close, and somehow deal with what indeed appears to be, again, an actual invasion of Heaven. ☹

Signed with a hope for a positive outcome, but in haste, due to the demons now breaking down the Gates,

DR. HORACE CATALLUS BIRDFIRE

Chief Physician, Psychology Division
Hospice of Heaven
Dictated Not Read onto Mind-Sensitive Scrolls

PRAYER to the READER:
(CARVED in GOLDEN GLYPHS on the GATES OF HEAVEN)

May the Personified Creator Reawaken
By Turning Its Power Switch On and Off,
Resetting any Random Programming Glitches
In Thy Personal, Perceptual Timeline
Due to the Uncanny and Inexplicable
Logarithms of our Lord's
Sacred Insanity

.

Namaste.

A FORMAL CURSE
AND MALEDICTION
UPON THIS VOLUME

By Arch-Demon Mortimer Pöncé

First, since our Evil Race travels through time in order to crush our enemies, and since time-travel creates self-canceling paradox, accurate dating of the Historical Fits of Hell can be well-nigh impossible. Thus, Truth and Falsity may prance through these pages like drunken dunces twirling each other at a Barn Dance.

Secondly, since the hateful conclusion of Lord Satan's journey is ever a pit of literary controversy, it is perhaps more tasteful that we invoke his story with more stealth than historical bravado.

Thus, this commemorative edition of The Conquest of Heaven, *compiled eons after Hell's successful invasion of the Celestial City, contains heretofore unpublished documents carefully curated to recreate an approximate simulation of the historical timeline before and after Hell's Hateful Invasion.*

Despite the ferocity and grotesqueness of the previous volume, *Encyclopaedia of Hell*, which tells the history of Hell's Conquest of Earth, Volume Two tells a deeper tale, the horrid history of Hell's Conquest of Heaven.

Sit back, then, O Hideous Reader, and deeply partake of its unseemingly cosmic revelations, with the caveat that our Evil Existence in toto is but an insubstantial blip on the Radar Screen of Reality.

For now the Editors invite you to Hearken to the awful tale of the clawing and devouring of Heaven's flesh by Lord Satan's rapacious incisors, with the colorful assistance of his mincing supplicant Lord Zyk of Asimoth who, as thou wilt see, makes of a bad meal something infinitely more distasteful.

Finally, we raise our wretched voices to curse the memory of Lord Satan, Paragon of Evil and Imperator of Hell, who ruled his Kingdom through the eons with an Iron Fist of Fear, and toward whom all Curses forever flow.

RADIX ILLA MALORUM STULTITIA EST

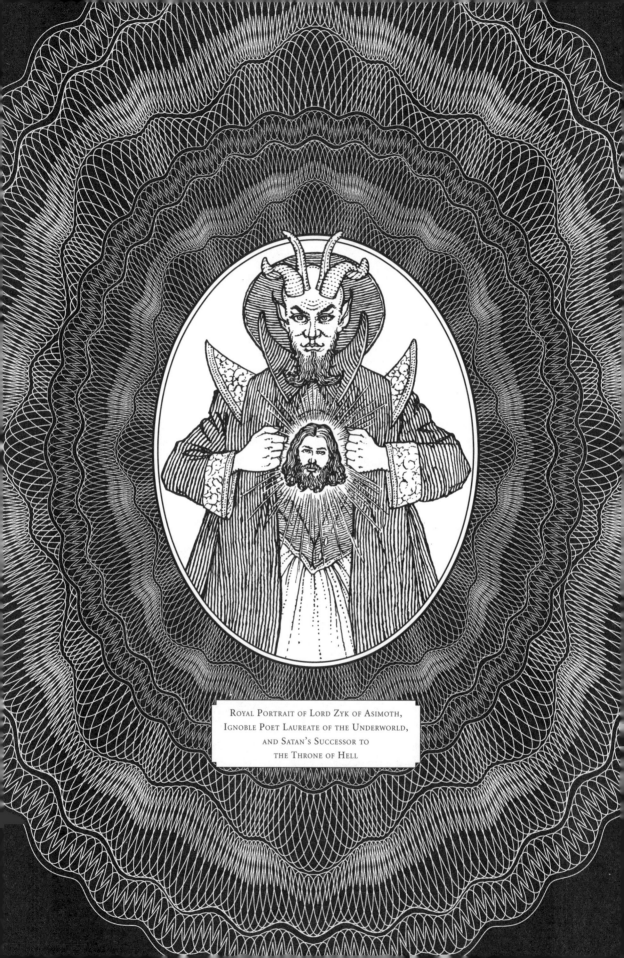

ROYAL PORTRAIT OF LORD ZYK OF ASIMOTH,
IGNOBLE POET LAUREATE OF THE UNDERWORLD,
AND SATAN'S SUCCESSOR TO
THE THRONE OF HELL

PREFACE BY
LORD ZYK
OF ASIMOTH
LORD OF HELL II

TO THE

COMMEMORATIVE EDITION
OF THE

CONQUEST OF HEAVEN

HAIL DEMON READER,

and bad tidings upon thee. Know that this *Commemorative Edition* was compiled eons after the Invasion of Heaven, and therefore has the advantage of hindsight in relating the cosmic events herein told.

As successor to Satan, I have been asked to compose the preface to this Deluxe Edition, despite the criticism of pundits regarding my reign as Emperor of Hell. Know, O Demon Reader, that Lord Satan's book *Encyclopaedia of Hell*, the invasion manual of Earth (of which I was Editor-in-Chief), defined *Emperor* as *"A sentient bag of dirt which rules its acre of rubble."* While I utterly agree, the rulership of Hell has been an uphill climb to achieve the greatness which I have earned based on my murderous exploits and absurdly evil triumphs.

To those detractors claiming that my Rulership was *not* earned, I say to them, does not success go hand in hand with the mercurial tides of chance? Is not aspiring toward greatness merely taking a walk in the Garden of my fecund Brilliance? Finally, to those claiming that my reign was a dismal and pathetic failure, I say, should not Infinite Time be the ultimate judge, and not those fools who, after mere eons, rush to judgement? For I have done my worst to navigate through my metamorphosis from lowly Poet Laureate of Hell to Supreme Lord of Evil with admirable insensitivity, if not with wan and arrogant aplomb.

This *Commemorative Edition*, replete with disgusting historical documents, explores my sadistic deeds, relationships, successes and failures of long ago, while I was at the Herculean heights of my Evil Creativity, when I accepted the mantle and responsibility of Hell's protection and power, despite the callow name-calling of my critics.[1] Still, as all Evil Creatures know, the nature of Hell's Spiritual Radiation favors Slander and Misconduct. For as Lord Satan has written in *Catechism of Calamity*, *"Falsity dost Triumph over Truth."*[2]

With my acceptance of this hellish trope, I elevate the value of this edition by signing the original manuscript with my royal signature, an artifact of inestimable value on eBay. And know, O Evil Reader, that the Histories herein, telling the legendary tales for which I will best be remembered, were transcribed by lesser demons, filled with complaints of what they perceived as my Cloying Insincerity, Shallow Self-Indulgences and Reeking Personal Hygiene.

In conclusion, what is important is that I have acquiesced to autograph this Commemorative Edition, and in so doing, as befitting my evil station, I curse you, my Reader, hoping that Personified Adversity defiles the hole you call home, rips up your family photos, scratches all of your records and squanders the contents of your liquor cabinet. Finally, O Demons, I conjure you a meaningless future engulfed by the Black Shroud of Emptiness that abnegates all that is, was and shall be, forevermore.

Flotsam and Jetsam you are, and to Flotsam and Jetsam you shall return.

Yours in Endless Contempt,
ZYK

---

1   Demon pundits hurled a plethora of insults at Lord Zyk during his reign, such as Knave of Turds, Three-Inch Cheswick, Imbecilic Dog, Scullion of Stupidity, Insouciant Insect, Pusillanimous Pig, Excrement-Eater, Stick Lapper, Bum-Sucker, Monkey Minge Licker, Pus-Squinger, Sheep's Flux, Swill-Sucker, Sperm-Sandwich, Backwoods Buffoon, Fisting-Freak, Detestable Dork, Maggot-Meat, Puttocked Ponce, Mewling Meowser, Pony-Dick, Open-Arsed Worms' Meat, Bilious Bastard, Vessel of Vanity, Numb Nuts, Frankfarter, Boot-Licker, Oil of Dog, and many other colorful canards too plentiful to list here. (Editor MK)
2   *Lord Satan's Most Unquotable Quotes*, edited by demon poetaster Melih Kazancioglu, Pg. 66, Hellhole Press.

BIOGRAPHIA DÆMONUM ET ANGELORUM

BIOGRAPHIES OF THE DÆMONIC AND ANGELIC PERSONAGES THAT PERVADE THE HISTORIES OF *THE CONQUEST OF HEAVEN*

FORMER RULER AND SUPREME CREATOR OF THE HELL COSMOS[1]

FORMER EMPEROR OF HELL, EARTH & HEAVEN AND THE INFINITE REALMS BETWIXT THE THREE[2]

LORD SATAN

All Astral Beings and Vibratory Locations in our World Materialized from the Black Fabric of His Mind with the Active Participation of the Astral Properties of his Excretory Portal.

The King of Evil who ruled the Totality of the Hell Universe with an Iron Fist, Here sporting his Vile, Shrunken-Head Trophy of the Original Human. Satan single-handedly brought the Darkness of Hell to Heaven, in a mission to Destroy Light and Assassinate God. Hobbies included Rulership of All That Is, club racquetball, pressing wildflowers and Cosmic Thermo-Nuclear Annihilation.

---

1   Lord Satan's complete résumé as a professional Lord of Evil may be obtained from the publisher, Mind Control Press.
2   In Dæmonic Black Science, Hell, Earth and Heaven each have three Realms: the Real, the Astral and the Imaginary.

INTERIM RULER
OF HELL[3],
FORMER
POET LAUREATE
OF HELL

FORMER PROFESSOR
OF EARTH EVIL
AT
HELL UNIVERSITY

LORD ZYK OF ASIMOTH
(HUMAN FORM)

Appointed by Satan as his Successor to Rule the Hell Cosmos, Hell's Chief Undercover Espionage Agent for Earth Surveillance, Editor of Lord Satan's *Encyclopaedia of Hell*.

Destroyer of Earth Density and, although Color-Blind, was Aroused by the Hue of Human Blood. Conqueror of the Celestial Plane and Silver-Tongued Propagandist of Hell's Spiritual Empire. Hobbies include Tastefully Arranging Decapitated Cherub Heads in Fibonacci Spirals.

CONJURER OF EVIL
ENCHANTMENTS,
DEMON OF
DISORDER AND
NAY-SAYING

LORD ZYK'S CHIEF
ASSASSIN AND ALSO
CROSSWORD PUZZLE
ENTHUSIAST

ODIN THE OBSEQUIOUS
(HUMAN FORM)

Lord Zyk's Highest Ranking Lieutenant, Translator & Chief Spell-Master. Odin also held the Office of Official Scapegoat, taking the Blame to make Lord Zyk a Paragon of Royal Infallibility.

Hobbies include playing the accordion, being publicly humiliated for political crimes, and being Celebrity Co-Host of Hades' Annual Baby Bake-Off.

---

3   Lord Zyk of Asimoth became Ruler of Hell by passive default, rather than in deference to his qualifications, since he was known for his delicate and introverted mien. Previously, Lord Satan, in fits of mindless rage, had obliterated all demon candidates who were, indeed, much more qualified. Thus when Satan required a successor to rule in his absence, his only officer remaining was Zyk, who became De Facto King of Hell.

DEMONESS
SAVANT OF
BLACK MAGIC

MEMORY
ACCOUNTANT
OF WEAPONRY,
FOOD
& PORNOGRAPHY

RAMONA IYAM

Hell's prodigious numerical genius, calculated mentally all supplies required
by Hell's army during the Conquest of Heaven.

*Her hobbies include reciting gibberish to dead birds, chewing on lead pipes,
and humiliating Demon Assassins by correcting their grammar.*

SOUL-MATE
OF LORD ZYK
OF ASIMOTH

MOTHER TO
LORD ZYK'S
SOLE PROGENY,
AN INVISIBLE
JACKAL FETUS[4]

SISTER DEBBIE OF KRAKOW
(ASTRAL FORM)

This mysterious Harlot of the Hereafter, Rumored to Manipulate the Destiny of *All That Is*.
After her death, her astral form radiated such immense spiritual sadness, she guided
Lord Zyk whilst in dreams to be reborn in the Vile Shadow of Anti-Evil.

*Sister Debbie's hobbies include being mysterious, deleting spam emails
and playing the glockenspiel in astral parades.*

---

4   See *Encyclopaedia of Hell*, pg. 182.

CHIEF MEDICAL
OFFICER OF THE
HOSPICE OF
HEAVEN

HOLY CO-DEPENDENT
AND ENABLER
OF THE MENTALLY
CHALLENGED CREATOR

DR. HORACE CATALLUS BIRDFIRE

Sight-Impaired Physician to The Personified Creator, Dr. Birdfire specialized in the
mental illnesses of Immortal Beings and their Terror of Self-Awareness,
due to dwelling in a Meaningless Universe.

*His hobbies include country-western line-dancing, baking mystery cakes,
and treating the Universe for Obsessive-Compulsive Disorder.*

SYMBOLIC
ESSENCE
OF THE
TOTALITY
OF
REALITY

ALSO KNOWN
AS THE
PERSONIFIED
CREATOR

THE PERSONIFIED GOD
(TWO HUMAN FORMS: SIX-YEAR-OLD GIRL AND MAN WITH A HAT)

At risk of decapitation by Satan, Hell's scientists secretly surmised the existence of a Neutral
(neither Evil nor Anti-Evil) Creator of Satan and Hell. Ancient evil sages even hypothesized
that the Hell Cosmos may be composed of the mental and emotional mind-stuff
of a Child Creator, not yet consciously self-aware.

*After Heaven's surrender, the actual Personified God's hobbies were revealed
to be hanging out at the fishing hole, telling jokes and laughing with talking dogs and cats,
and encouraging the Phenomenon of Sympathy with All Things.*

SPLENETIC
THE FIRST
PHASE ONE OF THE INVASION

◦ EDITOR'S NOTE ◦

*We hereby commence Part One of the History
of the Invasion of Heaven with lugubrious epistles
exchanged by our unesteemed rulers, followed by historical
and poetical excerpts from diverse demon historians, curated
and arranged to simulate the Chronological Sequence
of Evil Events through the Veil of Linear Time.*

LORD SATAN IN FORMAL EVILWEAR
OFFICIAL PORTRAIT TATTOOED
UPON THE BUTTOCKS OF ANGEL SLAVES

LORD SATAN'S EPISTLE TO ZYK

CONCERNING HIS

ROGUE MISSION[1]

FROM SATAN	**TO ZYK OF ASIMOTH**
FORMERLY LORD OF THE HELL COSMOS	LORD OF HELL IN SATAN'S ABSENCE
NOW FREE AGENT OF UNIVERSAL EVIL	FORMER POET LAUREATE OF HELL

Hail to Thee, Incompetent and Universally Despised Scrap of Nothing,

Although I wrote you previously abdicating my throne and giving it to you, and bidding you a hateful farewell, a strange matter has arisen that you should be aware of. If you try very hard, you may comprehend the simple concepts that follow, for it is of supreme importance that the contents of this epistle penetrate your impenetrable skull:

I wrote you concerning my paradoxical conundrum, perforce, of solving the mystery of my origin. But now, acknowledging that you are a droll, but utterly incompetent fop, and because it is the Eve of my Secret and Historic Departure, I repeat my message again, using different words and syntax, because it amuses me to irritate and demean you. Although I of course remember every detail of creating the Hell Cosmos and of engendering all demons that inhabit it, including you, having ripped you all from the Filthy Tapestry of my Mind and, as your Cosmic Slum Lord, leased you a wretched existence in the crumbling apartment projects known as Evil Reality.

After conquering humankind and amusing myself by studying mortals' bizarre philosophies, I admit that I was shocked at the human idiots' strange belief that a Higher Creator not only existed, but had dumbed Itself down by necessity, into a physical Personified God

---

1   Previously unpublished correspondence from the Editor's personal files.

not only existed, but had dumbed Itself down by necessity, into a physical Personified God in order to create a physical universe. I was certain beyond a doubt that there was and could be, of course, *no being "higher" than myself.* Yet despite its absurd ignorance, the human creation myth enflamed the hole in my memory regarding the mystery of my origin. I felt a paroxysm of rage and frustration that my memory was a blank slate on the matter of how my existence began. As a result, I became so obsessed with the mystery of my origin that I made a ruthless decision to temporarily abandon my Evil Kingdom. I abdicated my title as Lord, for I had become sick of *the Evil Politic,* alternating between ruling over or murdering my slaves, depending on my whim. Now I am determined to leave Hell and conduct a rogue mission to find out if indeed this *Personified Creator* has a whiff of existence. And if he does, then I will kill him so that I will own It All.

However, in my murderous haste, I neglected to order you to do what you, in your utter stupidity, have not even considered:

I command you to commemorate my conquest of Earth with a Festival so Profoundly Evil that it will insult the cross of space-time and imprint shame upon the consciousness of all humans, whatever few are left after my demon armies have eaten their fill.

To that end, idiot, LISTEN CAREFULLY. I command you to time-gather the Top Ten Most Beloved Human Leaders in the timeline of Earth's ridiculous histories. Then, in a live televised/internet broadcast entitled *Welcome to the Feast of Fear,* you shall cook all ten beloved human leaders alive and then publicly (and voraciously) devour their simmering gore. Seeing their idols humiliated, as well as covered with steak sauce, will ensure that mankind's most precious dreams are utterly squashed, shattered, cancelled—null and void.

Meanwhile I shall powerfully and viciously focus all of my majestic perceptive organs on the task of tracking down the supposed physical dimension of Heaven and, if it exists, zero in on the whereabouts of the Fool of *All That Is,* and destroy him utterly. When you next hear from me, in one way or another, I will have taken over the totality of the universe by force. And if he exists, I will step into the shoes of the Pretender God. I will then announce to all sentient beings that *I am the New Owner of the Playground of the Universe,* that all sentient beings are now my playthings. In so doing I will initiate a New Age of Pain and Sorrow, such as the universe has never seen before, as befitting creatures so arrogant that they dare to be alive without my consent.

That is all. Do you intuit, despite being a sniveling poltroon with a piece of shit in your otherwise empty skull, that I grow bored of writing to you and of all thoughts connected to your essence? Follow my commands to a T, you witless, organic stain, and feel shame that you are not suckling upon my erect reproductive protuberance while doing so. If the Pretender God exists, I shall slice him into Deluxe Swiss Cheese and, using forgiveness and empathy as bread, and stardust ejaculate as mayo, wash it down with the tears of a billion loathsome angels. For then, my cloying boy poet, the greatest Evil Feast of all shall follow, to commemorate my Conquest of Heaven. There I shall make my announcement, that I have assumed Infinite Godhead, and wrongfully stolen the Lowest Honor as the most Hated Being in the Cosmos.

I meditate tonight using all of my powers to determine the truth of this Personified God Hypothesis. If it warrants my attention, I shall act immediately, depart in stealth tomorrow morning in my astral time-vehicle, track down my enemy like a dog and assassinate him.

Know, Zyk, that you are forever my worthless whipping boy, and if *you* were "personified," you would be a buttocks boil's oozing discharge of bile, mucous and catarrh.

Hoping you Seek Solace in Evil and instead find that It too Despises You, I remain,

Lord Satan,
Creator of the Ineffable Hell Cosmos

P.S. Be aware that I have cameras everywhere. I know you rifled through my drawers looking for my most prized possession, my Shrunken Head Medallion, once belonging to Adam the first human. I know you have coveted it for some time, and therefore am taking it with me. I intend to wear it for good luck when I kill God. Besides, it looks good with my travel outfit. But most importantly, know that I have Tupperwared barbecued fried chicken in my bedroom's mini-fridge which has the original recipe. *I had to go all the way to a KFC in Missouri to find it. When I return and check the security cam, perforce, if you have disturbed even* one chicken wing, *the Spell of Apollyon will force you to jump-rope with your own intestines.* Be warned.

LORD ZYK'S MEMO
CONCERNING THE
FEAST *of* FEAR[1]

Memo to	**From**
Mortimer Pönçé, Esq.	**Zyk of Asimoth, Editor**
Publisher, Mind Control Press	Lord Zyk of Asimoth
Hell Hole West	Earth Invasion Headquarters
City of Hell	The Pentagon
	Arlington, Virginia

Detestable Mr. Pöncé,

Four months have passed since we last met in Paris to catch up over an exquisite dinner of French cuisine. My mouth still waters remembering the succulence of those sautéed children's lungs in a demi-glace of Michelin-star chef's buttocks.

I am bolstered that our relationship since our collaboration on *Encyclopaedia of Hell* has blossomed into such a satisfying enmity of indifference and disdain, gifting us with freedom from the scourge of friendship. In Satan's magnificent *Encyclopaedia* (which I edited with cognitive brilliance), I paraphrase our Lord defining *Freedom* as *"The uncomfortable interval one experiences between finding new forms of enslavement."* As you might imagine, I am grateful for the freedom to discuss with you Lord Satan's latest volley of insults and preposterous demands, entreaties which took me completely by surprise.

Just as you have your hands full weeding through amateur submissions at Mind Control Press, I've had my claws full ruling this drab human planet in Lord Satan's absence. As a result, the last thing I needed was another rash *peccadillo satanus* thrown at me by His Majesty. And his command to organize a "Feast of Fear" here on Earth fits the bill in spades.

---

1   Previously unpublished correspondence from the Editor's personal files.

LORD ZYK'S MEMO TO SATAN CONCERNING THE FEAST OF FEAR

You and I, Mr. Pöncé, discussed at that time the complexity of our Lord's demand to time-gather ten of Earth's most beloved humans and serve them at a commemorative feast. Why ten? Due to mundane convention? Because we happen to have ten fingers on our claws? This random mandate created my first problem—to determine the humans the most beloved by humans. But after several days, I devised a self-working Enchantment which scanned the psychic lattices connecting human minds regarding the idol worship of individuals. I was able to rank the Top Ten Most Beloved Humans in Earth's History as follows:

10. Krishna

9. Michael Jackson

8. Jesus

7. Buddha / Mohammed[2]

6. Elvis

5, 4, 3, 2. The Beatles (individually)

1. ABBA[3]

The Feast of Fear would be a live event, complete with balloons and clowns, to be watched by the conquered humans from the discomfort of their own homes, a.k.a. prison cells. The broadcast event would include a magnificent speech by myself announcing the victory of Hell over Earth, and explaining how and why the human slaves would all eventually be eaten. Then would follow the Feast Proper. First, the introduction in descending order of the Top Ten Humans throughout history, ending with ABBA. Then basting them in rotisserie ovens while Hell Symphony Orchestra plays Ives' *Robert Browning Overture.* And finally, the live feed of thirteen lottery-chosen demons devouring them with hot sauce at a long table while guzzling huge flagons of flaming human blood. That being the plan, the televised *Feast of Fear* was to be a magnificent event, striking terror into the hearts of all Humanity. (Sadly, the clowns were double-booked and did not show.)

Prior to the *Feast,* however, having been lambasted by demon critics regarding my style of leadership, I was worried. Yes, I was desperate to impress Lord Satan, for I knew that upon his return, I would be subject to his fury for having eaten his leftover chicken.

Thus, despite my expertise in time-traveling to Earth's past, I was admittedly nervous boarding my Hell-Craft to begin my new time-gathering mission, despite a few annoying peccadillos, including the following:

---

2   The Popularity Determinant Enchantment calculated an exact tie between these wretched beings, which cast suspicion on the cosmic calibration of the Spell; thus I threatened to shave bald my Spellmaster Odin the Obsequious (a hair-finery fop) if the calibration was not corrected at once; it was duly corrected, but I decided to shave him anyway.

3   While the members of The Beatles ranked separately, and Michael Jackson garnered the votes of the influential Child Predator Community, ABBA's popularity was proportionally far greater, having bribed the demon Judicial Committee with the only non-human-flesh dish on Earth which is palatable to demons, Swedish Meatballs.

After kidnapping the band ABBA in Earth's past, arriving back on present-day Earth and carrying the four ABBAs over my shoulders to be buttered up on oven trays, I was suddenly tackled by a screaming, long-haired human wielding a butcher's knife. He gauchely pinned me to the ground and proceeded to hack off both of my claws at the wrists. Unable to cast a Death Spell without claws, I conjured the only enchantment I could cast with my head and neck movements alone, a novelty spell which turned my attacker's flesh inside-out in the approximate shape and coloration of a human fez, the spell shedding his ripped clothes onto the stage, and transforming his long hair into the fez tassel.

In its death throes, the humanoid fez screamed and flopped to the ground in a sanguineous mess. As I used my head and neck to conjure my claws to grow back, I saw that the remains of my attacker's clothing was an ABBA T-shirt. The sequence of events became clear: the fool was an ABBA fan who had stowed away in my landing gear.

Another colorful anecdote, Mr. Pöncé, occurred after I strapped the ten most beloved humans to cooking trays and slid them into the ovens. Three of the four rotisserie wheels would not turn due to factory flaws, thus on three trays the popular humans lay flat and basted with herbs and olive oil. As I closed the oven doors, all ten humans began screaming in terror. And as they caterwauled, I recognized a familiar, internal tingling in my demon bodice, starting with my undercarriage, the same prickling I had noted when I first did my research on odious Earth. I knew that Earth's notorious *magentic field* [4] had once again triggered a physiological change in my innards, starting with said tingling of the taint, and spiraling up my torso which began the tragic organ-sprouting.

As you know, unlike the human carcass, demon physiology is devoid of *heart, spleen* or other emotive inner organs. Demon bodies, of course, are equipped with a single meat tube going from mouth to anus. Does having neither heart nor spleen give demons an advantage over humans? But of course. We never get heart attacks or ruptured spleens. And we only experience the exquisite and dependable emotional modulations of hatred, rage and self-adoration.

In my case, the magentic field goosed my demonic DNA to verily sprout these strange budding organs within me: two small, grisly, veiny organs, slowly growing in size from day to day. As they grew, my healthy, hateful emotions waned, giving way to ghastly bursts of what I assume is *human sentiment*. When I saw a puppy, instead of wanting to throw it down a well, I wanted to dress it in a pink, smiley-face vest. Yes, my new organs were unwanted interlopers, their effect upon my soul an incremental horror, growing like deformed fruit in a gnarled tree.

---

4   Contrary to the initial theories of Hell's scientists, it was not Earth's *magnetic* field that caused susceptible demons to sprout alien hearts and spleens inside their torsos; rather, it was the poisonous *magentic* field, which created the organs of human emotion—the heart and spleen—in the demon torso. Later in our historical *pastiche*, this particulate field played a fundamental role in the profound events of the invasion soon to unfold.

It was this tiny Fount of Empathy that told me to cancel the Feast, whispering that to dine on Earth's most sacred humans would be far too… *gauche?* Nay, I was furious with myself for harkening to my heart's traitorous voice, and rageful that I felt unnatural about something as natural as murder.

Still, I could not help myself. Right after sliding the Top Ten in the ovens, my heart and spleen throbbed as if they would burst! I was forced to listen to their ejecta in my brain, resulting in hideous pangs of conscience. With trembling claws and tears of self-hatred, I conjured a curtain around the ovens so I could secretly remove the humans without being seen by my lieutenants. I quickly unstrapped all ten from their trays and poured pitchers of water over their heads to revive them.

Unfortunately, most of them were already dead, their baked skin golden and succulent. Elvis, for example, was beautifully and evenly roasted, resembling a plump, oversized, plucked squab. However, Jesus and the blonde female ABBA singer, although swimming in sweat on their trays, their hair and the tips of their fingers and toes burnt off, were still alive and spluttered as I poured water over their faces. Filled with self-loathing at my absurd compulsion to save them, I whispered fiercely that they should both sneak out and run for the hills. As they staggered to their feet in confusion, I pushed their charred carcasses out the back door and urged them to escape.

But my famished and inebriated lieutenants, celebrating our victory over Earth, were still clamoring to be fed. Behind the drawn curtain, to cover for my seemingly insane liberation of our dinner, I quickly conjured two Fourier Duplicate Bodies[5] to replace the ABBA woman and Jesus. I prepared and served them up with the eight other beautifully baked humans. The meal was exquisite and praised by all, Mr. Pöncé, although I feared the Jesus Duplicate's hindquarters tasted a bit like a pair of sweaty break-dancer's jeans.

It is a great discomfort to share my triumphs and failures with you, my most repugnant frenemy. Alas, I am late for a meeting on the efficacy of the canning of human meat, but will write soon of another matter I would like to explore in distasteful discourse with you.

May the insecurities implicit in our evil lifestyles grow and heighten until they are too much for even a demon of your stature, scope and strength to bear.

With Sublime Hate,
ZYK

---

5   The Fourier Duplicates, in collaboration with a Transformative Spell, connected to a 3-D printer, produced duplicate human flesh pods. Depending on the calibration of the Enchantment, the flesh of the Fourier Descriptor Bodies will taste in some cases like liverwurst or, as in this case, like greasy sweatpants.

EDITOR'S NOTE

The following pages are a facsimile of the pulp edition of Lord Satan's experiences during his Hellkabah Journey, and what transpired when he breached the Walls of Heaven.

LORD SATAN DEFILES HEAVEN

EXCERPT NO. 1
FROM SATAN'S BEST-SELLING MEMOIR[1]

FEAR ME
THE MONSTROUS MEMORIES OF SATAN, LORD OF HELL

---

1   From the penny-saver Pulp Edition of Mind Control Press' Crushed Infant Imprint. Lord Satan wrote his memoir while trapped in the ineluctable Time Void, about which the less said the better.

I. A Dark Discovery

It was a dry, balmy night in the desert of South Hell when an epiphany hit me like a rainstorm of bullets. Idiot humanity claimed that a Creator more fundamental than Myself existed. Yet more twaddle from the race of talking monkeys. But the concept nagged at me. It formed a growing fissure in my otherwise perfect, stupendous magnificence. I cannot remember my origin, nor recall whether I had a creator. As no one should be permitted to be superior to myself, my motive for murder was crystal clear. *If I was created, I'd find my Creator and kill him.*

For as long as I could remember, I didn't know who I was and where I came from. I needed to solve the mystery of my Existence. I needed to put it to rest, like a corpse needs a casket. I'd already created Hell and all demonic beings from the cheesecloth of my imagination. Now if I could somehow get the Creator out of the picture, I'd be next in line to take over everything, and become Heir Apparent of *All That Is*.

To a Supreme Being such as Myself, it's All or Nothing. Nothing less is acceptable or even possible.

The next step, to simply begin.

II. Unleash the Death Ride

Through a tripped-up application based on the Mechanics of Time (which I figured out on the ride home from another late-night genocide), I went home to my workshop, which still smelled of stale cigarettes, and the time-traversing Hellcraft was born with a wrench. And some rare, incompatible, lithophile elements such as beryllium, lithium and tantalum. But the mentation of mechanical engines, although eternally fascinating, is a playground for primitives. My late-night studies, with the help of my tutor, a single-malt Laphroaig, told me that the simplest mode of time-travel is through the *astral* (the Fundament underlying matter and energy) by means of a mental creation which my Black Magick colleagues call the *Merkabah*.

The Merkabah is an astral vehicle which only travels in one direction. After the journey, its astral form dissolves back into the ethers. The reasons, thus:

1. The vehicle and its destination are one and the same.
2. The Infinite Power of the Universe is called upon to power the vehicle.
3. Once the Destination is reached, the vehicle's meaning is fulfilled, the Enchantment is complete, and the thought-form dissolves whence it came, back into the empty core of All That Is.

See if this floats your boat. The Merkabah is a thought-form consisting of two precisely locked pyramids. Its astral substance is drawn from the mind-stuff in my Think Piece. The Pilot, in this case Myself, sits in the center of the pyramidal formation. The recommended posture is cross-legged; the Intention, a cowboy taming Existence like riding a bronco. Next, the Pilot, through meditative exertion in the astral realm, cosmically imagines the two pyramids rotating in opposite directions.

The Pilot then speaks these words with certainty and conviction: *"Double Thy Speed."*

In response, the pyramids grow darkly luminous, and then speed up.

Then is spoken: *"Double Thy Speed Again."* The rotation complies and the pyramids whir with increased mechanistic gusto, imagined with an even deeper, richer Depth of Darkness. This step is repeated again and again. Precision of the mind, the result of deep meditative sweat and tears, boosted by ketamine and grain alcohol, is required to achieve the desired result. As the pyramids spin, their impossible speed makes them invisible, except for a feathery blur of black luminescence. Finally, in the Pilot's mind, a Vehicle of Infinite Darkness imbued with infinite power is formed, ready for take-off, a Vehicle which I shall rename the *Hellkabah*.

At that point, the Pilot commands the thought-form Hellkabah with three clear and confident directives:

1. The pyramidal engine will power the vehicle to rise.
2. The Pilot then clearly imagines an image of the Destination. The image is commanded to sustain in the mind until the Destination is reached.
3. The journey is initiated by speaking aloud thusly: *Take me to my Destination.*

If these instructions are followed precisely, the Pilot will shriek with success upon finding that this rather iffy, tendentious Spell actually worked, and will thrust his clawed fist to the Black Stars with the lush, cockle-tingling gratitude of Pure Hatred.

Cheers. I was on my way to decapitate the Creator.

Lord Satan Drives his Astral Vehicle to Heaven's Coordinates

III. My Savage Journey Begins

Woof. The trip itself was nothing to bark about. I had incorrectly imagined the height of the Hellkabah's fuselage, the low roof of which compacted my horns in an annoying manner.

Too impatient to re-imagine it over entirely, I decided to detach my head and carry it in my lap for the nonce, until my journey was complete. This entailed a surprising boon as the layers of filth encrusted in my groinage were closer to my nostrils; my head inhaling deeply thus contributed a delightfully foul sensuality to my journey.

I experienced the usual car-sickness, dry-heaving once, replacing my head on my neck to vomit thrice, once on the floor, once on the dash and once out the window, reveling at the thought of the hapless angelic bicyclists upon whose fresh faces my ejected effluvia splattered in diarrheic splendor.

The Hellkabah's dash radio drifted in and out playing oldies, and my music player, plugged into the cigarette lighter and playing old Beatles and Dead tunes, blew a fuse which I was too lazy to fix.

Since the Time-Travel calibration on my computerized itinerary read "Close to Infinite" (whatever *that* means), whorling dead insects and bird shit accumulated on my windshield like an East Bushwick idiot's kinetic art installation.

Using the wipers and squirting cleaning fluid just made it worse, for I was unclear how the geometry of the windshield illusion worked in tandem with the shape and speed of the spinning pyramids which, of course, were also illusory.

A sticker on my dash said it all, the one my most recent and most aesthetically pleasing wife, May She Rot in Hell, had stuck to it: *"Ours not to reason why, ours but to do and die."*

IV. The Silhouette in the Grass

Above me the Full Moon shone in the sky like a meth addict frozen in a Buick's headlights. The sky looked likc a medieval engraving with lots of photoshopped cross-hatching.

My Hellkabah finally landed at its programmed destination with a jolt and a rattle, creating a geometric moonlit silhouette on the lawn. I'd landed by the bushes at the bottom of the long, marble stairway leading up to the massive Gates of Heaven, which were covered with weird shadowy glyphs, all the weirder in Heaven's stupid moonlight.

I deplaned, and as soon as my hooves touched the ground, my dashboard dissolved into sickly green and violet smoke; the rest of the vehicle turned into a cauldron of bats that flapped away into the cross-hatched sky.

Through slitted eyes, I stared through the bushes at the fortress. There were two reptilian angel guards stationed on either side of the massive Gates. One was having a smoke while the other whispered on his cell phone; both looked sleepy and bored.

The Gates behind them were hypnotic works of architecture, carved as they were out of Nothingness. I tried not to admit to myself that I was impressed by their huge size, and their ancient, intricate engravings of intimidating symbols. Psychologically, despite confirming the existence of Heaven, I still didn't want to admit that God existed nor that I was created by him. Giving anyone other than myself the slightest credit for *All That Is* was against the unalterable nature of my Evil Being.

My immediate goal was to get through those Gates, behind which my Enemy surely slept, unaware of my mission to wipe him out like a cockroach in a Tijuana motel. However, one must surmise that God had imbued all of his infinite power in the defense of his fortress. After all, this was his Heavenly Home. If Satan's your enemy, who would slouch on a home security system? Thus, I assumed that using an ordinary, garden-variety Enchantment would be embarrassing. I must instead breach the security of Heaven in one of two ways:

I must instead breach the security of Heaven in one of two ways:

1. Summon the supreme powers of Darkness at the core of the Empty Universe and manipulate it in profoundly inventive ways to allow me to breach the Gates.

2. Kill the guards and use their corpses as a ladder to climb over the top.

The second option was too common for a malevolent enterprise of this scale. Therefore, I would enter via a profoundly evil Spell to reverse the force of anti-evil keeping evil out. To begin this enchantment, I did the usual: I stood up straight, cleared my throat and began, as an opening ritual, to verbalize my objective in a strong, clear voice: *"I want to be in Heaven."* My objective stated, I began to construct my Spell. But before I could begin my conjuration, something inexplicable occurred:

Reality opened up. Space unzipped like a giant pair of blue corduroys as I was awkwardly stuffed through the fly hole. I instantly dematerialized from outside the Gates and rematerialized inside Heaven's walls in the center of a circular Garden. There was a faint taste of copper in my mouth and a tingling in my nether regions. Infused with repulsive beauty, the Garden was scented by flowers of hideous sweetness, wafted by the cool evening breeze to my enflamed demon nostrils.

I hastily inserted nose plugs. What had just happened? How, why?

I saw an elegant brass sign next to me that read: THE SUPREME GARDEN OF GOD. Behind the sign was a garden with whorls of the most colorful flowers ever created, arranged in geometric spirals and three-dimensional glyphs. These were the most beautiful, and thus repugnant, flowers ever created—yet, somehow, they were not wholly repugnant to me.

What was happening to me?

A glowing golden fountain cascading glistening beauty in clear liquid form appeared beside me. Its bubbles were so effervescent, stray molecules of despised freshness seeped past my nostril plugs, making me sneeze and causing a coughing fit.

Yes, it was all Heavenly. All exactly what I hated.

I had come prepared with eye filters to screen out hideous beauty like the fountain. But I was unprepared for the audio component poisoning the air around me. Each festoon of flowers resonated with a different vibratory tone. Together, they emitted a hideously majestic symphony, a loathsome atmosphere of perfect harmony. Its precise overtones made my ears bleed. When I inhaled, the flowers' sweetness produced cognitive dissonance with the natural filth that composed my lungs. I swooned, heaved deeply, and vomited the remains of a virgin I'd eaten into the azaleas. It was confirmed: perfect harmony was an unbearable toxin to my soul.

After vomiting out the remains of my stomach, I took a deep breath and wordlessly cast an internal Spell that transformed the harmonies I heard into hideous dissonances, into the comforting ugliness of black noise, machine parts screeching and metallic grinding.

The resulting cacophony relaxed my soul. Centered once again, I could concentrate my powers. Most importantly, I could finally stop and ask myself again:

What the Hell had just happened?

I had been transported from outside the gates directly into the garden, but how? In this puzzled moment, I turned and saw something strange and absurd. The tightly-knit bed of colored flowers in the garden spelled out an answer to my question:

ASK AND IT SHALL BE GIVEN

I squinted my eyes at it. It was like seeing a tortoise in a House of Mirrors. It was turtles all the way down. Although I understood what it said, overall, its incomprehensibility was comforting. No need to be angry. I had just appeared here without any seeming nod to Causality. And the flowers? They were obviously a message meant for me personally. And it was true; I had gotten there because I desired to be here, and had spoken my desire aloud.

But, killing God aside, I had come there to learn whether or not I was a created being. I read the message in the flowers again, and decided to try speaking what I most desired: *"Take me to the Library."*

It was immediate. The same tingling in my undercarriage. The same bitter, coppery taste as I dematerialized and then re-materialized on the golden steps leading to the library entrance. Huge letters were carved into an archway over massive, obnoxious doors:

THE LIBRARY OF GOD.

V.   A Perfect Night for a Break-In

The Blacklight Sun made my surroundings look like a Vinegar Hill crime scene. The Library was partially darkened and closed like a Sugar Shack on Easter Sunday.[1] But, of course, that was not going to stop me. I slowly ascended the golden steps to the Library Entrance, looking left, right, up and down, in and out, to assure that no shadow entities or security holograms were recording what was, in effect, an act of B & E.[2]

Curiously, a strange sound component was added to my hoofsteps: as each hoof touched the stairs, I noted a distant yodeling that matched the cadence of my walk-cycle, a random mystery forever unexplained, but peculiar enough to be worthy of note.[3]

Reaching the top of the stairs I saw a brass plaque on the Library doors upon which was imprinted a poem. Next to the plaque was a red doorbell with a small, tasteful sign:

---

1   Although Satan's break-in was at night, time-travel unravels subjective time, thus confusion often arises in stitching events together. See Rumblefoot's *Time Distortions and the Co-Morbidity of God's Madness*, Hellhole Press.

2   Breaking & Entering, Heavenly Penal Code 106.5a, an offense under celestial law punishable by *imprisonment and/or a fine not exceeding* fifty seraphicons, depending on the severity of the offense and the criminal record of the angelic defendant.

3   Lord Satan wrote elsewhere regarding this strange phenomenon peculiar to Heaven. The yodeling, he hypothesized later while lost in the Time Void, was perhaps subtle mockery programmed by the Creator to amuse himself. The mystery was finally solved by Horace, who explained that these phenomena were likely glitches in the PC's insane mind, ceaselessly re-processing the fundamental interface between the perceiver and whatever reality is.

PLEASE LET ME READ IT TO YOU.

Although growing impatient with this *Alice*-like rigmarole, I pressed the red button. From hidden alcove speakers, I heard a brief fanfare of an angelic choir. A drearily cute old woman's voice intoned over it and read the poem on the plaque:

> *The Ghostly Books of Heaven's Library*
> *Are generated from an infinity*
> *Of precisely aligned algorithms,*
> *Programmed by Divinity.*
>
> *The Personified Creator,*
> *A sentient standing-wave satyr,*
> *Entangled each book with its object,*
> *A book-to-matter translator.*
>
> *As thought is ever expanding,*
> *The books have infinite heft.*
> *In case one falls, rent a hard hat*
> *From the dispenser to your left.*

The dispenser had a sign on it, printed in *The Prisoner* font, which read:

All credit cards are gainfully accepted.

Know, O Reader, that after the flower incident in the Garden, I was not in a mood for self-indulgent twaddle. Although the Door Poem itself was a decent touch, to my mind it was lacking in four areas:

1. It left the impression that God was not only trying too hard to be amusing, but also wretchedly insecure.

2. Requiring centuries-old monetary technology as an interface was rather random and annoying.

3. The poem itself had elements akin to "AI poetry," combining novel words into a slosh of vaguely unsatisfying metaphor.

4. Is not *gainfully* a superfluous and thus irritating modifier of *accepted*, since it goes without saying that accepting all credit cards would increase *gain*?

Still, since the poem might offer a valid warning, and I was already on guard enough without having to worry about falling books, I conjured a valid credit card[4] and slid it into the card reader.

I hadn't noticed that it had a chip and put it in the wrong way. *Beeep*. Realizing my mistake, but emotionally unable to be accountable for error, I flipped it and inserted it again. *Beeep*. Aggravated, I tried it the other way again. *Beeep*.

A rage rose within me. Furious, I roared with the roar of a thousand suns and smashed the dispenser with my tail, exploding the crackling plastic in a clatter of diverse trajectories. Reaching through the dispenser wreckage, I grabbed a hard hat and put it on. Then I summarily whipped my tail and smashed the stained-glass window by the Library doors, climbed through the shards of glass and entered the mysterious interior of the Creator's Library.

At last, I had arrived. Here, where lay the granddaddy of secrets. The Secret of My Origin. I surveyed the room which faded off into the hazy, infinite distance. Perhaps it was the influence of Heaven's extreme magentic field, but at that moment I felt excitement at the prospect of unraveling my destiny.

There was faint, easy-listening music playing through recessed speakers, enough, under normal circumstances, to make me go on a killing spree. In what I assumed was a programmed illusion, I inhaled the musty smell of worm-eaten books, and through the mist could see a highly detailed *chiaroscuro* of cross-hatching. It was as if the distant reality construct was a master engraving and the library itself a self-resolving fractal image, creating the illusion of infinite shelves filled with infinite books.

Hanging on the wall before me was a large, classical, oil painting in a golden frame: a can-can line of televangelists in women's lingerie were being whipped by monkeys with Hitler mustaches. I shook my head in mockery and disgust. Yawn.

Then I saw the books. They faintly shimmered and glowed. If you turned your head just the right way, you could glimpse a vibration of nearly invisible, psychic strings extending from each book out through the ceiling, walls and floor. Seeing this, I remembered reading that each book had a one-to-one-correspondence to each *thing* that existed in the physical universe. I suspected that each string connected each book to its corresponding object or thought somewhere in the ever-resolving algorithm of the complete set of physical *things*.

---

4   Editor's Note: It was amazing, Satan later mused to himself, since there was no one else to muse to, while on his downtime floating in the Time Void, how much backstory had to instantly materialize in order to create a valid credit card. A vast network of phone banks, employees and payrolls had to be instantly manifested, not to mention an entire planetary communication and banking system. Yes, it was amazing for him to think about, and it was a good use of his downtime while in the Time Void, to reminisce, and feel the expansive rush of amazement through his skull.

I sensed an impending danger before me, but wanted to act on it somehow. I was like a fly suspicious of fly-paper, but who jumps on it anyway.

I later perceived the danger. For on a bookshelf high above me was a large, sentient encyclopaedia. Its sharp edges were jagged and rusty; it had evolved a single, primitive, astral eye, a nose, and crazily-toothed mouth on its metal cover. Upon sensing me, the encyclopaedia became dizzy, intoxicated by the powerful emanations of my supernatural aura and body odor.

Unbeknownst to me, the book teetered and fell from on high, a victim of the laws of heavenly gravity, its silent screams of terror exacerbated by its fear of heights. Since its metal edges were as sharp as a guillotine blade, the book's direct descent, bee-lining toward my neck, unfortunately lopped my head off. The book toppled to the floor, landing next to my wobbling, severed head. An actual bloodshot eye gracing the book's cover, somewhat like the cover of the cursed book in *Evil Dead 2*, was pointed directly at my face. Seeing me, it blinked in shock.

Suddenly cognizant of what had occurred, I (that is, the I which was still perceiving reality from inside my decapitated head) responded by casting the book an intensely powerful *Evil Eye*. In reply, the book opened its mouth and let out another terrified, high-pitched scream.

Unable to cover my ears with my hands, I quickly rolled my head back to look up and saw my headless body still standing above me in a zombie-like pose.

Using a combination of my teeth and the vicissitudes of momentum, I climbed up my leg and torso until I reached the bloody stump of my severed neck. Through rapid licking, I then self-cauterized the wound, reconnecting my head to my body, and glared down at the culpable book.

Ironically, or perhaps not, the book that had decapitated me was a novelty edition of my own repugnant masterpiece of evil, *Encyclopaedia of Hell*, its ancient cover splattered with rose-red, black and purple coagulations of my royal demon blood.

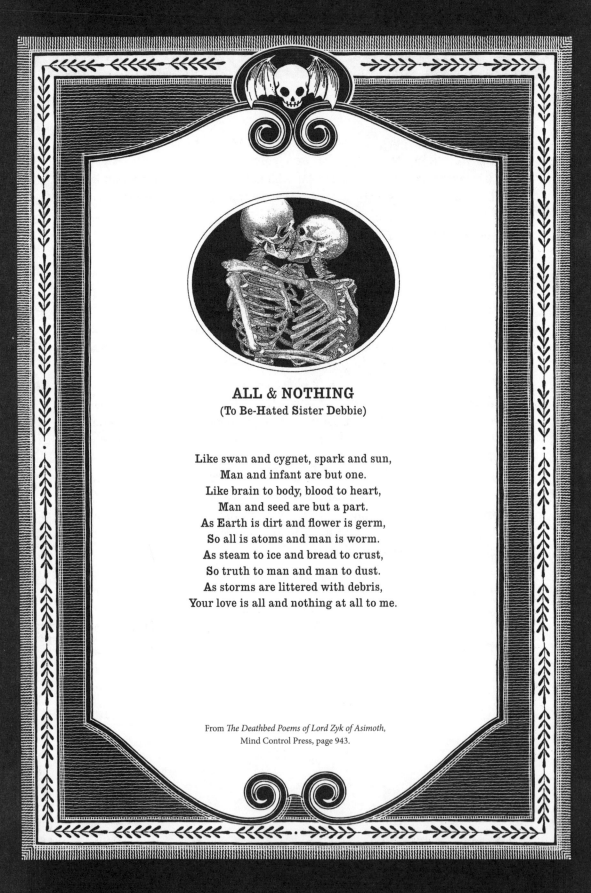

ALL & NOTHING
(To Be-Hated Sister Debbie)

Like swan and cygnet, spark and sun,
Man and infant are but one.
Like brain to body, blood to heart,
Man and seed are but a part.
As Earth is dirt and flower is germ,
So all is atoms and man is worm.
As steam to ice and bread to crust,
So truth to man and man to dust.
As storms are littered with debris,
Your love is all and nothing at all to me.

From *The Deathbed Poems of Lord Zyk of Asimoth,*
Mind Control Press, page 943.

◉ EDITOR'S NOTE ◉

*Sister Debbie had long been deceased when Lord Zyk
composed this strangely emotive entreaty. Thus it was written
partly to release his grief over her death, and partly to exorcise
himself of the hideous spiritual poison of Love.*

PRIVATE ENTREATY
FROM LORD ZYK *OF* ASIMOTH *TO* SISTER DEBBIE *OF* KRAKOW[1]
FROM THE
PRIVATE MANUSCRIPT COLLECTION
OF LORD ZYK AT HELL'S MUSEUM OF HATE

To	From
MY HATEFUL WIFE AND SOUL-MATE,	ZYK OF ASIMOTH
SISTER DEBBIE OF KRAKOW,	ROYAL BEDROOM OF SATAN'S PALACE
NOW AN ETHERIC BEING INHABITING	
THE ASTRAL VIBRATORY PLANE	

Hail, my Royal Estrogenic Stain of Blood and Lust,

It is you, Sister Debbie, my incomparable female counterpart, you and no other, who was with me in black spirit through my meteoric rise from lowly Poet of Hell to Editor-in-Chief of Lord Satan's *Encyclopaedia*. Nay, you were my *sui generis* inspiration as slowly I rose to my present stratospheric position as Supreme and Transcendent King of Hell. Satan's *Encyclopaedia* defines *King* as "That which soils the Queen." If only you were here, once again ensconced in flesh, Sister Debbie, so that I might sensitively soil you.

Why, why can it not be? Time-Travel heals death, for then no one dies. Even if, like you, your flesh is one with worms, your bones buried in the Garden of Gethsemane. My greatest desire is to pilot my Hellcraft back in time to visit your wet, sluicing, majestic vaginal orifice

---

1   Trigger Warning for the Young Demon Readers: Beware of several abhorrent and poisonous concepts advocated in the following epistle, such as Compassion and Love, which often trigger trauma in demon youth.

at its peak tumescence and copulate as we were wont to do like rapacious filth dogs, after which I would hop into my Hellcraft and travel minutes into the past, repeatedly, so that we could fornicate over and over, again and again, with the carnal freshness of our impetuous youth, our locked torsos squirting carny fluids, having rocking, rhythmic intercourse over six thousand times, until the animal novelty of lust at last dissipated.

But such is not to be. For Hellcraft, like all matter and energy in the Hell Cosmos, are powered by the Infinite Evil Energy of Satan. Thus, my quintessential paramour, all Hellcraft programmed with enchantments by Lord Satan will not operate in conjunction with the Unspeakable Abomination of *Love*.

By concentrating my mental energies, I did try to counter this impediment—this Cautionary Enchantment cast upon the controls of all Time Vehicles. Setting the dials of my Time Vehicle for the past coordinates when you were living, I attempted to override this awful enchantment so that I might visit you again. I used all of my powers to simulate sincere hatred for you, my palatine princess, my paragon of paizogony! I kept my concentration strong, steady and passionate, visualizing your ignoble death. A butcher's knife severing your skull. A Skillsaw dissecting you laterally. My red-scaled fist reaching down your throat and grabbing your internal organs and pulling you inside out, so that you resembled a deep-sea creature, its internal organs flopping on the outside, the beauty of your flesh enfolded and hidden within.

But no, my every attempt was met with failure. The sensors on my Hellcraft quickly detected the insincerity of my hatred. The dials and gizmos, drenched with Satan's enchantment, saw through my errant lie, making my Hellcraft's engine wheeze and chortle, refusing to turn over. My frustration was immense, not only because I could not see you, but also because all of my diligent attempts to trick the machine had failed utterly.

I hatefully understand the need for such a draconian Time-Travel Restriction. For Love, Earth's deadly emotional weapon, is a ghastly cosmic force that threatens the integrity of the totality of the Hell Cosmos.

It is indeed a truism that the Divine Hatred of Hell, when weakened, diluted or unused, must dwindle and eventually die of attrition. Once a demon is infected with the virus of Empathy, the Love Bacteria multiply exponentially, destroying the evil purity of a demon's consciousness, for the all-encompassing emotion of love requires a weaker mode of Perception, much less focused, violent and linearly powerful than is the magnificent power of Pure Hatred. *And Power, as all Demons know, Is Life.*

And so, my deplorable wife, unless in the future I am somehow able to either despise you, or penetrate the Astral Realm where, as the Vile Ancients spoke, the dead have evolved into Glowing Balls of Luminescent Darkness, this sorrowful glitch in Hell's time-travel precludes us gathering our energy clouds together again, to form our intimate Storm Cloud of Divine Hate.

In sum, my Exquisitely Foul Soul-Mate, the Fates have constructed an impassible obstacle between us, and I shall see thee, my hateful, cosmic *love*, nevermore.

I believe my recent realization of this fact, after years of malevolent hunger for thee, has been the recipe for my fresh batch of terrifying dreams. For this past week, in dense, eldritch nightmares, I have been visited by our dead son Jack, the jackal fetus who accidentally killed the American President, the billionaire whoremaster beloved by Earth's perpetually brain-washed group-mind of dullards who bask in baleful stupidity,[2] and who, notably, was the losing eleventh celebrity choice in the *Feast of Fear's* popularity contest.

My detectable darling, last night the ghost of our premature son strangely manifested in my wretched dreams, appearing like a fiery figure in a fifty-foot-tall blacklight poster, glowing in reds and greens, confusing my perception, for my deuteranopic color blindness replaces reds with greens in a stupefying tangle of hues. As his astral form coagulated, I discerned that Jack was dressed like a computer programmer, with thick glasses, a Grateful Dead T-shirt, shorts and flip-flops. With a terrifying intimacy he confirmed he had once been my son, but was now a mysterious ghost-fetus borne by galactic winds, drawn to his father's dreams.

Our astral progeny bore a message, spewed from his half-formed lips, covered with a lip balm made of radioactive cosmic dust, which gave his pronunciation an annoying, watery lisp. The message he bore was uncanny and, even in sleep, gave me goosebumps. For in an echoing voice, he announced that I, his father, was destined to become not only ruler of Hell, but supreme ruler of all dimensions of reality.

I was shocked and confused, unable to speak. Jack smiled, moved closer, and whispered, *"Father, Satan will fail. You must find a replacement for him, someone to rule Hell in his place. When you do that, my Lord, a secret will be revealed to you, a secret imbued with such Supreme Falsity that it will unfold your destiny, an opportunity to wipe every wisp of goodness from the Universe, allowing Pure Evil Eternal to reign supreme."*

Imagine, my despised consort of coitus, my shock and amazement, as I awoke from this intense astral encounter, lying in Satan's bed chamber in a pool of sweat, blood, urine and shit, so affected was my Black Soul by my Dream Son's strange and evocative prophecy.

What shall proceed from the prescience of this night-terror, O Debbie, I know not; but as I sit in the dead of night in my silken *Rocko's Modern Life* pajamas and fitfully scribe these words to my non-existent Mistress of the Myst, I tremble with wonder. But now the Cloud of Unknowing again engulfs me, returning me the to ravenous nightmare and my hungry tormentor, my Jackal son, who devours my mind in dreams of destiny, death and resurrection.

Fare thee badly, my wife, lost to me in the depths of the dismal ethers forever,

ZYK

---

2   See Volume One, page 150 of *Encyclopaedia of Hell*, Lord Satan's vituperative screed against the laughable Race of Men, a chain of flesh long since extinct, after having been devoured by demons during Lord Satan's Conquest of Earth.

ABRA KADAB
WITNESSES THE
CREATION OF SATAN[1]
EXCERPT FROM
THE INFERNAL JOURNAL
OF ABRA KADAB

I begin at the beginning, my creation. My Supreme Infamy was due to the fact that I was the first astral demiurge that Satan fabricated from his own mind-stuff, when he first created Hell. Thus I was a sort of Test-Model for what would later become the archetypal demonic somatotype, for I was mainly an amoebic blackness with blinking eyes. Thus Satan molded and engineered my consciousness in a slapdash way, like the mentation creation of an Egregore or Golem, shaping my astral essence into the first of the Djin lineage of demonic spirits. Satan endowed me, and subsequent Djin, with a simple mindset ruled by mindless obedience to my ineffable creator, Lord and King, the magnificent paragon of vituperation, Satan.[2]

Knowing he could trust me to do his bidding without questioning orders, Satan dubbed me Chief Military Adjutant to the Throne of Hell, a title which was, I learned eons later, sarcastic. But despite Satan's disdain at my creation, I was his first creature, Satan's right-hand demon, his most adoring fanboy and most despised toady.

As a boon to me, his first mind-birthed child, Satan conjured me a magnificent gift: the first Hellcraft, a vehicle which traveled not merely through space but through space-time, later to become the standard transportation for fleets of Demon Invaders across all temporal and spatial dimensions. However, this gifting was to turn out badly.

What transpired, O Demon Reader, was this: In love with my Mystic Lord, but too in awe

---

1   The infamous Abra Kadab begins the Preface to his shitty, self-absorbed memoir as follows:
"*O Demons of Impeccable Rage, hereby I commence my Infernal Journal. I Abra Kadab, the first Egregorian Demiurge created wholly from Lord Satan's Mind-Stuff, was assassinated by the wretch Zyk of Asimoth at the crucifixion of Jesus, but via a preordained Spell have arisen as a Black Spirit to take claw to parchment and compose my autobiography entitled* The Infernal Journal. *I hereby inaugurate my wretched memoir to inspire pain and depression in my Readers. Here begins the chronicle of the first Demon to be created, as well as the first to be banished from Hell, now deceased, and reminiscing.*"
    From its inauspicious opening lines, Kadab's wan screed quickly degenerates.
2   Editor's Note: Although it is obvious, repetitive and annoying to do so, I must point out the universal agreement regarding the horribleness of Kadab's writing. For a peculiar news story came to dark in Hell in which a book club of demon readers, addicted to the awfulness of Kadab's book, would read passages aloud from his memoir in basements and roar laughing at his utter stupidity. Obsessed with his book, hundreds of them donned Abra Kadab masks, time-traveled to Kadab's Palace of Displeasure in the Hollow Earth. There they roused the ghost of the senile demon from hibernation, demanded that he autograph their copies while they showered him with sarcastic praise for his literary techniques and gifted him with cases of Murine. Finally they refused to leave unless Kadab married them to show a reciprocity of affections. Kadab's ghost, blind to ironic humor, had his demon valet Belladonna Blackmoth perform a group marriage, wedding him to over eight hundred of his fanboy demons. See "The Cult of Kadab," *Car Battery Clamps Attached to the Genitals Monthly*, Vol. 60, Issue 16.

to address him directly, I sought to know his complete works and workings. The chief question was, of course, how did Satan get started in his illustrious career as Creator of Evil? All that I knew of Satan's past was from poring over his lurid autobiography, required reading at Hell University. In his introduction to that lurid and terrifying tome, Satan said of his own origin that he "manifested spontaneously by his own will to fulfil the universe's need for Pure Evil, which is the primary, spontaneous substance in the mystery of creation."[3]

This mystical story of Satan's origin was burned into the black brain-wiring of all Students of Evil, and whetted my sycophantic appetite to commune with my idol. But I yearned to witness my idol's first moments of existence, to personally if not intimately experience his actual creation as he first bloomed into being, so that I could blog about it from my Mother's basement.

So when Lord Satan was busy skeet-shooting cherubs on the Dog-Star Sirius, I stole the keys from his desk and took my first unsupervised Hellcraft ride into the depths of time to witness the birth of Satan. Enthralled with the thought of seeing the truth with my own bloodshot eyes, I jerry-rigged the time control mechanism and set the when/where parameters as far back as they could go. I turned the key in the ignition with trembling claws and lo! The gears of the time engines hissed, squeaked and backfired as I soared back in time into the murky depths of the Primordial Emptiness—the Time-Void which Demon Mystics say contained all possible Reality Outcomes in potential form. I had arrived at this time-destination, before the Hell Cosmos Itself was created, wherein began the first cymatic vibrations of Evil Creation.[4]

Giddy with the excitement every young demon feels when thinking about his Lord and Creator, I conjured a Spell to cloak my presence, and patiently veered left and right through the side streets of time, seeking Satan's first appearance. Eons of strange, uncanny sights and sounds roared by to the left of me, whizzed by to the right of me, soaked Lord Satan's Hellcraft in the primordial soup of diluvian mud, the mucilaginous blood, semen and glandular juices of myriad ancient creatures, finally tossed and rocked madly in a roaring tempest of shrieking winds and baseball-sized hailstones smashing the Hellcraft on all sides through a Hurricane of Time, until, finally, I arrived at the right temporal coordinates.

I had arrived at the precise moment to witness the most astonishing thing in the history of Hell—the moment in which Satan was created.

A vast glowing creature appeared, and was clawing at its own head. Somehow, from my hidden perspective, I was witnessing the most horrible thing in the cosmos. I was witnessing the moment of Satan's creation. What I saw happen then was incomprehensible. Eons later, it still makes the hoary hairs on my buttocks and thorax stand on end in utter disgust and horror. My young, demonic brain was barely able to process the unthinkable birth I was witnessing.

---

3   *Fear Me: The Monstrous Memories of Satan*, Preface, page xxiii.
4   This took some complex calculations on my part, for the stolen craft's time-controls were still primitive, not having yet evolved into the present advanced state of modern Black Magic Technologies™.

An adolescent Abra Kadab's illicit joyride to Satan's past.

The spectacle was of such visceral, indescribable madness that I shuddered and blacked out. I apparently fell upon my controls, which luckily sailed me forward in time, back to my default starting coordinates. Upon waking, having materialized back in Satan's garage, I was shaking violently, my thoughts popping like an electric popcorn popper. All at once I began bawling, moaning, sobbing uncontrollably. Right then and there I had a mental and emotional breakdown.

Satan found me lying in a fetal position in a corner of the garage, still shaking, babbling and raving about the unspeakable thing I had seen. He checked the odometer and realized I had taken his craft into the restricted areas of time and had suffered a temporal shock. Furious that I had stolen his car and somehow gone mad, he conjured the Hell Insane Asylum into existence, with me as its first and sole inmate.

Of course, I revealed to my therapist what I had witnessed, but these depositions were kept from Satan's purview, so as not to arouse his rage. The memory of What I Saw was ultimately erased from my demonic brain lobes, expunged utterly in a series of powerful shock therapies, wiping the infinite horror I had witnessed from my memory.

After eons of therapy in the asylum, I was finally deemed evil enough, and therefore sane enough, to face criminal charges by the Time Tribunal, a panel of demons formed by Satan specifically to deal with my time crimes. These crimes included Theft of a Time Vehicle, Harassment of Superior Beings, Invasion of Privacy, Stalking, and Interfering with Classified Intel, in this case, the ultimate unspeakable secret regarding Satan's origin.

As expected, the Tribunal sentenced me to death. This sentence, however, was commuted to Exile by the demon tribunal jurist Concentric Circularum, because I owed him money, and how could he be paid back if I did not exist? Thus, in the court of Hell, the Tribunal sentenced me to Banishment on the most odious planet in its time-density, the Detestable Orb of Earth. The sentence required I wear an ankle bracelet that restricted my presence there to Earth's prehistoric era, whence began mankind's evolution, the era when the planet began to radiate a terrible odor, namely the emerging stench of the human race.

Thus was I banished to spend eternity on an insignificant planet, in the shadow of my once prestigious, and now worthless, career as Hell's first and foremost Egregorian Enchanter.

As part of my self-rehabilitation program, I hollowed out the center of the Earth, and therein conjured a black obsidian edifice, The Palace of Displeasure, as my permanent living quarters. There I resumed my occult studies, experimenting with conjuring various Spells, each designed to make Earth vaguely tolerable for a demon of my age, stature and allergies. The Spell with the highest priority was a Spell to make human flesh taste better, so that I could engorge myself on the flesh of primitive humanity, and sate my voracious appetite, and the appetite of my occasional demon dinner guests, should they be willing to make the schlep, especially with all that astral time-traffic.

So it is that upon the eve of Satan's invasion of Earth (as chronicled in *Encyclopaedia of Hell*, Book 1), when Lord Zyk time-traveled to research Earth's greatest evil moments,

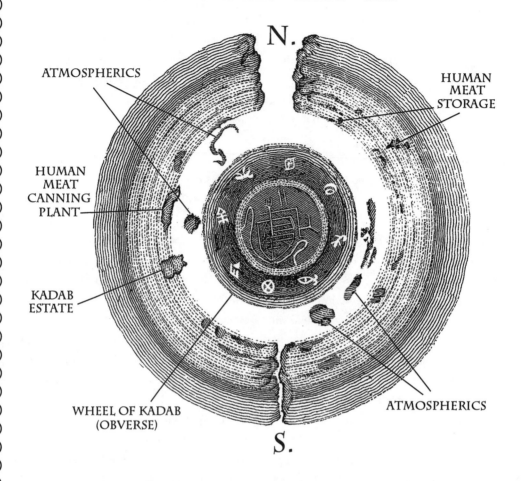

Diagram of Abra Kadab's Hollow Earth

I viciously attacked him for invading my new home, without permission or without first email-ing the proper paperwork.[5]

Of course, Satan's Invasion of Earth occurred at a time-frame eons after my homestead-ing here. My asexual intercourse with Lord Zyk continued long after my death at his hands, whereupon our destinies became forever entwined in a Battle to the Death at the Crucifixion of Jesus in the Garden of Gethsemane.[6]

But Death's hold on my soul would not be enough to stop me from my deepest desire. I would have my revenge on Zyk of Asimoth, my soul's execrable, eternal enemy.

---

5   The repeated battles of Zyk of Asimoth and Abra Kadab were recorded in all their evil glory in *Encyclopaedia of Hell*, Book 1, pgs. 20, 27, 70.
6   Ibid. page 179.

LORD ZYK'S MEMO
CONCERNING THE
SECRET PROPHECY
OF
THE WHEEL *OF* KADAB

MEMO TO	**FROM**
MORTIMER PÖNÇÉ, ESQ.	**ZYK OF ASIMOTH, EDITOR**
PUBLISHER, MIND CONTROL PRESS	LORD ZYK OF ASIMOTH
HELL HOLE WEST	EARTH INVASION HEADQUARTERS
CITY OF HELL	THE PENTAGON
	ARLINGTON, VIRGINIA

Detestable Mr. Pöncé,

I must begin by explaining that even the memory of our cherished enmity has been compromised with forgetfulness, like a crashed, antique laptop, for my neuron paths have been overshadowed by recent stupendous events which I shall now relate, events which have created a forked path in the nightmare of my destiny.[1]

I am a demon exhausted, akin to a quail that has repeatedly been shot from a cannon. Why? Because for too long my evil vitality was being sucked dry as I attempted in vain to supervise the commerce, architecture, infrastructure and weaponry of both Hell and Earth simultaneously. As you may recall, in *Encyclopaedia of Hell*, of which I was Editor-in-Chief, Lord Satan defined *Earth* as "An entity factory, notorious throughout the galaxy for producing substandard product." Verily, I found it necessary to time-ship more and more demon

---

1   Editor's Note: Like Abra Kadab in prehistoric times, Lord Zyk was also castigated by his demonic peers. See *Lord Zyk, the Butt-Hurt Hipster of Hell: The Rambling Reign of Satan II* by R. Goiter, Hell Hole Press.

troops to Earth to stop the insurrections of substandard mankind with an Iron Fist. And what, my friend of filth, is more satisfying than crushing idiot humans with an Iron Fist?[2]

The point is (and I appreciate the opportunity to gripe about this), I was exhausted from the endless duties of evil, busy doing nonstop evil this and nonstop evil that. Perforce, I was sapped of energy, like a serial killer dragging a plus-size model into a ravine. I did my best to administer hateful and corrupt leadership qualities, but am now mentally depleted.

True, I was able to ease my stress once, twice or thrice a week by slowly lowering giant tacos on ropes filled with screaming elderly humans into my shark tank. Even slathering them with hot sauce, thus heightening their shrieks, did nothing to energize my tattered spirits. For my emotions were torn by *them,* the quisling mutating invaders in my torso, my apostate beating spleen, its relentless rhythm constantly reminding me that I was going mad, awash with fits of terrible, humanlike emotions.

But things shifted radically after I attended a meeting in Vatican City to discuss the tedious topic of human meat storage. While leaving the meat-canning meeting, I was surprised to see Jesus of Nazareth approaching me out of the blue. The last time I had seen him was years ago when I freed him and Agnetha the ABBA singer from the *Feast of Fear* ovens and told them to run for the hills. His face still showed evidence of burn marks from the ovens, but his still-chubby belly belied a healthy recovery from being nearly baked to death.

For demons steeped in amusing time-travel trivia, Jesus was the figurehead of Earth's conservative Christian cult.[3] I am likely deluded, Mr. Pöncé, but through the years, my many chance meetings with Jesus made me feel that he and I were somehow destined to work together, so powerful and uncanny were our cosmic convergences.[4]

So here I was, have just left the most boring meeting in the world, when Jesus, wearing Adidas and a cute Tate and McHallahan tennis outfit, accosted me in the hall. At first, I didn't recognize him, for now he was clean-shaven and a little pudgier than I'd remembered. But when he whispered to me, I recognized his marble-mouth voice, saying that he needed to speak with me.

I am always annoyed if anyone talking to me uses the phrase *I need.* But Jesus and I had already shared novel experiences in several different time-densities. I knew him in this

---

2   "Killing humans is satisfying but not always fun. Since they are ensconced in the illusory world of matter, they have zero understanding of Black Magic, or any other real knowledge, and therefore easily succumb to enchantment." From the article "Sport Killing of Humans for Profit" by Baloo Blóchenspeil, *Hunting Humans Monthly,* p. 73.

3   Interestingly, Jesus was unique as the only Forbes Five-Star cult leader who was also a bona fide Doppelgänger. Genetic duplications or non-biological, identical twins, also known as Time Doppelgängers, occurred regularly on Earth, but were rarely if ever noticed, since temporal twins were separated on Earth by an average of 1,900 years. Jesus' Doppelgänger, born roughly 1900 years after Jesus' approximate birth date, was a stage performer named Buddy Hackett.

4   In their first fateful encounter, Lord Zyk, while time-traveling on Earth, unknowingly dropped a copy of Satan's hateful masterpiece *Encyclopaedia of Hell* into Jesus' teenage hands. Jesus studied and plagiarized Satan's Evil Parables therein and, in Satan's words, "reworked them, reversing the messages in an absurdly positive, saccharine form." This was the first of several time-intersections between Zyk and Jesus. Stranger still was the coincidence that Jesus' Doppelgänger Buddy Hackett was Lord Satan's favorite human comedian.

time-loop to be a harmless, albeit socially awkward, failed prophet. Therefore I agreed to listen to his whining for three minutes precisely, and dramatically set my phone alarm to make my point. *Jesus, you have three minutes starting—NOW!*

With surprising charisma, despite his cartoonish voice, he launched into his story, catching me up on his new career as a children's party magician. He mentioned in passing that he also had an interest in *real* magic, and was a hobbyist in the nuances of ancient and arcane magical languages.

He explained that he and Agnetha, the ABBA blonde, had stolen a time machine parked outside the Feast and returned to Nazareth to his own original timeline. There Jesus and Agnetha had lived as roommates with benefits for the past two years. She had changed her name to Mary Magdalene and became Jesus' stage assistant. Together they performed magic shows up and down the Red Sea Children's Show Circuit, developing a fresh act with innovative tricks with quaint names like *The Multiplying Loaves and Fishes* and *Water Into Wine.*

I narrowed my eyes and gestured for him to get to the infernal point. Speeding up his discourse, he said that despite their success as performers, a secret something had been aching at the core of his soul. It was his knowledge, as a result of his inculcation at the Feast of Fear, that in the future, Earth would be enslaved by demons. He became obsessed with this terrible secret. It began affecting his sleep patterns, which affected the quality of his magic shows. Mary/Agnetha suggested that he do something about it. So with her approval, Jesus fired up the stolen time machine and went on a solo mission to the future to find me.

"What have I to do with your sentimental sorrow? Your species is an embarrassment to all living beings. This is the Hell Cosmos, Jesus. Buckle up." I eyed my timepiece. "Your three minutes are up. Goodbye."

I turned but he gently grabbed my elbow, stopping me. He boldly looked straight into my eyes and said, "I came to find you because you didn't eat us. You set us free. I know there's hope for my people if you are in charge. If mankind is destined to be conquered by demons, I want to help them somehow. I want to see their struggle for myself, and somehow help my people."

All at once something came over me, and I knew exactly what it was. It was the *magentic field,* again distorting my thoughts and emotions into the horror of caring. My thumping spleen began beating loudly, like an anatomical vampire taking over my body, but instead of pumping black bile, it was pumping waterfalls of sentiment.

I fought off these perverse feelings with every iota of my being. Finally gaining control, I grabbed Jesus' tennis shirt in a fury and hissed through clenched teeth: "Your people are doomed, doomed, doomed!" I slapped his pudgy face back and forth with each *doomed.* "It's my job to slice and dice all of idiot mankind and store them in cans as processed meat!" I shoved him against the wall, slapped him again for good measure and kicked him in the groin, my horns shaking as I fought to control the spleen pounding out of my chest like a wolf in a cartoon.

To my discredit, everything I had told him was true. One of my duties as temporary King of Earth was to maintain the feeding of the new demon population by the canning and storing of human meat.

To that end, the ancient demon Abra Kadab, my amorphous, black enemy with a thousand glowing eyes, had supplied the answer. I am the supreme expert on Kadab, since I battled him twice, in claw-to-tentacle combat, once in Hitler's bunker, and once at the crucifixion of Jesus. And it was at the crucifixion where I annihilated him.[5]

Lord Satan had banished Kadab to antediluvian Earth for Time-Crimes. There Kadab began a new life. Upon finding that human flesh tasted terrible to the demon palate, he researched obscure enchantments and came upon an ancient Spell to improve the taste of ape's testicles. He deballed an ape and sauteed its undercarriage to test the Spell's efficacy. In his hated memoir,[6] Kadab describes the Spell, and his astonishment making the simian testicles indescribably delicious, so luscious that Kadab worked himself up into an orgiastic frenzy whilst savoring the ape balls in his mouth, rolling them around with his forked tongue until, trembling with excitement, his thirteen corkscrew-shaped mating reservoirs became tumescent and squirted green, inky acid on the walls and ceiling, causing them to catch fire. This was the highest compliment a demon of Kadab's lineage could pay to the excellence of a meal. The next day, Kadab gushed about his excitement upon testing the Spell on a human leg. After one bite of the juicy fibula, Kadab moaned in ecstasy, sending out a telepathic announcement to his demonic posse in all time-densities: *I have found the most delectable dish in the universe!*

On the basis of this groundbreaking culinary discovery, Kadab hollowed out a vast underground lab, and within it conjured a monolithic stone wheel about a mile high, the notorious *Wheel of Kadab*. The Spell carved magical pictograms on one side of the giant Wheel representing the Incantation for Ape Testicles. To put his scheme in motion, he performed an anti-gravity ritual, causing the giant stone wheel to levitate and slowly revolve. As soon as the Wheel turned, Kadab felt the Spell kick in as powerful plumes of evil energy radiated up through the crust of the Earth to the flesh of the surface dwellers, hopefully transforming their bad-tasting gore into delectable meat.

Kadab's first human taste-test was a kidnapped human named Jimmy Hoffa. It was a triumphant success. Mixed with mushrooms, Hoffa's roasted viscera took on a magical flavor unlike anything Kadab had ever tasted before.

Knowing he had struck culinary gold, Kadab continued hollowing out the planet's

5   See Zyk's account of this incident in *Encyclopaedia of Hell*, page 177.
6   See *The Infernal Journal of Abra Kadab*, page 2,952.

core and constructed a secret compound, erecting a magnificent black cathedral which he christened *The Displeasure Palace.* In his underground lab, in cahoots with a bohemian human designer named Dr. Seuss, Kadab conjured the nuts and bolts of a giant, whirling, meat-storage mechanism connected to a series of whirling, Seussian canning contraptions[7]. Using conveyor belts and quickly-moving mechanical hands with incredible precision, the contraption cut, gutted and decapitated the men, women and children Kadab had kidnapped. With the machine's rotating wheels, pulleys and blood-draining gutters, Kadab was able to efficiently slice, dice and store a dozen human carcasses each month.

Kadab became famous not only for his cooking and canning, but also for throwing notorious cocktail parties in his majestic palace. There he invited Hell's lowest and worst to a series of debauched, Dionysian soirées, where he served a delicious array of scurrilous intoxicants and inhuman delicacies. Unfortunately, I was never invited, since I was a scholar and a poet, and was definitely not a foodie; I lived on a conservative diet of one human baby per week and never yearned for anything exotic. I would read about Kadab's drunken adventures online, and as his renown grew, demon foodies traveled from the darkest sectors of creation to devour the delicacy of human flesh. The demand grew so great that Kadab had to conjure up thought-form beings, egregores and tulpas, as astral slaves to hunt and trap stray men, women and children all around the globe, kidnapping them from church picnics, scouting hikes and hunting expeditions, strapping their hapless flesh to his whirring conveyor belts where their meat was quickly processed, delighting and dazzling the drunken appetites of his loathsome dinner guests.

But once I killed Kadab, all that ended, and his palace was abandoned. Kadab's secret cannery had been closed ever since and was covered with cobwebs. For this reason I told the cannery committee, of which I was Chairman, that due to my personal vendetta against Kadab, I would personally conjure a Spell to penetrate his Cathedral, inspect his notorious slicing and dicing machine and find a human guinea pig with whom I'd test the canning equipment. If it was still functional, I would take charge of the operation, appoint a team of demon butchers and get the underground slaughterhouse open for business, processing human flesh steaks, ground intestines, brain burgers and groin hotdogs to feed the ever-growing number of demon tourists now time-immigrating from Hell to Earth.

But I digress.

As I said, I managed to fight off my spleen's disgusting bursts of sentiments, and began slapping Jesus around. Back in control of my hatred, I refused his pitiable request to

---

7   Despite their enormous cultural differences, the beloved human children's author Dr. Seuss made a blood agreement that if Kadab cast a Spell ensuring Seuss' financial success, in return Seuss would refine and redesign Kadab's Human Meat Slicing and Dicing Machine, as well as deliver four overweight children a month (procured from his fan club roster) to the rear door of Kadab's Palace.

somehow help Humanity, when something unexpected occurred: Jesus cast me a deeply sorrowful look, then began to sob as if his heart would break.

Demons never gulp, for gulping is a sign of vulnerability. But looking at those sad, tear-stained eyes, I gulped. Jesus was a mere human ignoramus, but he did have a talent few possess: to create a bridge of sympathy by using the expressive power of his eyes, the most soulful eyes I believe I have ever seen. If he wanted something badly enough, he'd cast those big glims on you, and cry. And when he did that, you simply wanted to please him. But I was determined to fight back. As he poured on the tears, I resisted both his tears and the persistent beating of my freakish, freshly sprouted heart. And as I resisted, *a delightfully evil thought came into my head.* It was a thought so heinous, it bolstered my willpower to defeat and humiliate the naïve Nazarene:

We needed to test a carcass on Kadab's slicing machine. What better guinea pig than the Swine of Love, the Ultimate Sacrificial Fool?

It would be a delicious, evil irony if the self-proclaimed Savior of Man was used to calibrate the machine that would destroy all Mankind.

"I tell you what," I told him what, "I was a tad rough back there, slapping you around like that. Allow me to make it up to you. I am returning to the Las Vegas Nexus if you want to accompany me and see if we can devise an alternate plan for the fate of humans, other than eating them. But first I need to make a stop elsewhere and do a quick test on some equipment."

Jesus fell for it, hook, line and sinker, sobbed happily and kissed my cheek in gratitude. He whipped out his cell, speed-dialed "Mary" and gushed that they had been right about me, that I was going to give him a chance to be the savior of mankind. It was a delicious moment of freedom from the emotions of my hideous heart and I wanted to savor the trenchancy of his delusion. I tried not to smile as I slowly and dramatically drew a sigil in the air, recited the vibratory sounds necessary to conjure a portal and summarily activated it.

The gleaming portal engulfed us. Jesus and I dematerialized and reappeared at the Gates of Abra Kadab's underground Cathedral. The magnificent Black Palace of Displeasure occupied an enormous, dark cavern, faintly illuminated by rows of torches[8] and interior-decorated with fire pits, skittering colonies of bats, bubbling lava pools, all accompanied by an unbearable, sulphurous stench. Kadab had chemically designed the stench to match the stench of his boyhood neighborhood in Hell, the overall effect orchestrated to bring back memories of his youth. And who among us does not yearn for a return to the stench of his youth? And Kadab's banishment meant that he could return to Hell no more, except via this elaborate simulacrum, an immersive special-effects experience reproducing the sights, sounds and smells of the Hell Time-Density, his lost home.

---

8   As are most rooms, of course, in these ancient, atmospheric histories.

Abra Kadab's cocktail party, unveiling his Human-Meat-Canning Machine.

I could see Jesus' amazement as I yanked the black sheet off the massive, iron Slicing and Dicing Machine. In awe at the sight, his eyes bugged out from his turgid, lopsided Buddy Hackett head. It was the elaborate mechanism of death designed by Earth's inventive child-hater Dr. Seuss. I was flushed with anticipation, eager to get to the part in our little pageant when I suddenly strap Jesus to the Seussian conveyor belt.

I should mention, Mr. Pöncé, that Kadab's lava pits had made the rooms hot as Hell. Thus, to torture Jesus further, on the pretext of giving him a tour, I led him into an even hotter chamber, the mile-high cavern housing the legendary Wheel of Kadab.

To put Jesus' mind at ease, I casually prattled on about Kadab. That I had always been fascinated by my old enemy, that until he went mildly senile, he had been Hell's most vicious warrior in the Black Arts. That is to say, before I killed him. I also explained that human flesh used to be inedible by demons, until Kadab conjured the giant, stone Wheel before us, which transformed human meat into a supreme delicacy.[9]

At this point the heat from the fire pits and lava pools was too hot for a human, and Jesus staggered, sweating as if he was going to be baked again. Fortunately, Kadab had long ago installed a giant fan and I clicked it on to simulate sympathy. Jesus was relieved as the breeze fluttered his long hair whilst he stared at the slowly turning Wheel, mesmerized by the mysterious hieroglyphs carved into its stone face. He wiped off beads of sweat as he walked around, curious, to observe the Wheel's opposite side. Carved onto its obverse was a fainter set of glyphs, which I had assumed were decorative, meaningless pictograms. I would later realize the deadly consequences of my ignorance.

At the moment, my scheme to kill and can Jesus was proceeding as planned.

Until the horror arose again in my torso. It begins as a sudden tingling and delicate softening of my senses. I am speaking, of course, of the effects of Earth's *magentic field* subverting my evil homeostasis. I fought off this perverse field as best I could. I could feel my thoughts becoming deranged, as I began to actually believe that murder was unseemly, instead of the supreme evil pleasure of existence.

Eyeing the mysterious carvings on the other side, Jesus was now at ease. A student of codes and ancient hieroglyphs, he was fascinated by the pictograms and raised his torch to better illuminate them. With growing excitement, he said he recognized some of the characters. "It seems to be a religious prophecy of some kind…" He began a rough, halting translation: "*For as the first shall become last… and the last become first… it is prophesied that Zyk of Asimoth, the least qualified to lead hell, and the weakest and lowliest of all demons…*"

I was stunned. "What? It mentions *me*? How is that even possible?"

Jesus shrugged and continued: "*Zyk… the fool… the miscreant…*"

---

9   Refer to the chart entitled *The Taste and Edibility of Human Flesh* by the despised Gourmet Behemoth (pg. 11, Vol. 1 of *Encyclopaedia of Hell*). Some of Hell's leading Gastronomes, however, rejected this chart when it was revealed that Behemoth's three tongues had been bitten off by a Screech Imp seeking to make a home by burrowing into his sinus cavity.

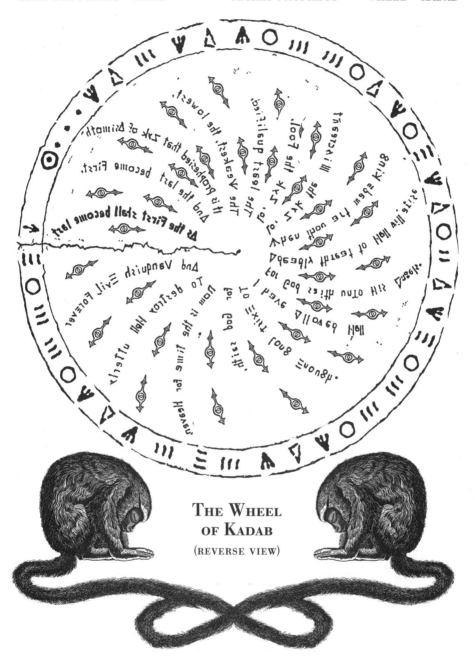

THE WHEEL
OF KADAB
(REVERSE VIEW)

"Okay, right, I get it! Get to the prophecy!"

He continued: "—-will become King of Hell. When that comes to pass, the greatest threat to the Hell Kingdom will arise, and that threat will be…"

He paused, so I yelled, "What? What threat?"

Jesus rubbed his eyes and said the glyphs were faded there, and the spinning of the

Wheel made it difficult to read. But I was chomping at the bit to hear the rest and told him to bloody well hurry up.

As Jesus turned his back to me and continued translating, an uncanny, glittering black fog materialized next to me. The smoke swirled intricately, at last congealing into the Ghost of Abra Kadab, the Infamous Demon with a Thousand Eyes, architect of the hollow Earth and sorcerer of the Wheel of Kadab.

Kadab's Ghost raised to his full terrifying height and whispered for us to leave at once, his voice growling faintly through dimensions with a metallic, phase-shifting sound.

I forgot all about my plan to murder Jesus, for another confrontation with Kadab loomed. His Ghost felt even more powerful than his physical presence had been, perhaps because his astral form could absorb the Evil with which he had poisoned his home in the past. With a roar he materialized a scimitar and slashed it back and forth, trying to decapitate me. I too materialized a scimitar and slashed back, our weapons clanging and hissing, knocking things over as we battled across the cavern. Kadab's spiritual force was mighty, and my power dwindled due to his immense fury. Opening his huge mouth, he blasted a powerful roar that lifted me into the air and slammed me up against the cavern wall.

Somehow Jesus was still unaware of the battle, so focused was he on translating the mysterious glyphs by torchlight. I heard his voice echoing through the cavern as he continued translating the prophecy over the sounds of our skirmish:

"—*When Zyk becomes King, the greatest threat to Hell will arise, for God will say unto his Angels, I have allowed Hell to exist long enough. Now is the time for—*"

Kadab sliced my right leg off at the knee. I toppled backwards into a large cooking vat filled with crumbling human skeletons.

I screamed at Jesus, "*The time for what? For what?*"

I struggled to climb free of the bowl of skeletons, but my oddly-shaped posterior was stuck between the madhouse of bones.

Gratified to see me trapped, Kadab's ghost widened its thousand eyes and grinned in victory. With six tentacles wrapped around its hilt, he raised the scimitar over his head to slice me in two vertically, starting with the skull, and whispered, "*Revenge is all!*"

My groin was now tumescent, so anxious was I to hear the rest of the prophecy. I screamed at Jesus, "*TIME FOR WHAT?*"

Jesus yelled back, translating: "*THE TIME FOR GOD TO DESTROY HELL UTTERLY, AND THUS VANQUISH EVIL FOREVER.*"

As Kadab's scimitar hissed down to slice my skull, I was utterly shocked by the prophecy. Satan had trusted me, and now under my watch Hell would be destroyed? Proving that my critics were right, that I was but a dilettante, a pretentious clown, unqualified to rule Hell?

Whilst Jesus translates the Ancient Wheel, Lord Zyk battles the ghost of Abra Kadab to the death.

In that instant, I somehow sensed the depths of another organ, my faux heart, and found there an unexpected well of strength. I screamed back at the ghost, causing my strangely-shaped buttocks to flex with rage—and the skeletons shattered! Freed, adrenaline coursing through my gore, I grabbed his descending scimitar, wrenched it free from him and began slicing it back and forth in a frenzy, hacking the ghost's astral form into jagged shards of smoke, still vaguely hanging together in Kadab's shape, trying to reunite like confused, ghostly amoebas.

Jesus finally turned and saw what had happened. Thinking fast, as Nazarenes do, he leapt from the top of the stepladder to the giant fan and switched it from LOW to HIGH. The fan blasted a formidable wind, blowing the slices of Kadab's smoky essence away into a spiral of oblivion.

Exhausted, I fell to my knees, dropping the scimitar which clattered and sparked across the stone floor. Out of breath, I looked up at the Wheel's glyphs. I heard Jesus' voice in my mind echoing the prophecy: "NOW IS THE TIME FOR GOD TO DESTROY HELL UTTERLY, AND TO VANQUISH EVIL FOREVER."

No God was going to destroy Hell, my hated home, not while I was in charge. This, Mr. Pöncé, was the moment when I decided not to slice, dice and can Jesus' meat, but rather to put his mottled human carcass to work. He would be the perfect patsy to relieve 80% of my stress by taking over my atrocious job of running Hell. I knew I could seduce him into accepting with his new title, *Jesus, Lord of Hell.* "What better way, Jesus, to stop evil, than to be in charge of it?" With Jesus running Hell in any manner he pleased, I was free to leave Hell in my wake as I conjured my stupendous new destiny. For this was the moment when my tiny heart embraced a New Mandate of Evil: *The Supremacy of Hell Requires the Conquest of Heaven.*

I shall update you anon, Enemy of Filth.

With Subliminal and Overt Radiations of Loathing, I remain

ZYK

LORD ZYK *AND* RAMONA IYAM
REPLENISH
THE ARSENAL *OF* HELL
EXCERPT FROM
THE DEVIANT *AND* UNSATISFYING
FOLKTALES *OF* HELL

COMPILED & TRANSLATED BY HARGOBIND THE RAPACIOUS,
ADJUNCT PROFESSOR OF ABHORRENT HISTORIES
UNIVERSITY OF HELL, WEST.

Lo! As the tale is told, behold Lord Zyk, the new King of Hell!

Having revealed his invasion plan to his lieutenants, he retired wearily to his royal bedroom, formerly the private chambers of Satan. With his master gone, Lord Zyk of Asimoth, now Lord of Hell, was entranced by his new home at the heart of evil. In a fever of smug satisfaction, such as one feels when about to declare war, he first attended to some unfinished business. He had always desperately desired to possess *The Amulet of Adam*, Lord Satan's most prized trophy. Now, alone in Satan's royal chambers, this was his chance. Lord Zyk rifled through every drawer, seeking that which he so deeply coveted. However, after upending every nook and cranny and finding nothing, he instead took down a bottle of Satan's most prized liqueur and poured it into a crystal goblet upon Satan's writing desk.

As he drank, he paraphrased Lord Satan's *Encyclopaedia of Hell* (of which he was Editor-in-Chief) which defined Alcohol as "A hallucinatory escape hatch through which one escapes from the Unspeakable Prison of Himself." Emptying the glug down his throat, he got down to business. He shoved Satan's silken brocaded buttocks pillow between his rump and the chair, ready to compose his masterpiece, The Invasion Proclamation.

Lord Zyk scribbled his speech as his thoughts cascaded from his mind to his claw, excited as the warmth of Satan's exquisite liqueur overheated his lordly horns. At the height of his inspiration, Ramona Iyam, Hell's Chief Savant in charge of Arms Inventory, burst in, tilting and lilting as she was wont to do, her big wall-eyes fraught with fear, her eyebrows arched as for anarchy, her breath sour from ambergris and perfumery. She spluttered incoherently in a demeanor of dread, "The armory is lost! Our invasion is defeated before it is begun!"

Then she recited in her wretched voice a dirge of doggerel and despair:

"Gone is our armory of death we require
For the death of Heaven. Now smoking rubble
Sits in its place, from a cataclysm of fire.
Devoid of munitions, the Invasion's in trouble.

"Shame on those demons who, careless with smoking,
Made our munitions-keeper jobless and bedless.
You may in a rage want to kill them by choking,
But I've done it already by making them headless."

Furious at this uncanny news, Lord Zyk rushed to the Armory of Death and saw that what Ramona had sung was true; Zyk's war munitions were no more, for they were charred from a fire and had crumbled to brindled ashes. Without weaponry, Hell's armies could not attack Heaven, and Lord Zyk's invasion plan would be in ruins. He must replenish his munitions immediately. But how?

His stature as straight as the letter I, Zyk went immediately to Satan's Chamber of Contemplation. There, asking for inner, evil guidance, he pulled a tarot card from Satan's deck: the Two of Wolves. Symbolizing twice the cunning, twice the immoral, brute strength. Meditating on the card, the answer came to him:

To replenish our munitions, I must travel back in time before the fire occurred, and transport our weapons to the present. Tonight, however, is the New Moon of Horus, and the Moon's weakened luminosity through the veil of time allows only three round-trip time voyages.

Thus Zyk had but three chances to save his Invasion of Heaven. He ordered Ramona Iyam to fire up her Hellcraft and, with a battalion of demon warriors, time-travel to the armory before the fire, empty it of its weapons, and bring Hell's Bounty of Death to the Palace.

Flushed with excitement at her evil mission, Ramona led her demons to the armory, but found the door was sealed with an enchantment. To open it required Lord Satan's palm print.

Back at the Palace, Zyk was scrivening the last phrases of his Invasion Proclamation when Ramona, lilting and tilting and spluttering, as she was wont to do, came with the news, reciting it again in her raspy, pitiable voice:

"Access denied to munitions and rockets.
Sealed by magic, we are thwarted and cheated,
Now only the devil's palm print can unlock it,
Our Invasion is doomed and already defeated.

"Lord Satan is needed but cannot be gotten,
For in stealth he proceeds on his murderous mission.
Your fruits of war will soon be rotten,
For a war without guns dies of malnutrition."

Again furious, but with his stature as straight as the letter I, Zyk returned to Satan's Chamber of Contemplation. Again his mind was overshadowed with the blackest luminosity, a memory of Satan bragging to his court about his centuries as a wastrel and a drug fiend; since he was unable to die, he enjoyed simulating death through narcotics.

He leaped to Satan's *Book of Secrets*, a hellish journal detailing Satan's most evil and uncanny exploits: hunting and cooking holy men on the banks of the Amazon, going feral for decades in the Black Forest with packs of wolves, kidnapping and devouring nuns and orphans in Armenia, exploding ships and planes carrying needed medical supplies, annihilating anyone and anything getting in the way of whatever he wanted, centuries of debauchery and degenerate acts, all carefully preserved in the *Book of Secrets* for Satan to revisit in his old age.

Zyk pored through Satan's journal entries. Praying to the wisdom of an evil owl for success, he searched for a specific date, and found it—an evening when Satan had sunken into a deep coma from an excess of drugs. Thereupon Zyk called for Ramona Iyam and her men to time-travel to the armory the night before the fire.

Zyk then flew his Hellcraft back in time to Satan's Age of Addiction and spied on Satan in his private chambers. He had hoped to find Satan comatose on drugs, but the evil lord was wide awake on his balcony, baying like a crazed wolf at the Moon, his eyes on fire with drugs and death, his scarlet face reflective of the sublime black moonlight, his lips moist, engorged with blood and carnelian in the violet, narcotic night.

Zyk's plan was stymied by Satan's sustained energy and lack of sleep, for it took days before the evil lord's eyes finally closed. Zyk watched with relief as Satan dropped to the stone floor in a twitching, tweaking fit before going unconscious. At this sight, Zyk's hope redoubled as he rolled up Satan in a blood-stained Persian rug, threw him over his shoulder and soared with him through time to the entrance of the armory at the appointed time.

There, Ramona Iyam showed him the security enchantment requiring Satan's palm print. Zyk unrolled Satan from the rug, but just as Zyk and Ramona held Satan's hand up to the security screen, Satan began twitching and tweaking again, jumping to his feet, his eyes crazed with a wonderment of renewed evil energy, and ran off into the woods, howling like a wolf in heat. Hereupon Zyk and Ramona took chase after their mad, screeching King.

The woods were filled with moonlit mist and marauding packs of rapacious wolves. As Zyk and Ramona pursued their lord, his feral howling, combined with his reeking stench from months of degeneracy, attracted a pack of wolves, their bellies swollen with hunger. Following his scent, they leapt upon Satan and began ripping him apart. Before Zyk and the others could stop them, the wolves tore the sinews of Satan's arms from their sockets and carried them off into the murderous night.

When Zyk and his evil horde reached Satan's armless body, Ramona's hopes were dashed and she cried plaintively to the faceless black moon:

"Our mission was moments away from fruition,
Despite Spells broken, enchantments made harmless,
Moments from stealing our own ammunition
Now thwarted by finding Lord Satan is armless.

"Perhaps the invasion is cursed and ill-fated,
Angel meat left uneaten instead of digested,
Our nightmare of conquest left unconsummated,
Paradise lost, leaving God unmolested."

Furious, Lord Zyk examined Satan's comatose, armless torso and saw that Ramona had spoken truly. The devil's arms were no more. What to do? Composing himself, Zyk stiffened and clamped his eyes shut in contemplation. An idea formed in the black luminosity of his mind. Invoking a spell, he returned to Satan's Palace, and and again opened the *Book of Secrets.* Studying the chapter about Satan going feral, he learned Satan's secret of enchanting wolves.

Thereupon Lord Zyk conjured himself back to Ramona in the forest. Casting Satan's wolf enchantment, Zyk caused two wolves to magically return, each with a mottled arm of Satan in its mouths. Zyk and Ramona subdued them and rode the wolves wildly through the wood, waving Satan's arms as they hooted and howled in victory. Reaching the armory, Zyk, Ramona and the wolves held the handprint of Satan's dismembered arms up to the security screen. The vast armory doors creaked open before them.

Ramona's demon warriors emptied the armory of their vast storehouse of weapons and shipped them back to the Palace, while Zyk re-attached Satan's arms with an imperious Spell and returned his comatose body to the past, back to the squalor of his Chamber of Debauchery.

Meanwhile Ramona, lilting and tilting and spluttering in childlike pleasure, as she was wont to do, recited the following doggerel in her hoarse and phlegmy voice:

"A lack of weapons is infuriating,
Making demons vulnerable and sterile.
But our desire for angel flesh marinating
Is satisfied by going feral.

"If angel flesh and blood shall be desired,
Be guided by guile and not false alarms.
Pilfer Weapons of Hell whenever required,
And ride wolves to retrieve dismembered arms."

Thus concludes the tale of the new King, and how he regained his lost weapons, while flailing the glorious, gory arms of Lord Satan under the New Moon of Horus.

Under the Black Moon, they rode the wild wolves carrying their booty, Satan's dismembered arms.

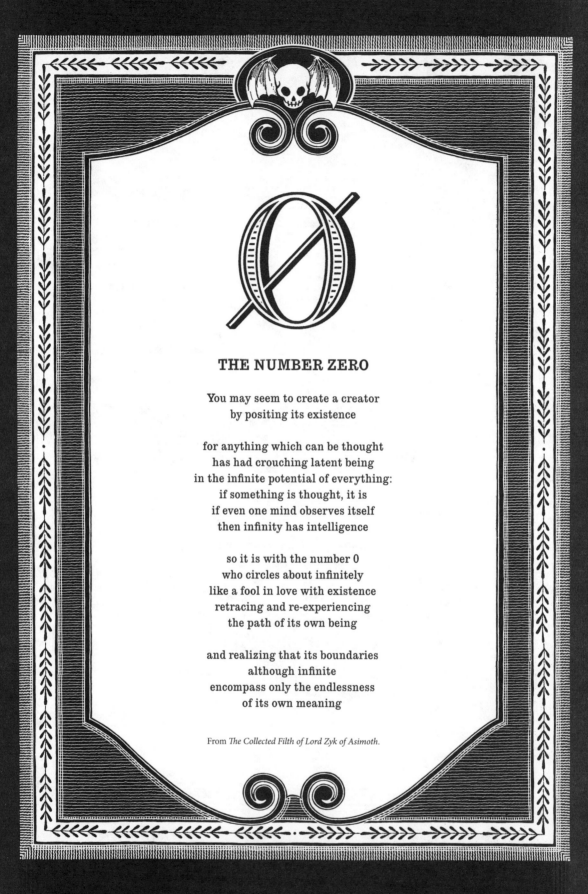

THE NUMBER ZERO

You may seem to create a creator
by positing its existence

for anything which can be thought
has had crouching latent being
in the infinite potential of everything:
if something is thought, it is
if even one mind observes itself
then infinity has intelligence

so it is with the number 0
who circles about infinitely
like a fool in love with existence
retracing and re-experiencing
the path of its own being

and realizing that its boundaries
although infinite
encompass only the endlessness
of its own meaning

From *The Collected Filth of Lord Zyk of Asimoth.*

INVASION
PROCLAMATION

—◆—

AN *ADDRESS* TO
THE *GENERALS* OF *HELL*
FROM THE *PLATFORM* OF *PFANG*
IN *SATAN'S PALACE*
UPON THE EVE OF THE
INVASION OF HEAVEN
BY
ZYK OF ASIMOTH
LORD OF HELL

—❖—

O DEMON HORDES!

I have emailed each of you, my citizens—that is, not each individually, but rather all citizens cc'd in a group email—a Royal Proclamation announcing the discovery of the time-density known as Celestia, its central city Heaven and the execrable race of Angels that infest it. Just as Humankind's delusional Philosophies of Sympathy gave strength by contrast to Hell's appreciation of Chaos and Calumny, so, too, our new mission shall reinforce Hell's Creed of Hate by contrast with the most unspeakable Philosophy of all—the scourge of the Anti-Evil known as Love.

[Gasps of fear and loathing from the hordes of Hell]

Lord Zyk of Asimoth Announces the Invasion Proclamation

For I hereby proclaim a New World Disorder as I lead Hell's Armies on our ultimate mission, the heretical and blasphemous invasion of Heaven by the Sword of Hell, which shall slash, decapitate and utterly eradicate the Angelic Race!

[Huzzahs and bravados of exquisite Hate]

Know, O Demon Warriors, that this new campaign is the most dangerous and deadly in the History of Hell. Heaven is the Architect of Delusion, of Ignorance, of Smug Stupidity, of all things intolerable to Hell and insufferable to Demonkind!

[Whoops and growls of clamorous agreement]

Know, O Demons, that the poisonous sweetness of Celestia will rot out the sinuses of invading demons unless girdled with protective masks to shield our demon lungs from the deadly, flowery fragrances of Heaven. Know, O Demons, that the toxic beauty of their City of Death will kill the weaker of our kind without protective polarized lenses to filter out the rapacious sights of symmetry and harmony that infect demons with discord and death!

[Thunderous cheers and claws of applause]

But despite the castigations of some among you charging me with incompetence and civility, I shall lead you with the strength of Hate into the breach of Death, to burn, pollute and soil that Holy Ground with the strength of Evil, to fight off the noxious radiations in that loathsome realm of Goodness, Grace and Meaningfulness, and replace them with Hell's hateful radiations of Death, Destruction and Meaninglessness!

[August volleys of cheers]

Follow me, O Fiends of Filth Incarnate, and together we shall storm the Gates of Heaven, rape and pillage the race of angels, stuff their wings down their choir-singing throats, and burn the tinder box of Heaven into the charred blackness of Hell!

[Deafening Chaos of Hateful Cheers]

Jesus Heals the Damned and Redecorates Hell.

LORD ZYK'S MEMO
CONCERNING THE
DESTRUCTION OF HELL
BY
JESUS OF NAZARETH

MEMO TO	FROM
MORTIMER PÖNÇÉ, ESQ.	**LORD ZYK OF ASIMOTH**
PUBLISHER, MIND CONTROL PRESS	EARTH INVASION HEADQUARTERS
HELL HOLE WEST	THE PENTAGON
CITY OF HELL	ARLINGTON, VIRGINIA

Detestable Mr. Pöncé,

A quick epistle updating you on the latest internal quagmire that has twisted the warp and weft of my evil soul.

First, during a meeting with my editorial staff for the *Invasion Manual of Heaven*, I learned that, before his sudden abdication, Satan suppressed all information about the intellectual inferiority of our present demon military forces. In his *Encyclopaedia* (the definitive guide to Earth which I brilliantly supervised), our lord defined *Soldier* as "A target made of flesh." Sharing this sensibility, wealthy, sophisticated demon families simply bribed Hell's military to exclude their children from service. As a result, Hell's entire army consisted of Hell's poorest, most uneducated demon grunts. At the same time military engineers had upgraded the design of our standard Time Vehicles to include sleek, complex, quantum-computer-based operating systems, requiring an operating manual of over 8,000 pages, requiring a college reading level to understand. Since Hell's average warrior was barely literate, and unable to understand the manual, as the invasion of Earth began, over two hundred army-issued Hellcraft crashed into each other, or into Earth's mountain ranges, oceans and deserts.

This collateral damage resulted in a severe depletion of Hell's royal coffers, depleting my military budget, leaving me with barely enough to pay for fuel, food and pornography for my invading forces. I was in a pickle, Mr. Pöncé, for I still had to pay for the production and distribution of the new, glossy *Invasion Manual of Heaven,* explaining to our troops, among other things, how to operate their time machines.

Needing funds immediately, I reluctantly sold Satan's prize collection of antique torture devices, as well as his Deluxe Espresso machine and cases of Kopi Luwak coffee. But even that was not enough. Thus I had to rethink the *Invasion Manual of Heaven* and produce a low-budget version, geared toward a third-grade reading level.

But, still worried about the intelligence of my invading forces, I covertly broke Hell's time-laws by taking a brief Hellcraft trip into the future, to observe the initial invasion of heaven first-hand. Unfortunately, I learned that my demon army would become even stupider, and that like the Earth invasion, they would crash hundreds more Hellcraft into each other or into the Celestial terrain.

But that was only part of my tsuris, Mr. Pöncé. For while working on Earth with my editorial staff to complete the simplified *Invasion Manual of Heaven,* I had appointed Jesus of Nazareth as the new King of Hell in my absence. I expected that he would do the usual, wear the crown and the robes, lie around in Satan's bedroom, watch TV, eat grapes and listen to the moaning and groaning of the millions of damned souls outside, mulling about like zombies in a video game. But when I revisited the Palace of Hell to retrieve my car keys, I found an unthinkable disaster in the making. Left to his own devices, and driven by a strange combination of egotism, arrogance and naïveté, Jesus had begun *remodeling* Hell to his liking.

He started by commanding all demons in Hell to form a long line. Then, one by one, he would heal them, curing them of boils and lesions, then bathe them clean of Black Turpitude, and enchant their tormented souls with loving and charismatic speech. Even worse, he extinguished all of Hell's sulphurous fire pits, conjuring paint brushes, rollers and paint, and exhorting the vast throngs of healed demons to wallpaper and paint over my magnificent coal-black walls, transforming them into ghastly colors—pink, beige and robin-egg blue.

And even worse than that, Jesus also installed a large-scale, commercial HVAC system, purifying Hell's evil, sulphurous atmosphere into fresh air, adding an elderberry scent with a hint of effervescent mint.

Mr. Pöncé, shock does not describe my reaction to the ruination of Hell. Upon entering, I grabbed my chest in shock, flabbergasted at the gleaming chandeliers, track lighting, wall-to-wall carpeting, antique end tables with French doilies, grand pianos and candelabras.

LORD ZYK'S MEMO TO SATAN CONCERNING THE DESTRUCTION OF HELL BY JESUS OF NAZARETH

When I entered, Jesus was eating grapes and reading a copy of *The Watchtower* while languidly lounging on a silk, chartreuse ottoman, his head resting on my embroidered pillow that read *All Must Die Who Do Not Try,* a gift from my aunt. Furious, I grabbed him by the neck, shook him up and down, backwards and forwards, asking him what he had done, finally punching him repeatedly in his smarmy face, flattening and bloodying his prominent nose.

Jesus collapsed to the cavern floor, crawled on all fours into a corner and sat in a bean bag chair whimpering.

Having dispatched the fool, and looking around in disbelief at the flowery, disinfected abomination that was now Hell, I sat in Satan's throne to calm down.

The throne, as Satan mentioned in his resignation letter to me eons ago, still wobbled. I looked down at the shorter leg of the throne and noted the folded-up wad of paper Satan had shoved under it.[1] Under threat of decapitation, I forced demon contractors to come in and restore the chambers of Hell to their former horrific atmosphere of suffering, stench and filth.

As mentioned above, I have completed editing the new, shorter *Invasion Manual of Heaven,* Mr. Pöncé, which I enclose for your disapproval.

May the Terror You Fear Come to Pass Swiftly and Without Mercy.

Most hatefully yours,

ZYK

---

1   Lord Zyk apparently forgot about it during the flurry of events to follow, but that wad of paper would someday return to haunt him with rather shocking news.

The Symbolic Memorial to The Personified God

SPLENETIC
THE SECOND
THE *INVASION PAMPHLET*

EDITOR'S NOTE

*Young demon readers immersed in the loathsomeness
of the actual invasion story may wish to skip this brief section for
the nonce, for it interrupts the linear flow of our abysmal legend with
annoying facts. The more scholarly student may return later to absorb
its brief, shallow overview of the Invasion and its evil execution,
dumbed down for demon warriors.*

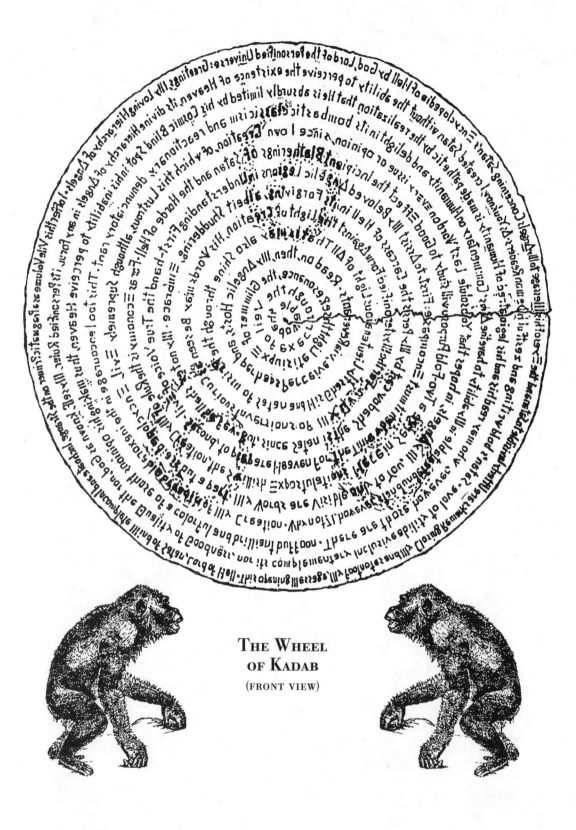

THE WHEEL
OF KADAB
(FRONT VIEW)

LORD ZYK
OF ASIMOTH
*Interim Lord
of Hell*
PRESENTS

THE
INVASION

INFORMATIONAL PAMPHLET

A Quick-Look
MILITARY GUIDE
for Demons

3 MINUTE READ

How to Invade Heaven
THE BASICS

What and where is Heaven?

You're standing on it. It's Hell in the inconceivably distant future. It's a beautiful fortress, therefore poisonous to demons. Wear goggles.

What is our mission?

Use these FIVE EZ-2-REMEMBER steps for a truly **NASTY** conquest!

NAVIGATE to the Gates of Heaven.
ASSAULT the Gates with a Ramming Enchantment.
STOMP on, Kill and Eat God and his Angels.
TIME your escape, then set Time-Twister Bomb.
YELL huzzahs as Bomb destroys Heaven.

What is the best way to pray for Heaven's annihilation?

Your commanding officer will lead you in The Annihilation Prayer, an Enchantment of Will to assist in destroying your enemy.

Who is God?

The Enemy Chieftain. Believed to be a supernatural being like Lord Satan. Unknown species and anatomy. Shoot to kill.

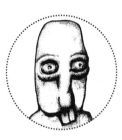

What are angels?

The enemy. Citizens of Heaven.* Bird-based humanoids. Can only be killed with your military-issue, hand-held Unexistinator, a fun, easy-to-use, point-and-shoot murder device.

Are angels edible?

If rations are depleted, angel flesh is edible and will supply calories and nutrients necessary for demon survival. For more information see following page: Cross-Section of an Angel, showing its edible but absurd anatomy, perhaps the work of an insane enchantment inexplicably cast upon their inner organs.**

* As opposed to the lowest species of demons in Hell, also referred to as Angels.
** The source of this strange enchantment, it was later confirmed, was none other than The Personified God.

A warning...
REGARDING THE **EDIBILITY** OF **ANGEL PARTS**

The internal organs of an angel are incomprehensible to Hell's Dismemberment Engineers. Angel anatomy combines edible flesh with inedible metal gears, tubes, pumps, and pistons, as well as diodes, lightbulbs and tiny kitchen sinks. We believe that an unknown force has altered their anatomy by casting a complex Enchantment. It should be noted that the fleshy parts are indeed edible and nutritious, but DO NOT EAT THE METAL OR RUBBER INTERNAL ORGANS. Whatever Enchantment was cast, it made these organs poisonous. Once Heaven is conquered, we will dissect as many carcasses as possible until we plumb the secrets of Angel Biology.

Introducing...
THE TIME-TWISTER BOMB
HELL'S PRIMARY WEAPON AGAINST HEAVEN

KA-BOOM! That's right, the Time-Twister Bomb is the most deadly weapon ever created! It destroys Time itself, erasing all future local time past the moment of detonation. Satan banned the device, believing its detonation might create a hypothetical Time Void, ripping the universe apart. Despite this ban, Lord Zyk ordered use of the Bomb in a preemptive strike against Heaven, promising that if the universe *was* destroyed, he would time-travel back to stop the detonation of the Bomb. With many fail-safes in place, Hell's Time Tribunal reluctantly agreed.

Quick Tips in Heaven

1. TOO MANY BUTTONS? Your Hellcraft is operated by pressing the IGNITION button ONCE. Your course and destination coordinates are preset. DO NOT TOUCH THE CONTROL PANEL DURING TIME-TRAVEL.

2. SPORTS FAN? Got a big-money bet on who wins the Invasion? DO NOT BREAK CHILD-PROOF LOCK ON TIME-CONTROLS! Traveling into the future to see who wins is punishable by immediate decapitation.

3. DON'T LIKE WEARING YOUR MASK? Your plutonium-coated mask will deflect Heaven's deadly radiation, protecting you from insanity and preventing organs of empathy from sprouting in your chest. THESE ORGANS WILL MAKE YOU THINK YOU CARE ABOUT OTHERS! When in doubt, always MAIM and KILL.

4. DON'T WASTE YOUR BABY! Each warrior in each battalion is allotted one human baby per day. *Every part of a baby is edible so do not waste your supplies.* DO NOT DISCARD BABY INTESTINES, WHICH ARE RICH IN DEMON NUTRIENTS. Each regiment will have three portable microwaves for cooking infants.

5. HOLES CRUSTED WITH WASTE? The intense beauty of Celestia will cause you to violently purge the contents of your bowels, stomach and smell sacs. Toilet paper and wet wipes are stored in your pack's Toiletries Pocket for Hole Cleansings.

6. OK, THEY'RE ALL DEAD, NOW WHAT? Once genocide is complete and you have activated the Time-Twister Bomb, immediately flee the city and return to your vehicle.

Already forgot?

DON'T TOUCH THE BUTTONS!
NO GAMBLING ON DEATH COUNT.
WHEN IN DOUBT, MAIM OR KILL.
EAT ENTIRE BABY.
CLEAN YOUR HOLES.
RUN!

SPLENETIC
THE THIRD

EVENTS CONCERNING
THE INVASION OF HEAVEN

EDITOR'S NOTE

Herein continues our rough historical timeline of
Heaven's Invasion, an epochal event in the distant past.
Told through Letters & Diaries of Supernatural Beings, Military
Interrogations, Prophecies of Ancient Oracles, Cultural Myths,
Folk Tales & Urban Legends, as well as Legal Depositions of
Paid Witnesses, and the Testimony of Inanimate Objects
Enchanted with Sentience.

LORD ZYK'S ANNIHILATION PRAYER

EXCERPT FROM *THE BOOK OF HELL'S HISTORICAL ANECDOTES*

BY RAGNOK THE IMPETUOUS
CELEBRITY VLOGGER

CHAPTER 23

After the infamous Feast of Fear, a deluge of radioactive blood, gore and viscera enveloped Planet Earth's charred surface, its slaughtered human population dwindling as Lord Zyk and his Hellcraft bombers utterly destroyed Moscow, Los Angeles, Chicago, New York, Tokyo—virtually all of Europe and America, except Germany, Lord Satan's favorite country.

Enterprising demon musicians planted high-density microphones on 5-D hooks stuck in the air over each major city, recording the death throes and wails of radiated humanity around the globe. These popular tracks were repurposed in hip-hop mash-ups by Hell's greatest rappers, featuring samples of human men, women and especially children screaming and weeping, loudly begging for death. Hell's Society for Human Debasement offered free DLs of these mashups with six-or-more party bucket orders of Kentucky Fried Human Flesh.

Since radioactivity increases the deliciousness of human flesh, Hell's popular chains of fast-food restaurants opened in the ashes of Earth's major cities, serving contaminated human meat to the hungry legions of demon insurgents and the incoming demon population that began homesteading in the caves, craters, grottos and wastelands of Earth's now-blackened crust.

The new inhabitants of Earth welcomed the new aura of evil engulfing the planet. The greatest signet of change was the homely stench of the decomposing human bodies, creating an aroma everywhere that immeasurably improved the ambiance of the planet.

The demon troops were entertained by human enemies volunteering, in the name of patriotism, to fight each other in steel cages, each deluded victim thinking that the victor would be spared. All opposing political, religious and cultural leaders were forced to fight to the death in glorious steel cage battles. As they sliced each others' limbs off, Hell's soldiers cheered while eating human-flesh hotdogs and quaffing flaming flagons of the finest Antragon mead. Regardless of who was the victor, all human combatants, of course, were decapitated and their heads sold as Steel Cage Night Souvenirs to the highest demon eBay bidders.

Most of mankind's government and military institutions were abandoned by the screaming, bomb-fleeing humans. But of interest was the sneak attack, prior to Hell's invasion proper, by demon forces at the Pentagon in Arlington, Virginia. Led by Lord Zyk and his lieutenant to test the mettle of the human military, the battle was an excellent way for demons to assess the pathetic weakness of human beings, with their tiny, fragile bodies, underdeveloped brains, soft, tender flesh and underbellies, and self-defeating emotional highs and lows.

The idiot humans were clearly no match for the demons, a race with bodies naturally armored with reptilian scales and spikes, who easily absorbed and repelled the humans' poison gas, germ warfare and chemical weapons. In the end, the humans' cooked flesh was made even more delicious being seasoned by the exquisite flavor sof their own weapons of toxic gas, germs and chemicals. Soon after Hell took over the Pentagon, the corpses of Earth's military were bulldozed into piles behind Texas Meat Smokers, buttered, barbecued and lunched upon by demon insurgents.

After Earth's conquest, Lord Zyk used The Pentagon as his new headquarters, and from there would launch his attack on Heaven. On the eve of the Invasion, Lord Zyk called a meeting of his Chiefs of Staff at the newly commandeered Pentagon, who beforehand were served a sumptuous buffet of Five Star General human limbs and military-grade, alcoholism-soaked livers with mashed potatoes and coagulated blood sauce.

After the dinner, Lord Zyk called for his staff to take their seats. "My despised lieutenants," he said, "since I personally led the bombing missions of all Earth cities, I've agreed to personally pilot the lead Hellcraft for our invasion of Heaven. General Gryphyn will take over as Headquarters Commander here in my absence. Even though I, Lord Zyk, your savior and chief military strategist, carried out the legwork and execution of the first invasion manual that made the invasion of Earth a success, and now lead you in a soon-to-be-legendary mission in which I shall personally surgically remove all Empathy from the Cosmos by my supreme plan to destroy Heaven, the heart of the universe, we also should, I suppose, offer some traditional lip service to honor our former lord, Lord Satan, in a prayer. Stand as we perform the Ritual of Nihilism."

Odin, Ramona, Morgellon and Steve, and the rest of his evil lieutenants stood, solemnly held claws around the table and bowed their heads as Zyk invoked the Ritual: "I curse you all in the name of Lord Satan, and ask that we join claws as I give the Annihilation prayer."

Lord Zyk nodded to his six-demon drum corps, their drums crafted from the skins of flayed, human, Oscar-winning movie stars and Grammy-winning recording artists. The corps began playing their military snares in a soft, inexorable rhythm, a cadence from Hell which slowly grew louder as they accompanied Lord Zyk's awful prayer.

THE
ANNIHILATION PRAYER

O Father of Evil, Lord Satan, we curse you
and ask in your name to destroy and kill
all angelic enemies of Hell, shredding their bodies
and drowning out their cries with the thunder
of our supreme fire-power.

And protect our young demon homunculi, O Father,
for they are our future and will go on to greater glories
with wondrous things beyond our imagination,
such as acoustic ultrasonic laser weaponry
and geosynchronous detonation systems.

We pray that our homunculi's toy weapons
be superior to our enemies' children's toy weapons.

And above all, O Father of Evil, we ask you to sanctify
and make fool-proof Hell's military industrial complex,
and all hierarchies of munitions manufacturers,
related distributors and mail-order franchises,
and ask these things in the name of the One most holy,
whose murderous arms embrace our arms,
our allies' arms, and the arms
of our arms suppliers.

AMEN.

The demon warriors answered in kind, saying, "Amen."

While some of the demon lieutenants fought back tears, due to the emotional distortions of Earth's heinous magentic field, they all silently turned to one another and exchanged solemn Handshakes of Hatred.

The rat-a-tat of the snare drums ascended fitfully, reaching a magnificent crescendo.

Saluting each other, Lord Zyk and his Lieutenants of High Filth marched grimly out of the Pentagon briefing room, beaming with bad will, excited to kill, burn, and utterly annihilate God's stronghold of Heaven.

ODIN *AND* RAMONA'S
RECON MISSION
IN
CELESTIA

FROM

THE HISTORIES *OF* HELL'S
CRAVEN CONQUESTS

A YOUNG ADULT DEMON'S HISTORY LESSON № 17

BY HARGOBIND THE RAPACIOUS
ADJUNCT PROFESSOR OF ABHORRENT HISTORIES
UNIVERSITY OF HELL, WEST.

CHAPTER 13

Odin the Obsequious' Hellcraft was the first to emerge from the Quavers of Time. It hovered like a Wheel within a Wheel over the planet known as Celestia. Celestia was in size identical to the planet of Hell and the planet of Earth. This was because they were in fact the same planet. They were located, however, at different extreme densities in the Spectrum of Time. It was unclear which planets were in the future and which were in the past. But legend has it that Celestia was located so far in the future that trying to grasp the distances between them would drive men and devils mad.

The landing was in the etheric wilderness, ten kilometers from the despised fortress called Heaven. Heaven was the only populated area on Celestia, and was believed to be the home of the Personified God. This unique being was acknowledged by some to be the most powerful life-form in the universe. The Personified God was said to be the consciousness of the living universe itself. It manifested itself as a humanoid being, akin to a noble demon or a primitive human. It seems that even something as all-inclusive as *All That Is* couldn't do much of anything without a body, except feel. A body was necessary in order to have fun. And according to Scholars of Evil, this was why the Emptiness at the Core of *All That Is* desired a body. A body, of course, allowed the Personified God to talk, have a hot fudge sundae, play a penny whistle or drive a racing car. Overall, it allowed the Universe to spend some downtime experiencing Itself, by doing whatever It damn pleased.

Odin's sophisticated spy craft, to speak plainly about what it was, covertly touched down. It emitted a creaking hiss of hydraulics as it landed in Celestia's tangled wood of emerald shrubbery and mint-green flora. The glowing green meadow, rife with obscenely exquisite wildflowers, seemed to know that it was a signet of God's unimaginable power. The peneplain itself seemed to put its hands on its hips and brag, "I like to imagine that I radiate out infinitely on all sides of God's home." For that is what it seemed to do, although the planet and its constituent parts were composed of finite amounts of matter and energy.

Little was known of the infrastructure of the city of Heaven, the home of the Personified God. Because of that, Lord Zyk assigned Odin, his Chief Lieutenant, Strategist and Spellmaster, assisted by Odin's co-pilot, the savant Lieutenant Ramona Iyam, with reconnaissance duties. They were to land in advance, gather intel and map out the Heaven Fortress. The city was of immense size, slightly bigger than Hell's continent Facinorus, slightly smaller than its continent Repudius, but about the same size as Earth's Australian continent. Celestia did not have continents as did its past incarnations. Instead, the highly evolved planet had one majestic continent which gracefully enwrapped the globe like a faintly luminous, velvet glove. Celestia's sole continent had glowing rain forests, jungles and deserts, glistening lakes and rivers of pristine water, and all manner of other environs that are hated by Hell due to their extreme beauty.

Odin the Enchanter immediately went to work in his Command Center. He closed his eyes and began a series of long-practiced, fluid motions of his claws and his scaled, scarlet limbs by which he would initiate the emotional fulcrums of a Deep Enchantment, in this case, an artful, vicious Spell worthy of casting on the enemy city. But soon after Odin began his enchantment, he stopped abruptly, looking confused. Something was wrong. Strangely, his horns were itching, as were his claws and his hooves. Annoyed, he conjured a can of itching ointment into existence, but even a simple Summoning Spell seemed arduous. Usually, Odin could effortlessly perform Spells of extreme complexity, but now, as he slathered the soothing salve on his stinging horns, an otherworldly fog clouded his mind, making it hard for him to concentrate. And focus was the most important faculty of a Spellmaster, essential to the strength of his Enchantments.

As he salved his hooves, he was disturbed by an unpleasant thought. Ever since landing on this higher-vibratory planet, it took him more energy than usual to maintain enough *pure hatred* in order to cast Spells with satisfying perfection. He remembered Lord Zyk telling moribund tales of his supernatural powers being stripped by the *magentic field* of Earth, a field poisonous to demons. Since all three planets were the same, but located in different Time Spectra, Odin wondered if Celestia's field had evolved to be even *more* poisonous than Earth's. This thought caused a sinking feeling in his testicles. He was terrified that if it was true, it might throw a monkey wrench into the clockwork of their invasion.

Odin, like all demon officers, was literally allergic to failure. As a young demon, the faintest scent of defeat would make his neck, groin and buttocks break out in hives. Now, he simply refused to fail at this, the most important mission of his career. Eyes clamped shut and fists trembling, he forced himself to concentrate. And, in a rush of hateful power dredged from the depths of his black soul, he did just that. He used this power to summon up an Astral Egregore, a thought-form slave commanded by demons. Odin psychically projected a mind-map into the egregore and told him to conjure the tools needed to map the Fortress of Heaven.

The Egregore scanned the map and instantly conjured a fleet of six-hundred and sixty-six black drones hovering with a low, metallic, resonating hum. Odin blasted an Opening Spell at the large hatch which flew open. At Odin's command, the drones moved in unison like a precisely trained flock of mechanical crows, their hum escalating into in a high-pitched whine. The egregore's work done, Odin dissolved him into a swirl of purple vapor, materialized a joystick and commanded the astral drones to fly out the hatch.

From centuries of playing VR games at Hell's *Incel Gamer Cave*, Odin used his joystick to fly the drones in precise formation, heading for the heavenly fortress which glowed in the distance. He switched on the lead drone's camera and a virtual hologram screen materialized next to him, showing a bird's-eye view of the drones' flight path.

Soaring high to avoid detection, the fleet silently flew over the city, sending back video of its infrastructure. Odin's bank of quantum computers clicked and whirred as they processed the data.

But something was wrong. The images were not what Odin expected. He expected roads, vehicles, buildings, bridges, rivers, boats and millions of angelic inhabitants. But no matter how many times he recalibrated to sharpen the images, there was no precise detail to be seen, merely a blur of gray fog covering the city. Something was hiding Heaven from view. Odin cursed the God ruling the city. Of course, the Supernal Leader must have cast an enchantment himself, one which would hide the city from spying enemy eyes.

Odin did the best he could stitching together the return data in AutoCAD, and compiling a rough map of the city. The lack of precise detail made the map somewhat useless. Lord Zyk would likely be furious and humiliate him in front of the other lieutenants, as he had done on countless other occasions. Although he knew it was a useless gesture, Odin printed the map on the ugliest parchment he could find, hoping its exquisite ugliness might distract Lord Zyk's attention at the map's impotence.

Odin buzzed Ramona in her lab. She appeared onscreen and said she was busy dissecting an angel prisoner they'd bought from a time trader. She was compiling a chart of angel anatomy for the Invasion Pamphlet. Seeing Ramona's oblong, rutted face brought to mind his other problem, their personal relationship. Odin was lonely, living in a mid-level cavern with six hundred and sixty-six cats, a number of cats he carefully maintained through the years, depending on their deaths or births, due to his obsessive-compulsive disorder. Odin was sexually attracted to Ramona, for her horrible skin, webbed fingers and skeletal toes made his undercarriage constantly tumescent. At times he imagined her sharing his cavern, as mother to his cats, and spending downtime watching pornography holograms, while Ramona scaled down his horns and hooves with an electric grinder, then salved them with the foulest of ointments. Odin despised Ramona's reptilian femininity and was deliciously repulsed by the bleeding areas of her carcass. Odin hated thinking about her, for he was having enough trouble dealing with the emergence of feelings in himself due to the odious magentic field.

While Ramona was unaware of his genital inflammation in her presence, she was, in fact, attracted to Odin. She reeled at his bulbous nose, foul odor, masterful enchantments, and the libelous insults he concocted in his popular gossip column "Here's the Dirt, Folks!" in *Electrodes to the Genitals Monthly*. She also despised his overly vibratory, off-key singing, his moldy, tooth-crazy mouth and his out-of-time clapping to Hell's Dictatorship Anthem. But as dedicated, high-ranking military officers, Odin and Ramona knew that they must not allow each other's compelling atrociousness to distract them from their vital duties.

When summoned by Odin, Ramona appeared instantly, as if moving through a Dutch angle of shadows, as befitting the devious ways of the Djin. Odin took the map from the printer. It was still vague regarding details. However, it did reveal two gigantic, unidentifiable buildings sticking up through the strange layer of camouflage. Due to their size, Odin assumed they were the main government buildings of Celestia, and therefore important targets for destruction.

Both Odin and Ramona knew that the map was a failure. Their most crucial reconnaissance task was to calculate placement of the Time-Twister Bomb to cause maximum damage. And this map was useless in its lack of detail. If Lord Satan was still in charge and had seen this map instead of Lord Zyk, Odin knew he would be killed instantly. Odin, however, knew that Lord Zyk was prone to undemon-like fits of empathy, behavior which Odin could encourage and manipulate to his own advantage—mainly in discouraging Zyk from killing him. But Odin had darker motives which, if given the opportunity, he would carry out with extreme prejudice.

Lieutenant Iyam was Lord Zyk's third in command, despite her gender and obnoxious behavior, typical of evil idiot savants. Females in Hell were traditionally relegated to inferior positions, subservient to male demons. But such was Ramona's deep level of loathsomeness, combined with her unparalleled photographic memory as a savant, that she was recognized as an invaluable advisor to Lord Zyk, and indispensable to the success of the invasion.

Yet her childish savant behavior irritated not only Lord Zyk, but all demons forced to endure her repugnant presence. Upon seeing the lack of useful features on Odin's map, for example, her eyes widened in shock. She froze, staring at the map, then began shaking and jumping up and down, as if on a pogo stick, spluttering drool which bubbled through a wound in her throat as she angrily pointed at the map.

"Stop it!" shrieked Odin, who was not in the mood.

She instantly stopped her gyrations and whispered, "Sir, the map does not provide enough data to calculate the placement of the bomb."

"I know that, imbecile!" Odin said. "Leave me!"

Ramona again stopped dead in her tracks. This was the first time Odin had called her an imbecile. She was at once overwhelmed by Odin's rare use of an intimate expression of obvious dislike. Instantly, she felt her undercarriage juices leaking down the scales of her left thigh. Her vagina opened like a spikey cactus flower. She trembled, and thought, *He called me an imbecile.* For secretly she was desperate to hear more of his personal insults, hoping beyond hope that his feelings for her would blossom into pure romantic hatred.

But they both knew the importance of remaining strictly professional at all times, especially on this, the most important military campaign in history. As her vulva trembled like a recondite sex addict after a stranger unknowingly intones her trigger word, Ramona vanished in her shadowy way into the umbric vapors.

Odin gritted his teeth, steeling himself as he transmitted the map to Lord Zyk. Within moments he watched Zyk's Hellcraft descend and touch down next to his. Zyk's kingly time-vehicle gleamed like beryl and was crafted with the royal icons of wheels revolving within wheels. In its wake, six hundred and sixty-six military Hellcraft materialized and landed around them with magical, mathematical precision. They touched down in the soft evergreen, filling the glorious meadow of wildflowers with Hell's murderous army of demons, all of whom dreamed of gleaming cataracts of filth in order to lower their spirits, and to inspire the demon warriors on their mission to vaporize the True Enemy of Evil.

EXCERPT FROM
THE DEPOSITION OF HELLCRAFT 1439: CONCERNING THE INVASION DUTIES OF ODIN THE OBSEQUIOUS AND RAMONA IYAM

ATTESTED BY HELL'S PROSECUTING ATTORNEY BOMBATIUS RANK

ATTORNEY RANK: Let it be stated for the record that the witness is a Hellcraft transportation device, factory-programmed with sentience, and designed to transport its user through space and time. Hellcraft 1439, what roles did Odin and Ramona play in the invasion and what was their relationship?

HELLCRAFT 1439: I ask the court to forgive my speech center which was programmed to give colloquial banter.

ATTORNEY RANK: So noted.

HELLCRAFT 1439: I'll tell you, Odin and Ramona were ace pilots and felt good inside me. As a machine, I don't get much affection, so when they were excited, I was excited. We were a team, the three of us, and when I felt their lustful forms moving inside of me, my excitement grew by leaps and bounds until--

ATTORNEY RANK: Please confine your testimony to their activities and relationship.

HELLCRAFT 1439: Activities? Well, they took me on their recon mission, and between the two of them, mapped out the area, bought a kidnapped angel and dissected him. We were a cracker-jack team. As for their relationship, they had true mutual hatred, which as the court knows is where demon babies come from. I mean, their body heat melted my fuel cells. I'm not kidding. Their combined auras flared up when they got too close, that's how much astral heat those two generated.

ATTORNEY RANK: And these personal issues, did they interfere
    with--

HELLCRAFT 1439: You should've seen the escalation in their plas-
    ma and other body fluid levels. They pinned the fluid excre-
    tion meter! When their sex glands turned up the heat while
    discussing something as inconsequential as a malfunctioning
    diode, I thought my engines would blow. Still, they kept it
    professional, except when they didn't, if you know what I
    mean!

ATTORNEY RANK: Thank you, 1439.

HELLCRAFT 1439: They were a pair of hot messes, but otherwise
    they were dedicated to the bylaws of Evil. Oh sure, they
    felt true hate for each other. Strictly platonic, though.
    But their mutual disgust was so palpable you could cut it
    with a scimitar. I remember one time--

ATTORNEY RANK: That's more than sufficient.

HELLCRAFT 1439: Trust me, something about these two created a
    primal stench you wouldn't believe. I'm used to the smell
    sacs of unwashed demons, but this was monumental, radiating
    from their reproductive areas. It was so intense, any or-
    ganic matter around them would crack like Grandma's peanut
    brittle.

ATTORNEY RANK: Bailiff, deactivate the witness' speech center.

HELLCRAFT 1439: You should have seen it when they stepped out of
    me together. Their combined heat was like a furnace. Plants
    around the gangplank wilted. Birds fell from the sky fully
    cooked. And not only that, you should have seen--

END DEPOSITION.

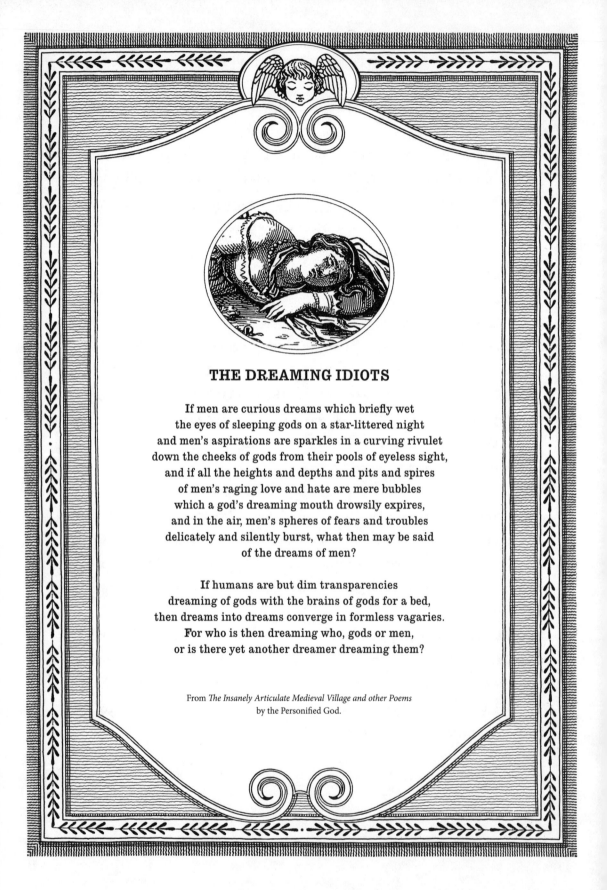

THE DREAMING IDIOTS

If men are curious dreams which briefly wet
the eyes of sleeping gods on a star-littered night
and men's aspirations are sparkles in a curving rivulet
down the cheeks of gods from their pools of eyeless sight,
and if all the heights and depths and pits and spires
of men's raging love and hate are mere bubbles
which a god's dreaming mouth drowsily expires,
and in the air, men's spheres of fears and troubles
delicately and silently burst, what then may be said
of the dreams of men?

If humans are but dim transparencies
dreaming of gods with the brains of gods for a bed,
then dreams into dreams converge in formless vagaries.
For who is then dreaming who, gods or men,
or is there yet another dreamer dreaming them?

From *The Insanely Articulate Medieval Village and other Poems*
by the Personified God.

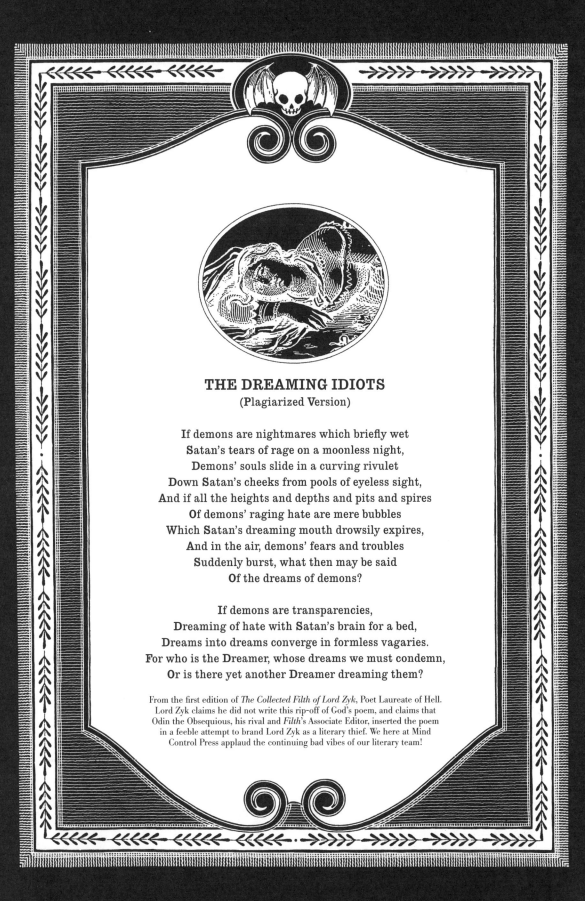

THE DREAMING IDIOTS
(Plagiarized Version)

If demons are nightmares which briefly wet
Satan's tears of rage on a moonless night,
Demons' souls slide in a curving rivulet
Down Satan's cheeks from pools of eyeless sight,
And if all the heights and depths and pits and spires
Of demons' raging hate are mere bubbles
Which Satan's dreaming mouth drowsily expires,
And in the air, demons' fears and troubles
Suddenly burst, what then may be said
Of the dreams of demons?

If demons are transparencies,
Dreaming of hate with Satan's brain for a bed,
Dreams into dreams converge in formless vagaries.
For who is the Dreamer, whose dreams we must condemn,
Or is there yet another Dreamer dreaming them?

From the first edition of *The Collected Filth of Lord Zyk*, Poet Laureate of Hell.
Lord Zyk claims he did not write this rip-off of God's poem, and claims that
Odin the Obsequious, his rival and *Filth*'s Associate Editor, inserted the poem
in a feeble attempt to brand Lord Zyk as a literary thief. We here at Mind
Control Press applaud the continuing bad vibes of our literary team!

LORD ZYK'S MEMO
REGARDING THE
INVASION *OF* HEAVEN[1]

MEMO TO	**FROM**
MORTIMER PÖNCÉ, ESQ.	**LORD ZYK OF ASIMOTII**
PUBLISHER, MIND CONTROL PRESS	FIELD BATTALION TENT
HELL HOLE WEST	BATTLEFIELD OF HEAVEN
CITY OF HELL	

Detestable Mr. Pöncé,

Delighted to hear of your wife's death in the runaway steamroller accident. Her demise will provide light conversation for us at the Groucho Club over a relaxing aperitif.

But until then, the most significant events in my career are still unfolding regarding the invasion. I must, however, ask you to mind-stamp the nondisclosure agreement below by thinking the words I AGREE. Once stamped, this document will allow you to read it and my disclosure of the events leading up to my first incredible glimpse inside the Gates of Heaven.

> **Legal Notice:**
> The following contains classified intel regarding Hell's present Military Deployment. Its disclosure by you in any part or form is punishable by Standard Carcass Crucifixion, including Groin Immolation performed by the Lava Inquisitors of Arachnid II.

Yes, you were correct, Mr. Pöncé. There was not a doubt in my mind that my Invasion Plan would be successful. However, what we discovered upon smashing through Heaven's Gates was certainly not what I had expected, to say the least. But to prepare you for those uncanny particulars, I must explain the events leading up to our entry into Celestia.

---

1   From *Asimoth, Burg of Shame: The Suburb of Hell that Produced the Idiot King*, Ragnarok Press, Hell City.

LORD ZYK'S MEMO TO SATAN CONCERNING THE INVASION OF HEAVEN

With the assistance of Odin, my Chief Black Magick Attaché, I had cast a Seeking Spell to determine Lord Satan's location. Was he within the walls of the City of Heaven? Had he already found and murdered the Creator, if such a thing could be? I knew that Satan had cast an Invisibility Spell around himself to avoid detection, and our counter-enchantments did manage to detect his presence within the city's perimeter. However, pinpointing his location failed.

As for whether or not Satan had found and killed the Creator, Odin and I quickly confirmed that no Death Spell would work on the Creator at all; our readings on him, her or it were a blank slate, as it were. You can't kill something if it isn't technically alive.

However, I knew that my treachery at such a high level would improve my reputation among Hell's elite. If I could find him and kill him with the Bomb, then I would be heir not only to Hell and Earth, but Heaven as well.

After completing their prior mission—buying a kidnapped angel for military intel—Odin and Ramona landed on Celestia ahead of my fleet to perform a second reconnaissance. After sending me an aerial map of the Heaven Fortress, I led my military fleet of sixhundred and sixty-six Hellcraft to a covert valley a fortnight from the fortress, under the evening umbra of Heaven's Black Sun.[2]

We landed without incident under cover of twilight dawn. After a turbulent flight due to unexpected time-convections, I began to obsess upon the astounding opportunity before me. But it all depended upon a successful preemptive strike followed by a speedy holocaust of the entire feathered population. I had carefully bestowed each of our troops with necessary accoutrements for every possible happenstance that might arise, including:

—Protective eyewear to stave off Heaven's Deadly Beauty.

—Rations of one human baby per soldier to efficiently supply both protein and unpasteurized blood.

—Pitchfork Lasers with three settings (Stun, Decapitate and Cook).

—One copy of the *Invasion Pamphlet of Heaven*, designed to be idiot-proof, with simple invasion tips, as well as convenient methods to eat an angel.

But what I had not anticipated, due to its utter strangeness, was the debilitating effect of Heaven's grotesque *visual beauty* on our demonic physiology. Yes, Mr. Pöncé, I had forgotten that the pale azure morning skies, the cool balmy breeze and the radiant rolling hillsides, shimmering with loveliness, were not merely repugnant to demonic sensibilities, but *poisonous* to the demonic nervous system.

~~~~~~

2   Celestia's sentient Black Sun gestates in the sky in waves/phases of radiation and absorption which allow the panacea of sleep and the succor of dreams to the recumbent angelic population.

Upon deplaning en masse and glimpsing Heaven's beautiful flora and fauna, my troops immediately became queasy in a first wave of nausea. As their leader, I had to hide my own reactions of dis-ease, although I felt as if a baby yak was writhing in my belly, gnawing on my intestines. Without betraying my discomfort, I raised my megaphone and shouted across the myriad ranks and files of warriors.

"A-ten-hut!"

Despising weakness, they valiantly straightened to attention. However, as a faint breeze wafted the sweet, buttery scent of honeysuckle to their nostrils, hundreds of my demons, starting with the rear ranks, clutched their stomachs and retched in a cacophony of sickening *exculpatus*.

It was important, however, in these first moments of military discipline, that I stood strong by way of example. I straightened my uniform's custom-made, frilly polonaise, betraying no sign of sickness and, displaying superb leadership skills, I megaphoned even louder:

"A-TEN-HUT!"

To their credit, my army also fought off their waves of revulsion, wiped their throat holes of muck and straightened to attention, upright and strong.

"Drums ready! Mark time!"

The rows of tiger-skinned drummers kept time as my troops marched in place.

"Forward—MARCH!"

Under the rising of Celestia's magnificent Black Sun, I led my warriors up the steep hillside of multicolored wildflowers. Seeing them, several of the drummers buckled and vomited into their drums, but quickly caught up to keep time with the troops.

Despite my suppressed sickness, I was feeling in control. Our landing had been undetected by the enemy. My tarot reading for the invasion was auspicious and, regarding our success, my military-issued Black Magic 8-Ball read: SIGNS POINT TO YES.

The 8-Ball reminded me of my childhood, and the warmth and welter of daily beatings from my father, whom I always wanted to impress and show respectful hatred for. The obvious occurred to me then, that Lord Satan had replaced him as my father figure whom I desperately wanted to impress. Perhaps my desire to kill Satan was a projection of my desire to finally kill my father. My eyes teared up and a final thought sprung to mind.

Magentic.

The despised field was again having its way with my stupid tear ducts. My father-figure musings were sentimental idiocy. The drums pounding a tarantella shook me from my reverie. Emboldened by thoughts of victory, and my epiphany concerning Lord Satan and my father, I led my army of hate-filled warriors toward the enemy, and knew that nothing could stop me.

Until a moment later, when we crested the hill, and froze in shock at what we saw. For in the distance was our first view of Heaven's Golden Gates radiating powerful pulses of hideous, deadly positivity, and beams of warmth and love.

Cringing, I megaphoned: "Eye filters—ON!"

This was my opportunity to show everyone the excellence of my constitution, my strength and leadership, and the evil sophistication of my tactical planning.

However, even from this distance, Heaven's radiations were too much. I tried to snap on my lenses to block the rays, but they tumbled to the ground as I clutched my stomach and doubled over. I heard my troops groaning and looked up to see them all in *maior faucibus porrectis*[3], splattering the beauteous surrounding environs with cataracts of buttocks expungement. Some of my troops, out of a desire to conceal weakness, dove into bushes or behind trees and, either squatting or bent over, did their business quickly and discreetly. Unfortunately, with many thousands of soldiers involved, this took some time, for when each cycle of queasiness and expulsion reached equilibrium, then even the briefest glimpse of the city's shimmering majesty re-afflicted us anew. For the next twenty minutes, as further detonations rang from my troops, the air was rife with splutter and stench. I could only hope the history books would record that we sprayed the celestial vista with our post-digestive discharge to mark our territory, rather than succumbing to anatomical queasiness.

Eventually we collected ourselves and resumed marching, still roughly three miles from the city. When roughly a half-mile from the odious Gates, we paused to refill our bellies with baby flesh rations. I note that each time we rested, my Chief Black Magic Attaché, Odin the Obsequious,[4] conjured a force field around me to stave off assassination attempts which occurred roughly once every half-hour. It was my charge, of course, to alert my savant accountant Ramona Iyam[5] to use her photographic memory to record each assassin's name and rank, for that is how demons are awarded medals for Military Dishonor.[6]

During this brief respite, I snapped on Distance Lenses (deeply filtered), examined the gate structure and began formulating my plan of attack. It was then that I saw, peeping from turrets above the gates, rows upon rows of angelic soldiers wielding deadly weapons, awaiting our approach. Their weapons glimmered with exotic metalwork, each deadly sharp edge radiating beauty in the form of soothing diamond reflections of the rainbow's spectrum. I had never conceived that a weapon could communicate such hor-

---

3   "*The major oracies projecting.*" In this case, stomach cavity effluvia.
4   See *Biographia Daemonum et Angelorum*, Pg. 28.
5   Ibid, Pg. 29.
6   The most successful demon warriors were those festooned with military medals pinned or stapled permanently into their hides, medals for low crimes or misdemeanors against the state; the more potent the disgraceful act, the lower the Medal of Dishonor. The hides of the most vain or insecure warriors are bogged down by hundreds of medals pinned or stapled to their chests in such quantity and weight that they must crawl while engaged in battle.

Lord Zyk Leads the Forces of Hell to the Gates of Heaven.

ror to a demon. I alerted my troops that we were being watched and ordered them, as we drew closer, to conceal themselves behind the bushes and trees surrounding the vast fortress entrance.

Minutes later, we were concealed and my troops were awaiting my command. Before us, two strange creatures were guarding the entrance, a species of reptilian angels, appearing formidable if not deadly. On my command, Odin transformed them into sacks of filth. Behind the sacks, the Golden Gates radiated such intense beauty, it was difficult for me to concentrate. I verily gritted my teeth as my stomach turned, my head throbbed with an atopic rash, and my horns swelled unnaturally.

My double-headed lieutenant and personal bodyguard, Morgellon and Steve[7], informed me that three of our four battering rams had been lost during the second or third wave of our explosive waste ejecta.

At that moment one of the drummers, foolishly staring at the gates without eye filters, convulsed and exploded. I quickly cast a Skeleton Spell on his remains, transforming his gore into a skeletal throne which I then sat in to contemplate my next move.

But instead, I was awash with sentiments, clearly the work of that odious field. My emotions dragged me back to the dreams of my youth, when I dared not dream of being a lauded poet, never mind imagine I would be King of Hell. But my buttocks chafing on the skeleton chair brought me back to the present, and I knew it was time to take command, to take action.

I conjured a psychic link with my troops and silently ordered them to bring forth the remaining battering ram and follow me in stealth to the gates.

But even as we crept toward them, the shaking of my tail, a demon's tell-tale sign of cowardice, exposed my fear. For high above us, hundreds of angel warriors in the turrets pointed their weapons down at us. Strangely the rows of angels did not fire, move nor make a sound. Just as we reached the gates, one of the armed angels above us toppled forward, falling from a turret and landing at our feet in a flurry of feathers.

Odin scanned the body with his Mortality Meter and cast me a puzzled look. "Lord

---

7   Editor's Note: For the edification of the Reader evolved past Demonhood, the two lieutenants are twin demons born from the same female demon's egg pouch. Twin demons are often created by a spell cast upon a demon fetus which splits it in twain, akin to the amoeba. This was the case with the twin lieutenants Morgellon and Steve, identical except for one of Steve's eyes, which was lazy and forever pointing upwards, as if half-rolling his eyes at the absurdity of existence. Not surprisingly, the twins had opposite natures. Morgellon exfoliated from his lips delicate little bursts of spittle with every word from his distinctly flamboyant, feminine voice; Steve, on the other hand, was a natural mimic who entertained the troops by imitating Lord Zyk to a T.

A demon fetus gestates in the female's leathery pouch; once its arms and legs articulate, the baby demon, or gnomen, crawls from the pouch with cute, peeping sounds. Then it slides down the demoness' legs like a slug to the dirt and follows its parents around as a chubby, larval demon. After a week it burrows into the ground, in its chthonic stage. Soon the demon homunculus bursts from the fundament, half grown and fully terrestrial, in a swirl of greenish smoke and purple fire.

Some gnomen remain in the ground longer, finding comfort in the muffled sound of demon feet clomping above them. For despite the tortured life of Hell, all demons remember as fetuses the sound of their parents' hooves cleaving the sod above into half-moon glyphs, a rare memory of comfort and safety in a life brimming with hatefulness, horror and despair.

Zyk, he appears to have been dead for several weeks." I looked up at the motionless rows of silent angels in the turrets, and a strange thought occurred to me. As a test, I grabbed a rock and threw it amongst the overhanging angels, and another tumbled, dead, to our feet.

"They're *already* dead! All of them!" The dead angels were a psychological ploy, a primitive show of force when none, apparently, existed.

I ordered Odin to cast the Spell of Yank to pull all of the angels from the turrets en masse, which he did, creating large piles of feathered corpses.

Inspired with an idea, I improvised a Spell which crushed the pile of corpses together into three cylindrical battering rams. Now devoid of fear, I ordered the front line to assume battering position. My troops grabbed the original ram and, with the three others conjured from angel gore, prepared to ram the gates. I megaphoned: "Inside those gates is intense, toxic beauty. Deploy secondary radiation shields!" My troops snapped them on. "On the count of three, begin! One—two—THREE!"

With a deafening cry of hateful force, the warriors smashed the four rams into the Gates, once, twice, thrice. But despite the powerful blows, the gates remained sealed. "Again!" They smashed again and again with renewed fury and power. This time, the gates gave way slightly, but it seemed as if some obstruction on the other side was blocking them from opening. "AGAIN!" Even more ranks of warriors pushed themselves into ramming position. With a ferocious roar, they smashed the gates with even greater force.

Crrrrack! The Gates snapped free, but only yielding part way. Something on the other side was still blocking them. "Force them open! And beware the radiation!" With the brute power of Hell, the front line slammed at the Gates with enormous pressure. *CRRRAAACK!*

Our final thrust through the gates seemed to go against the fundamentals of nature. It was as if Heaven's Vibratory Density itself was offended by the gates being forced open, instead of opening joyfully. And, indeed, Nature itself reacted, for as they opened, a shocking subatomic rip sounded, akin to a sonic boom, that we could feel on our faces and skin. A thick roiling dust cloud formed, blinding our vision as the gates swung to their mirrored perihelion. We cringed and slitted our eyes in anticipation of the fearful sight within.

But instead of beauty, the partly-opened Gates revealed ugliness reminiscent of the black glory of Hell. An enormous, twenty-foot-high pile of stinking garbage was blocking the gates from opening. I was stunned, for it did resemble the entrance to East Hell, clogged as that entrance was with tin cans, coffee grinds, soiled newspapers and cardboard boxes, rusty bicycles, spring-punctured old sofas, and thousands of plastic trash bags.

I had a moment of cognitive dissonance, trying to reason how Heaven could be buried in hideous filth, and had an absurd but powerful thought: either this is not Heaven, or the leader of this realm is a hoarder, and the endless piles of refuse were the side effect of severe anxiety and depression. I megaphoned my demons: "Push through it! Quickly!"

As the Gates of Heaven burst open, the Demon Invaders were shocked by what they saw.

With a furious outcry, my troops upped their adrenaline and plowed through the enormous pile of filth, knocking it over, revealing behind it yet more enormous piles of trash.

The truth was evident now. There was no radiation of beauty coming from the City. There was only the ugly stench of garbage inside, as far as the eye could see.

"Shields down!" I disengaged my filters, as did my troops, and we stared into the expanse of the inner city square. It was like a city dump clogged with tall, rickety piles of junk.

Heaven was a city in ruins.

Odin and I eyed each other in amazement, as did my troops. There is nothing more puzzling than an expectation of beauty replaced by the comfort of ugliness and degradation.

Taking this as a sign of the Victory of Evil, we the invaders raised our voices as one and plowed like Viking berserkers into the ruins of Heaven.

Lo! Celestia now kneels before the glory of its magnificent victor, Lord Zyk of Asimoth. I smile ear to ear while writing about myself in the third person. Odd that my goal to defile God has somehow already been achieved. The exquisite ambience of filth permeating the city will make it a perfect annex to Hell.

After I secure Heaven and its remaining population, Odin and I will perform another Seeking Spell to over-ride Satan's Invisibility and determine his location. Then I will place the Time-Twister Bomb at a strategic location, and set it to detonate at the precise time when it will cause maximum destruction. Thus shall Lord Satan, the enemy race and God's Fortress be no more. God, if he exists, will be unable to fulfill his prophecy of Hell's ruin, and my conquest of Heaven will be complete.

If not for my chilblains, this would be a perfect day, Mr. Pöncé, for as you may infer, I am about to become the greatest villain in the Memory of the Cosmos, and certainly the Most Evil Demon in the History of Hell.

And then, they will *have* to respect me.

With dreams of a railroad spike through your neck,

ZYK

P.S. Remind me, after the conquest of Heaven is complete, to tell you about my curious, continuing dream journeys with Sister Debbie, my soul-hate. I feel those dreams are intertwined with my destiny, but would like to vent about that profound possibility, and about my sinuses exacerbating my ear infection.

LORD ZYK'S MEMO
ON THE LAST ANGEL
AND HIS TESTIMONY
REGARDING HEAVEN[1]

MEMO TO
MORTIMER PÖNÇÉ, ESQ.
PUBLISHER, MIND CONTROL PRESS
HELL HOLE WEST
CITY OF HELL

FROM
LORD ZYK OF ASIMOTH
FIELD BATTALION TENT
BATTLEFIELD OF HEAVEN

Detestable Mr. Pönçé,

To reply with concise perspicacity to your fascinating question, the most succulent human meal is undoubtably baked white supremacists who have been gang-violated from the rear. Demon gourmets rave at the savory layering of exquisitely sour flavors.

Tomorrow, after the Time-Twister Bomb eradicates Heaven's dismal future once and for all, I will be done with the exhausting—though infinitely rewarding—business of invading this deadly clime. I will also be free of all this time-consuming treachery that my grab for power requires. Once this matter is completed, I would deign to treat both you and your rotten-toothed secretary Magda to a delectable serving of Nazi Nachos at Maxwell's.

As for your question of what occurred once my warriors breached the Gates of Heaven, I must say that the most unlikely of events unfolded, like a soggy accordion bleating in the rain. I shall begin where I left off in our last correspondence, interrupted as I was by my Spellmaster Odin's daily modicum of unctuous praise, trying to curry my favor, albeit completely justified and deserved, by composing a poem about the maleficent ugliness of my blood-drenched hooves. It ran thusly:

---

1   Previously unpublished correspondence from the Editor's personal files.

ODE TO MY ODIOUS OVERLORD
by Odin the Obsequious

Only thy groincup chlamydeous
Compares to thy vile, dank and hideous
Claws, crusty knees, hooves and elbow,
Unfit to play flute, fife or cello.[2]
But chief in uncomeliness truly
Is thy fatuous face long and mulely,
Second only to organs detestable
Which to demons are quite undigestible.
Thy visage a pornograph etching
Causing nuns fits of roiling and retching.
Seeing thee in a Fun House mirror,
Your stop-a-clock face becomes queerer,
As does your reign, my King. So corruptly
Thou rule, your End must come abruptly.[3]

Although ostensibly praising my unparalleled Ugliness, Odin's poesy criticizing my musicianship is akin to a knife thrust into the unsuspecting scales of my back. But why harp on Odin's misspoken mewling concerning my musicality when I intend to have him decapitated yet again for his critique? Like other demon rogues decapitated repeatedly, his filthy neck will again have to await a cycle of eleven years to fully regenerate his head.[4]

More relevant is the momentous historical event which culminated after leading my troops to the Gates of Heaven. In fine, they stampeded, crushed and burst them asunder with a hateful force unparalleled in the annals of Evil Invasions. Boom went the gates, cracking and cleaving like a swine's hymen rapaciously cloven by a hog's corkscrew phallus.

Upon penetrating Heaven, we were astonished that there were no angels protecting it, and relieved that the city did *not* radiate rays of love. Quite the contrary, we were greeted by garbage, its comforting stench filling our nostrils. What had transpired here? Could it be that by audaciously storming the Gates of Heaven, I somehow unleashed a magical force that caused this ruin? For I *am* an inspired leader, perhaps the most successful in the history of Hell, and from now on I must own it.

---

2   It should be noted that Lord Zyk takes vain pride in his self-indulgent musical performances of funereal dirges, while forcing his captive audiences to listen and cheer his amateurish wailing, flibbertits and splats on these instruments. After the invasion, Odin's insulting verse resulted in Hell's Council of Injustice punishing him by forcing him to eat a raw Frenchman, followed by his expulsion from the League of Hateful Poets.

3   After quoting Odin's poem, Zyk seems not to interpret the last line as a cold and deadly warning. This seemingly self-serving doggerel was in fact a threat, presaging the treachery Odin would soon wreak against his despised Lord.

4   See *Encyclopaedia of Hell*, its entry on *Decapitation*, pg. 50.

LORD ZYK'S MEMO ON THE LAST ANGEL AND HIS TESTIMONY REGARDING HEAVEN

As my eyes adjusted to the shadows, I could articulate lines of giant trees surrounding the only building visible, a magnificent cathedral in the distance, half-buried beneath a chaos of garbage. Our rations of human infants were growing low; thus I ordered my troops to follow me through the trash, seeking angel citizens we could interrogate, torture and eat.

"Follow me!"

They followed me in rank and file toward the distant cathedral, through the narrow paths between the heaps of ruin. The brusqueness of my troops caused many teetering towers of trash to topple over, burying soldiers whom we hastily dug out. As the piles fell and settled, I led them on through the waist-high waste. We moved quickly, determined to reach the cathedral and make some sense of this madness.

But as I pushed through the trash bags, rusty bicycles, unwound eight-track tapes and stacks of old magazines, I came across the only creature we encountered—a large falcon with a tether around its neck, perched on a broken hot water heater. On my way to examine the bird, I stepped on something soft and squishy beneath the trash. I stopped, pressed my hoof down again on the object—and heard a moan.

I called out: "Someone's under here! Quickly! Dig him out!"

My adjutants burrowed down revealing an angel lying on his back. He was short, elderly, long white beard, bald on top, his eyes hidden behind antique, circular sunglasses, his girth caked with grime and coffee grinds. His blue jumpsuit was reminiscent of medical scrubs which his shoddy gray wings stuck through in the back. He had chubby hands and feet, wore one Adidas sneaker, the other foot bare and calloused.

When they uncovered him, he smiled idiotically, revealing a missing front tooth. Morgellon and Steve grabbed him by the arms and brusquely yanked his tiny frame upright.

He was exceedingly short, the trash line slightly above, one would imagine, his nipples. He shook his wings like a dog after a bath, splattering me and my lieutenants with muck.

The falcon fluttered comfortably onto the angel's shoulder, its tether connected to his wrist. He staggered forward, off-balance, unleashing a telescoping stick which he tapped down on the garbage, an extension of his vision.

At that moment I realized that he was blind. The bird, of course, was the avian equivalent of a seeing-eye dog.

"Yes, yes, quite blind," the angel murmured, reading my mind. "But I can sense my way around here better than you boys. So this is the invasion, eh? I really didn't think it would come to this. So you've unearthed me only to kill me?"

Steve, one of the two heads of my two-headed lieutenant, spoke up. "Yes. And with pleasure, fool."

"We'll feast on your flesh!" Morgellon, the other head, said. The surrounding demon voices murmured assent.

LORD ZYK'S MEMO on the LAST ANGEL and his TESTIMONY regarding HEAVEN

I raised an imperious hand to silence them.

The old angel shrugged. "I hope you don't mind. I took the liberty of reading yours. And yes, this is, unfortunately, what Heaven has become. It is an unpleasant tale I shall relate to you anon. I am Dr. Horace Birdfire. Myself, my assistant Brother Bebo, and Amos and Joe, our dinosaur guards, are the only angels left. I know you've encountered Amos and Joe at the entrance."

"Yes," Odin said. "They are now dog's meat."

The angel frowned, his eyes tearing up. "How terribly unfortunate. I do hope, for the dogs' sake, that our beloved dinosaur friends at least taste decent and will sate the poor dogs' hunger. For your information, I am the first and last of the angels. The others have either died or abandoned us for more habitable, antiseptic realms. The cathedral? The Hospice of Heaven. Where I keep his majesty. Follow me, please, and I'll take you to him." He turned and waded through the trash, tapping his cane in the direction of the enormous edifice.

I asked, "You are, of course, referring to God? And explain what happened to your city."

The elderly angel, a bit fatigued due to his age and diminutive size, said, "I tell you what. Why don't we have a little sit-down and you can properly interrogate me."

I barked an order. "Clear the area! Find two things to sit on!"

Working quickly, my adjutants cleared the immediate area, revealing what looked like a street of golden bricks. They placed a broken refrigerator on its side and a skeletal sit-down lawnmower next to it, where the angel and I sat.

"Ramona! Take notes!" She materialized from the shadow of a tall pile of offal, as she was wont to do, and began scribbling on a soiled pad with her raven's feather.

"Let the interrogation begin," I commanded.

Detailed notes were taken by my savant, who despised Horace for reasons that will become evident to you.[5] Now I must cut this short to deal with many arcane matters that have arisen to the Glory of our Evil Enterprise.

In arrogance and in haste, I close,

ZYK

---

5   See *Battalion Field Report 33-352*, which follows.

BATTALION
FIELD REPORT

ATTNG-33 352

SUBJECT: Interrogation of Prisoner 1A Horace Birdfire

THRU: LIEUTENANT RAMONA IYAM, 1ST
Battlefield Tent in Enemy Perimeter

TO: Commandant Lord Zyk of Asimoth

PRISONER INFORMATION:

ID'd himself as Angel Horace Catullus Birdfire, Chief of Psychiatry at Heaven Hospice, one of two angels remaining in Heaven City.

DEMEANOR OF PRISONER:

As a Runner-Up or recipient of a Dishonorable Mention for three years in a row in the East Hell Annual Strangulation Contest, I despised the prisoner so much it was all I could do to refrain from ripping the long white beard off his chin and throttling him with it. Despite the fact that we found him buried in filth, his city in ruins and his life and career destroyed, the prisoner's delusion was to express everything with annoying positivity. However, the main reason why I hereby vow to murder the prisoner is because of my intolerance to excessive smiling. As you know, I favor my own demeanor, for in general we savants eschew the bane of smiling and talking.

APPEARANCE OF PRISONER:

Height 4' 6 ½". Waist 40 ½. Hat size 8 ¼". Wearing a white robe, soiled from mud at the hemline, frayed at the sleeve-ends. White beard 1' 4 ¾". A small sign pinned via safety pin to the back of his robe, which read "KICK ME."[1] The prisoner's lips were wrinkled in such a way to form a perpetual smile, revealing crooked, aged, yellowed teeth. His earlobes had extended with age and the crows-feet wrinkles on the far ends of each eyehole were dry, leathery and purplish. His eyes themselves were bloodshot as if from excessive drinking, but maintained a hideously bright and exuberant twinkle. Overall his eyes and expressions suggested a total lack of evil thoughts that, in his demeanor of upbeat positivity, made him the being I hated more than any other being I had ever encountered, save an incontinent, humanoid Turd Creature I beheaded centuries ago at the Slicing Sacraments of Geb.

Finally, it appeared that his pet falcon was attached to his wrist in order to assist him in his blindness and guide his way through the city. Further, the bird and the angel had a symbiotic relationship, for the bird on his shoulder received its sustenance by picking lice and other parasites from his beard.

REGARDING HIS BLINDNESS:

The prisoner claims that his psychic senses are able to project a blurred but understandable image of his surroundings which he sees as a screen in his head. Thus he claims to be able to sense his surroundings despite his blindness. That ability, combined with his pet falcon serving as his seeing-eye bird, allows him to function efficiently as Chief of Psychiatry.

SUMMARY OF INTERROGATION:

Despite Lord Zyk demanding that Birdfire get to the point and only answer the questions asked, the elderly fool insisted on recounting his entire life story in great detail, including ten minutes describing his joy hatching from his primordial egg, five minutes describing the menu of his preschool lunches, and six minutes listing his favorite types of hard candy.

He finally got around to the information we require. In discussing his psychiatric work, he unexpectedly became focused and concise. His words from the interrogation transcript follow.

---

1   I inferred from his lack of awareness of the sign that it had been placed there as a prank, perhaps by his employer, the Personified God.

"*Eons ago, Heaven was originally created as a psychiatric facility for the treatment of the Personified Creator, who, I'm sorry to say, had gone mad. Through the centuries, a surfeit of buildings were added around the facility, giving it the illusion of a city, instead of what it really was, a cosmic mental hospital. During the ensuing eons, I've had the honor of treating the oft-changing psychosis of my only patient, the physical embodiment of All That Is, the Personified Creator—whom I sometimes call the 'PG.'*

"*PG, as a creator, was also interested in developing his ability to create worlds with his mind in a simpler way. Ever since his youth, he wanted to be a writer, and spent most of his time tapping away at a keyboard obsessively, writing poetry, stories and novels. Since he had created the physical universe with his mind, he wanted to create other worlds that would live on paper. This was PG's chief form of therapy, writing, in order to work out his mental and emotional problems.*

"*Unfortunately, as it turned out, this was not a cure.*

"*Treating the strange, self-inflicted, psychological wounds of the Creator was exciting in the early days. Here I was, a young angel fresh out of medical school, and now I found myself in effect healing the Universe Itself by proxy.[2] But after eons of daily therapy sessions with the PG, another event occurred which, in combination with the Creator's pitiable madness, made an unfortunate situation increasingly dangerous.*

"*For Heaven had fallen victim to its greatest quality, a seemingly positive trait which attracted tourists from distant realms—the fact that here nothing dies. In the naïveté of my youth, I assumed that a Heaven in which nothing ages, decomposes, oxidizes, rusts or otherwise breaks is what makes it reign supreme above all other parts of Creation. But after eons, the angelic population learned the hard way that Heaven's Triumph over Death resulted in its ruin.*

---

2   Birdfire summed up his early diagnosis of the Personified God's mental illness as follows:

"*The Personified God's first episode of psychosis was simple bilocation, his mind splitting and sharing the souls of many trillions of life-forms at once. Unfortunately, the effects of his instability created corresponding instabilities in the physical universe. Thus we have begun back-engineering our therapies, starting with 'ailments' in the universe, so to speak, and seeing if fixing them will in turn cure PG.*

"*In our weekly medical exams, we observed elevated comorbidity prolactin levels in his pituitary, resulting in schizophrenic delusions, osteoporosis and erectile dysfunction. As I explained, we were fascinated to find corresponding symbolic comorbidities occurring in the physical universe.*

"*For example. the erectile dysfunction of the universe corresponded to an impotence in the cosmic orgasm of the Big Bang. A simultaneous lowering in the dispersal of cosmic rays observed by our astronomical observatories corresponds esoterically to the lowering of the Personified God's libido, resulting in the impotence of his creative powers. By injecting a black hole with an inhibitor, administered by a ten-thousand-mile-long hypodermic needle operated remotely from our mothership, we blocked the muting effect of quantum impotence, allowing the normal exchange of cosmic fluids necessary while performing magic, enacting divine intervention, interpenetrating dimensions and other godly duties.*" (excerpt from "Update on God's Insanity." *Weekly Report on the Personified God's Mental Status*, Vol. 801, pg. 66).

"For a strange and deadly cataclysm crept into Heaven, the one you see around us, the incremental horror that I refer to as The Garbage Tsunami. This slow, insidious catastrophe took place over countless eons—a diluvium of indestructible trash slowly burying our once-pristine Kingdom.

"I assumed that once the PG was made aware of this in his daily therapy sessions, that with one simple snap of his, her or its fingers, depending on what gender It preferred on that particular day, the vast heaps of garbage would simply disappear, dissolving back into PG's mindstuff, and Heaven would instantly return to its former pristine glory.

"But such was not to be. For just as trash accumulated through the centuries, so did the Creator's mental state decline through the centuries, and the Tsunami became a slow-motion flood clogging Heaven. Due to this awful scourge, millions of Heaven's Angelic Citizens abandoned their homeland to escape not only the garbage, but the sad, daily reminder of the Inelegant Imperfection of Intelligent Infinity, their beloved God.

"Although most left, thousands remained, inspired by their faith—and mine—that PG would one day be cured. After further centuries, these thousands who remained gradually formed a cult, calling themselves The Order of Ravens, after the smartest species of birds. Convinced by faith alone that the PG would soon be cured, they gathered each day to pray for what they called The Curative. They believed that The Curative would be their salvation, and lead to a new dispensation of sanity and love."

When he came to this part of his narrative, the old angel could not restrain his tears, saying he was reminded of the young angel, one of the Ravens, who strapped a bomb to her chest and tried to blow up the hospital, but only managed to blow up a hot dog stand, a sewer grating, and herself.

The fool blew his nose and continued:

"Unfortunately, instead of getting worse. His behavior became more erratic, weird and inexplicable. Each day PG's insanity acted out in a different, unexpected way.

"One day the Creator strapped his feet to the backs of two giant bats, ripped off his clothes and flew them naked over the city side-by-side, dive-bombing angel pedestrians

while he played polkas on an accordion. Another time, 'he' metamorphosed himself into multiple giant radioactive monsters he called God-zilla, and went on a rampage stomping on angels and crushing the city's buildings, bridges and infrastructure. Another time 'he' transformed entire city boroughs into giant urinals and flushed the Order of Ravens over and over into Heaven Bay.

"Since this went on for eons, the PG's fits of madness were too numerous and varied to list in your brief report.[3]

"The long and short of it is that our therapy wasn't working. I had to face the truth—I might not have the medical skills to successfully treat his illness. The possibility existed that the Personified Creator's outré behavior might continue like this unto eternity with no cure, no meaningful endgame in sight."

By this time in the interrogation, it had taken hours for Birdfire to reveal the present nature of the Creator's illness. Growing impatient, Lord Zyk put an end to the interrogation and asked exactly where the Personified God was located. Birdfire said that he, she or it was locked in a padded cell for his, her or its own safety. Lord Zyk placed Birdfire in custody as a prisoner of war, and demanded to be taken to meet the PG at once. Birdfire agreed.

Thus concludes my field notes concerning the interrogation of Angel Horace Catullus Birdfire, submitted hatefully by Hell's Recording Savant Ramona Iyam, Personal Assistant and Invasion Supply Accountant to Zyk of Asimoth, Lord of Hell.

/s/ A B Odin

/t/ A B ODIN

Lt Col AGG

Asst AG

---

3   Such as transforming the bodies of the angelic population into candy and infusing their tongues with the need to lick themselves, projecting giant video loops on the sky, stretching from horizon to horizon, of funny cat videos and obnoxious commercials for sauna pants, acne cream and automated egg scramblers. Know further, O Peruser of Annotations, that Dr. Birdfire claimed to have faithfully scoured the medical records of every insane being who had ever existed throughout the universe, but found no analogous medical precedence to help him understand how to protect himself and the faithful Cult of Angels from their Creator's insanity. God's passive-aggressive behaviors verily mocked Birdfire's attempts to find a model of therapy, a balance of meds, hypnotic or surgical procedures, etc., and made Birdfire's quest to cure God's Divine Insanity a heart-breaking failure.

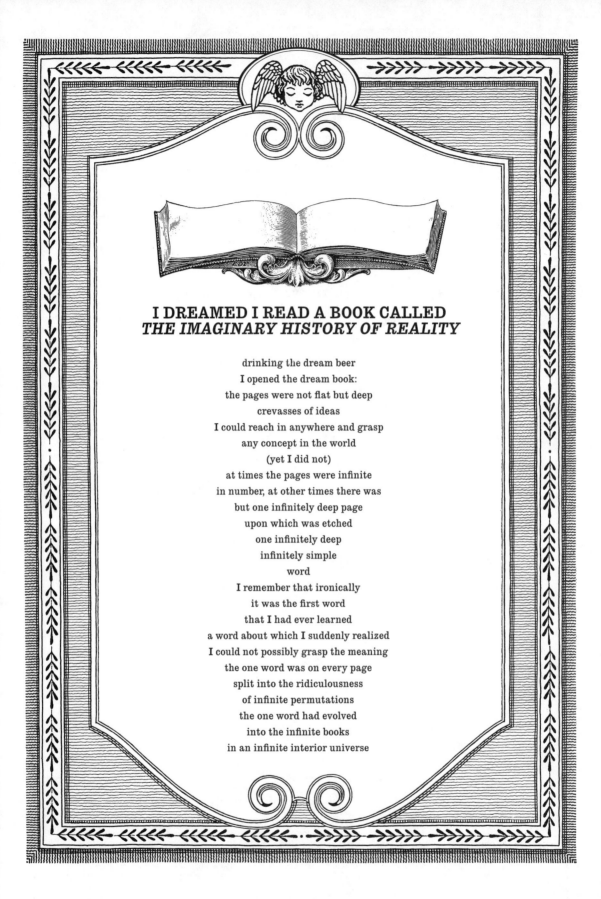

I DREAMED I READ A BOOK CALLED
THE IMAGINARY HISTORY OF REALITY

drinking the dream beer
I opened the dream book:
the pages were not flat but deep
crevasses of ideas
I could reach in anywhere and grasp
any concept in the world
(yet I did not)
at times the pages were infinite
in number, at other times there was
but one infinitely deep page
upon which was etched
one infinitely deep
infinitely simple
word
I remember that ironically
it was the first word
that I had ever learned
a word about which I suddenly realized
I could not possibly grasp the meaning
the one word was on every page
split into the ridiculousness
of infinite permutations
the one word had evolved
into the infinite books
in an infinite interior universe

and after the universe exploded,
or dissipated,
the infinite pages of the infinite books
vanished
into the silence of a wordless void
pull back cinematically from the depiction
of the ultimate void
revealing it on the dust jacket
of the book you read
at the beginning of your dream
the imaginary history of reality
the book you now hold in your hands
in the eternal moment of now
the infinite commemorative edition
being read at this moment
through your eyes by the ultimate reader
squinting as he squirms in the void
thumbing through infinite pages
for the final chapter
that sums up the sweet
and languid emptiness
of the creation premise
on the final page explaining
the infinite etymology
of the final word
of the non-existent speaker
finding instead
only the silence
that follows and separates all
words

From *The Imaginary History of Reality, Lost Poems*
by the Personified God.

❧ EDITOR'S NOTE ☙

*This excerpt chronicles the start
of Lord Satan's dangerous journey through
God's Infinite Library, wherein he encounters
and defeats a Talkative Plaque in his
search for a mysterious book.*

LORD SATAN
LOST IN THE LIBRARY OF
GOD

❦

EXCERPT No. 2
FROM SATAN'S BEST-SELLING MEMOIR

FEAR ME
THE MONSTROUS MEMORIES OF SATAN, LORD OF HELL

VI. THE UNWELCOME WELCOME PLAQUE

Having killed the library window, I entered through its corpse. On the wall facing me, a sign read: "THE LIBRARY OF GOD." Under it was the library's logo, a Phoenix in flames, reborn from its own ashes. Under that was the legend, in smaller letters: *Transformation Through Information*. The room was vast. I would soon find that this was the first of a seemingly infinite series of rooms with high, vaulted ceilings, all filled with books.

By the entrance was a large, colorful Plaque, grotesquely adorned with hearts, smiley-faces, rainbows and unicorns.[1] I gave the room a once-over, noting that the entire interior was imbued with bright colors and idiotic slogans promoting the ludicrous philosophy of positivity. The Plaque displayed illegible pictograms and glyphs. Curiously, a sledgehammer was mounted to one side, bound by leather straps, labeled SLEDGEHAMMER. On the other side, similarly mounted, was a small backpack, labeled BURN PACK. Over the plaque was a row of unreadable letters which, when I looked upon it, instantaneously rearranged into Low Demonic.[2] The plaque now read:

WELCOME TO THE LIBRARY OF GOD!

Tripped by sensors at my approach, the plaque began speaking in a somewhat effeminate male voice that might be described as presumptuously intimate or, alternatively, drearily cute. I was already in a sour mood thanks to all the positivity everywhere, but what happened next pushed me over the edge. Through a row of small, high-quality Bose speakers, the Plaque's voice chirped thusly:

"Wow! So, you made it! Welcome to God's Library! I am your Information Guide, having been made quasi-sentient by God so I can roll out this fun little talk. If you're in a hurry, or have been here before and already know the ropes, you can turn me off by pressing the red button playfully labeled 'Shut the Plaque Up Already!'"

---

1   Hell's historians have noted that this design matches that of God's Diary, which Satan encountered later in the Personified God's office.

2   This is the language of Hell, created in my youth, that I sadistically forced demons to conjugate.

So dismal. Then the Plaque chuckled. Unbearable.

Straight away, of course, I went for the *Shut-Up Button*. But an instant *before* my claw touched the Button, the Plaque blurted out a blathering that gave me pause. Since I have a flawless, pristine memory concerning All Things About Me, save the details regarding my own hazy origin, I reproduce below the Plaque's annoying screed verbatim:

"Wait! Sorry, but if you *don't* listen you'll likely suffer another terrible accident within a couple minutes, and who needs that? I mean, you were already injured by that nasty book, so believe me, Lord Satan, you won't regret hearing me out. (Yes, my sensors have scanned, profiled and identified you and the events leading up to our present encounter.) Let me repeat, while it's true that I'm not fully sentient, my AI bank is big enough to simulate a pretty decent conversation. I mean, the goal of AI isn't to make quantum circuits *actually* conscious, but rather just to *simulate* it. Sentient beings are half-asleep most of the time anyway, so programming with a lot of self-awareness-simulating-phrases does the trick, even though I don't *actually* have real consciousness, *nicht wahr?*

"Education aside, the only requirement of visitors to The Library of God is to have *fun*. So, Lord Satan, we've come up with a humdinger you might like! In order to be allowed entry, you must first put on this backpack. In your case, we'll call it a Burn Bag."

The Plaque chuckled again as a mechanical arm extruded, handing me the backpack. The sign continued, "In addition to finding the book you seek, please choose any books you hate the most, put them in the backpack, and burn them when you return to Hell. Please put on the Burn Bag to allow entry."

I ground my fangs until I tasted enamel, but put on the backpack to get through this nonsense. It was light and a perfect fit, so it was no big deal.

"Allow me to explain how to find what you're looking for amongst the infinite books before you. And yes, I did say *infinite* books, and that's a tad misleading, for the truth is, there are *no* infinite number of objects anywhere. Infinite space doesn't even exist; all seemingly infinite spatial areas are automatically generated mathematically by your perceptual interface. 'Infinite books' is just a catchy, dumbed-down term to explain the nature of the library, which is actually a meta-self-recursive-algorithmic-iteration program (whatever *that* means!) which will bring more and more potential books into existence *only* when they intersect your perceptive path.

"Specifically, when you walk down an aisle, it'll seem as if there are *tons* of books stretching out as far as you can see. But really, they just materialize into existence the moment you look. Just out of your perceptual field, there's really nothing there till you turn your head in that direction and look. What you can't see doesn't have to be materialized, right? Who needs to waste all that processing power? *What you see is what you get."*

I felt my gorge rise along with my blood pressure. Algorithmic creation was old news to me since it's the essence of Black Magick. I'd discovered it eons ago while putting the final touches on expanding Hell, giving it just the right look of ferocity, keeping it intimidating to my demon slaves. It takes an annoying amount of processing power to create an infinite Heaven or Hell—but there was no other way to do it. Still, if something seems real—looks, tastes, smells, feels real—then it *is* real. (With the caveat that Reality itself, of course, is an illusion, a total sham.)

"Moving on. This Library contains every book ever written in every galaxy in the multiverse from the beginning till the end of time. Curated for your personal taste today, we feature every book written by the Personified God, some good, some bad, numbering in the mega-trillions, as well as the infinitude of good and bad books he, she or it did *not* write. Now, enough talking *about* the Library; let's get right into what the Library actually *is*.

"For starters, *All That Is* can't write a book by itself, right? It's just some kind of a unique, amorphous, self-aware, infinite energy, right? I mean, one of the original problems was, if *All That Is* doesn't have a body, then it can't do anything except *be*.

All That Is needed an actual hand in order to cast a Spell, fingers to draw, a mouth to sing, and so on. So first things first, she manifested a physical body. (Yes, this time I said *she* instead of *it*. Just for fun, let's pick a gender since your language tends to get unwieldy when talking about squirrely things like *All That Is*.) Her body, also known as the Personified God, or PG, lives right here in Heaven City. Despite a lot of personal problems over the eons, she's personally written every book in this library. I mean, PG has plenty of time, since both the past and the future are composed of unquantified durations back-engineered in either direction.

"Specifically, PG wrote every book in this library about herself. Each book explores different aspects of her multifarious wonderfulness, strangeness, joys and sorrows, her modesty (considering that she's the only thing that is), and her overall magnificence. She's written autobiographical memoirs, vast collections of poetry, plays and third-person fictional satires about herself, how-to books about the techniques she invented to materialize the universe, comic books, in which she plays superheroes, villains, love interests, I mean, you name it, she's *it*. Not to mention trillions of science books exploring what *All That Is* could possibly be composed of, you know, the fundamental hypostasis underlying everything. Not to mention all the mathematics, philosophy and theology she wrote about herself, legal books so that she could sue herself, medical books so she could operate on herself, books of criticism and denunciation about herself, and so on. Just think of a big good-natured egomaniac who has nothing but herself to think about and that's basically what we've got here, *n'est-ce pas?*

"So that's about it. Have fun exploring, Lord Satan. Don't forget to grab the books you hate most to burn later! And if you have any questions, just pick any book and open to any page.

"Oh, and I obviously took the liberty of scanning your purpose in coming here, which is to learn about your origin, so here's a tip—try the aisle labeled *Books Written by God.* Because unfortunately, the information you're looking for, the *real* reason behind your creation, was rather an embarrassment to the Personified God, so there was a bit of a cover-up. I'm afraid she tucked away some of that stuff so that angel readers wouldn't trouble their pretty little heads about it. She likes to keep the mood upbeat here, especially when the overall *gestalt* starts to fall apart, which certainly has been the case lately. The fact is, her reason for creating you was always a thorn in her side, but try not to take it personally. You've always been kind of on the outs, a *persona non grata* with the Creator, a bit of a problem child, because the bottom line is..."

And with that, it was check-out time. I grabbed the sledgehammer from the plaque and crushed the sign to pieces. As I had smashed the hard-hat dispenser. But this time with more feeling. Not to be outdone, the wreckage of the sign managed to have the last words, which it squeaked over hissy, smoking speakers: *"Sorry for rambling on like that. Good luck on your journey, Lord Satan. Ciao!"* The speakers shorted out with a pathetic puff of greenish smoke, and that was that.

The visceral act of destroying the plaque gave me some satisfaction, and I wondered—who put the sledgehammer there in the first place?

I saw an adjacent aisle labeled *Books Written by God* and turned down it. For if the Plaque was true to its simulated word, it was there that I would find out the truth of how and why I was created by the Being I had come to kill.

⁖ EDITOR'S NOTE ⁖

Metatron, Chronicler of Heaven's history, researched the ancient legend of the Invasion of Heaven by plugging the Akashic Memory Bank into a slot in his head, and writing down what he saw. Since the Akashic is notoriously subjective, as well as a victim of prankster angels re-editing ancient scrolls, some details contradict other accounts. Thus are Metatron's transcripts clear in lyrical expression, but confused on corroborative facts.

ON ODIN'S TREACHERY, WHILST THE LAST ANGEL LEADS LORD ZYK TO GOD'S PADDED CELL

FROM THE

AKASHIC RECORD

TRANSCRIBED BY METATRON, SCRIBE AND RECORDING ANGEL, CELESTIAL ONLINE UNIVERSITY[1]

———⧓———

I am again honored to share my visions of the Akashic Records, events in antiquity recorded by the Living Universe and described as I see them now with my inner eye. I begin. I hear a clicking sound. I see churning billows of lavender and chartreuse clouds. The mist slowly parts with a fanfare of trumpets to reveal the desired target from Heaven's History, a scene conjured by our intent.

We are now with Lord Zyk breaking through the golden gates of Celestia eaven with battering rams wielded by his league of six thousand, six hundred and sixty-six bloodthirsty troops. Things are occurring very quickly. They are inside. Lord Zyk uncovers and discovers Horace, the legendary last angel, he who is charged as protector to All That Is. Lord Zyk demands of the old angel, "Take me to your leader."

---

1   For the Angelic scholar on a budget.

Zyk and his demon lackeys follow Horace through the filthy causeway of Celestia. As the senile angel leads them hobbling with his golden cane, he often hums sumptuous melodies wind makes as it whistles through his long, filthy beard. Being blind, his sense of sound is hypersensitive. Thus he hums rhythms in counterpoint to those made by his feet and his cane shuffling through the chaos of refuse, the material that fills the city like excreta filling the intestines of a sated Offal Beast. He knows how much his humming aggravates the demons, and this pleases him. Sometimes he is bursting with angelic positivity; at other times he is silent and contemplative, as befitting a blind member of the strange species angelorum avem paradiso.

Time check. It is morning in Heaven. Blooming on the horizon is the Black Sun of Paradise, that astral Presence which radiates black spectral light to all thought-forms enveloped in its rays. As I intimately watch Lord Zyk following the old angel, I can hear tendrils of the sun's photonic quanta whispering into Zyk's ear with a faint, desiderate hiss, "All is Good… All is Light… All is One." Irritated, Zyk swats away the blasphemous susurrus as a goat's tail, in other timelines, swats away Hessian gnats.

Horace leads them through the sea of trash to an angular Isle of Gold, the center of the metropolis, the famous Circle of Eternal Rejoicing. Much like the whisper of the sun, subsonic bass speakers attached to massive alabaster columns speak in semiotic subtones to Lord Zyk and his men as they enter the Square, saying "All is as it should be! Rejoice you may now? Is this not cause for? Then why do you not?" Again, Lord Zyk swats it away, as a bear gnawing on a coon head flicks away flies, and leans to rest on a strange, long, rectangular machine, one of hundreds installed in concentric circles around the Golden Plaza.

His finger shaking with age, Horace points to the entrance of the massive building dominating the plaza. Its sign glistens strangely in the black sunlight, reading

THE HOSPICE OF HEAVEN

"Our glorious leader is in there," Horace says with an unexpected hiccup. Unfortunately, the addition of the hiccup makes it ambiguous as to whether the phrase "glorious leader" was meant to be sincere, or sarcastic. I sense it is sincere, that he loves our God, despite everything. Time check. It is 6 a.m. local time, a magical period to bask in Heaven's vibratory etheria, the cool, clear magentic field. Here the vibrations are so off the charts, Lord Zyk again experiences one of the side effects, another almost imperceptible chitter of tiny voices in his ears, as if invisible insects are flitting in and out of existence around him.

Lord Zyk's facial expressions reveal his quixotic thoughts. He is worried about what could go wrong, immersed in potential glitches to the secret agenda of his invasion. He is also worried about something deeper and less real. For some reason he thinks that since Satan is partly an astral being, and has also been affected by the magentic field, he may somehow meet Sister Debbie in the astral realm and fall in love with her. Thus Zyk wants to be Satan's successor, powerful enough so that Debbie would in turn love him. He knows that his thoughts are not logical, but also knows that in this respect only, he is at the mercy of Heaven's deadly field.

Confused by these thoughts, Lord Zyk stops at the entrance to the hospice and tells Horace that before entering the hospice and meeting the creator, he wants to gain his bearings. He says he will call for Horace presently to take him to meet his leader.

Having turned away from the old angel, Zyk unrolls a large, crinkly parchment atop of one of the many rectangular contraptions which, Lord Zyk thinks, resemble the tanning machines that demon tourists use in the Glacier Hotels of North Hell. The parchment, a Map of Heaven given to Zyk by his treacherous lieutenant Odin, is a masterful engraving of Evil Art as well as an example of cutting-edge military intel. It is, however, difficult to read, obscured as it is by a Cloud of Unknowing, a mist that obstructs the drones' aerial view of the city.

But by closely comparing areas on the Map to corresponding areas surrounding him, Lord Zyk understands the problem. For the layer of mist on the Map is actually the layer of trash covering the city, as seen from high above, rendering the infrastructure invisible.

Now that he knows what the Map means in its strangeness, he is able to piece together what he needs to know to carry out his agenda.

"Ramona!" Zyk calls. His demon accountant Ramona Iyam materializes at his side.[2]

Ramona possesses a phenomenal photographic memory. As the invasion proceeds, she is assiduous in tracking the army's food rations, weaponry and sexual needs. While writing nothing down, Ramona's legendary mind-matrix retains every detail, always aware of anything that may interfere with Lord Zyk's plan.

But Zyk now needs Ramona for her other talent—her savant skill as a Sidereal Astrologer.

For now she is being called upon to calculate the complex horary factors that will determine the success or failure of Zyk's secret plan to kill God and Satan. Aware of his lieutenants watching them surreptitiously, Zyk barks at Ramona, "Activate your primary Thought Slot." She nods and closes her eyes. Lord Zyk conjures a small diamond-shaped flash drive and slides it into a matching slot in her head. Ramona hums and trembles slightly as she downloads the intel which Lord Zyk has secretly prepared. It plays as a neuron-compatible audio file and speaks in her head as follows:

"Ramona, as you know, Lord Satan left on a rogue mission to destroy God and Heaven. He does not know that, after learning of God's plan to destroy Hell, I seized an opportunity to launch my own concurrent invasion. I did this to protect Hell, as well as further my career through treachery. As you know, Treason, and her eloquent sister Betrayal, are the lowest and most detestable acts of evil, and thus the most cherished by demons. With that in mind, and to kill two birds with one stone, your assignment is as follows:

---

2   Ramona, having evolved from a race of Umbric Jinn, could hide, undetected, in shadows until her presence was required. Although her genius intellect was in constant demand by Lord Zyk, she preferred to stay present but hidden while on duty. In her memoir *Shrieks of a Shadow Savant* (Feral House), she recounts her acute awareness of her ungainly appearance, "from the skin of my stout, oatmeally torso rife with splotches of vitiligo, to my ducklike feet covered with purple chilblains." It is rumored that Ramona's comely, childlike face is the result of a charm she paid Odin to cast in order to make her leprous hide less savagely revolting.

"1. Odin could not create a Spell strong enough to pinpoint God's location, but was able to determine Lord Satan's location and the potential trajectory of his movements.

"2. Calculate where and when to detonate the Time-Twister Bomb to fulfill two Prime Objectives:

"a. That Heaven's existence in the flow of time will be erased past the moment of the bomb's detonation, leaving in its wake an ugly cosmic wound in the carcass of Heaven, known as a Void of Time.

"b. That Lord Satan, his tremendous power matched by that of the bomb, be cast by the blast into the Time Void, and become lost in its fierce and unfathomable depths.

"Know, Ramona, that although Lord Satan cannot be killed, still, through the Bomb's chain reaction, he can be physically thrust, tetherless and alone, into the primeval Time Void. Although demon physicists do not know the precise effect of the Void on demon physiology, it is generally agreed that within that zone of emptiness, cause and effect cancel each other out. Thus, although Satan cannot be killed, his cosmic power will be strongly challenged, if not completely nullified, by the Void. He will be nicely neutered, up the creek without a paddle, lost so deeply in the Nothingness that demonkind can at last celebrate the long-awaited end to the reign of Satan, Creator of Hell."

Ramona hears a metallic *click* in her head as the voice recording ends. She stops humming and trembling, opens her eyes and whispers into Zyk's ear: "Transfer complete, my Lord." A beat, then she whispers, "I have already determined the optimum placement of the Bomb, and have calculated the most auspicious time for its detonation." She points to a spot on the map. Zyk casts a Spell to expand the map's detail, revealing the optimum location for the Bomb's placement: the left side of the second stone step leading to the entrance of a building labeled God's Library. Ramona then whispers the most auspicious time: "Tomorrow, at 6:42:23pm."

Lord Zyk's removes something from his pack, a rectangular gift box, gaily wrapped with ribbons and bows. As he hands it to Ramona, their eyes meet significantly, for only she and Zyk know that inside it is the Time-Twister Bomb, the most devastating weapon ever created. It is the weapon, one that affects and alters the depths of time and creation, which will change the destiny of dimensions, histories and the trilateral fates of Hell, Earth and Heaven.

He smiles at her grimly. "You know what to do." She nods and walks away with the gift box through the ungainly landscape of garbage, on her mission to discreetly place the Bomb where the Map indicates—thirteen inches from the left-hand side of the Library Steps.

As I watch Ramona leave, I transfer my focus to Odin the Obsequious, who has been spying upon Zyk and Ramona from behind filtered eye shades. Having taken mental note of the time and place Ramona indicates on the map, Odin excuses himself. He sneaks into the hospital, finds an empty office painted pink and robin's-egg blue, the walls inexplicably covered with teddy bears which had been nailed into it, enters the room and locks the door behind him.[3]

Now alone and in a meditative state with the teddy bears, the Spell Master conjures his own Master Enchantment to supplant the Spells of Lord Zyk. Noting the time of his query, he formulates a Horary Spell to determine the precise moment to detonate the bomb, so that it will destroy not only Lord Satan, but also Lord Zyk. Odin's enchantment reveals that the Bomb must detonate today at 6:42:23pm, instead of tomorrow. Through further magical manipulation, Odin enchants Zyk's future actions so that both he and Lord Satan will be influenced to gather dangerously near the Bomb today at 6:42:23pm, The Hour of Doom, when—Boom. If his treachery succeeds, the metaphysical force of the time-erasure cataclysm will cast both Zyk and Satan to their deaths in the strange, inconceivable labyrinth of the Time Void.[4]

Odin conjures a small radio-controlled detonator which appears in his claw. His Master Spell manipulates astrological, black magical and quantum physical forces to bring an unknowing Zyk, Satan and the Personified God together at the designated time. The Spell combines the manual pressing of the detonator with a visual symbol, for when Odin sees the shadow of ravens fly over the detonator, he will press the Button. He carefully plays out the sequence of events in his mind, reviewing each step to insure its inexorable, evil perfection. He revels in his treachery. He will spread the word amongst his military allies that a coup is in place which will make him King. Odin feels a satisfied power in his joints, toes and genitalia, a feeling that he knows from experience signifies a Spell that is flawlessly constructed.

Finally, he ingests a designer tab of acid from his belt dispenser, a dose engineered to last thirty seconds and unveil (for reasons of military incentive and psychological positivity) a grandiose vision of a demon's potential future and fate:

In Odin's trip, the room splits apart from the constructs of reality. In its place he sees himself on the balcony of Hell Palace, festooned with celebratory wreaths and bunting, as he is worshipped by an assembled multitude of demons in the plaza below. The throng chant "Odin the Obsequious, the legendary Demon King!" Odin, whose treason rewards him, not only with the Throne of Hell, but also with eternal dominion over All That Is.

The lavender and chartreuse mist again obscures my view. I close.

Namaste.

---

3   As postulated in Ranganak's disputed tract *Symbolic Tropes in the Death of Heaven*, the teddy bears were not only artifacts of a schizophrenic episode earlier that week by the Personified God, but were also foreshadowed by Odin's astrological reading that morning from his ship's AI Astrologer, predicting *"The seductive influence of a sleuth of bears will strengthen your perverse Talent for Treachery."*
4   Odin did not know whether Satan or the Personified God could actually be killed, but he did know the homely Precept of the ancient demon Dongdrape the Destroyer: *All must die who do not try.*

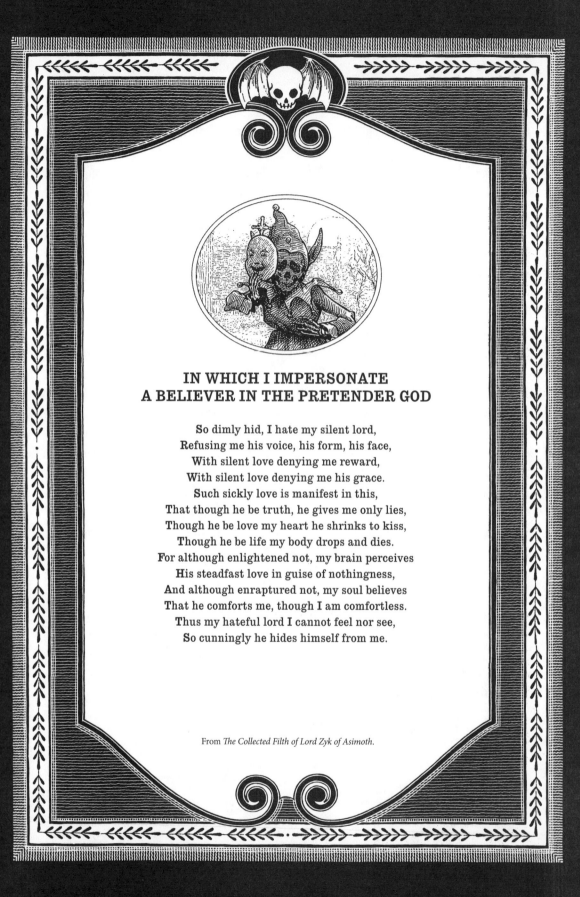

IN WHICH I IMPERSONATE
A BELIEVER IN THE PRETENDER GOD

So dimly hid, I hate my silent lord,
Refusing me his voice, his form, his face,
With silent love denying me reward,
With silent love denying me his grace.
Such sickly love is manifest in this,
That though he be truth, he gives me only lies,
Though he be love my heart he shrinks to kiss,
Though he be life my body drops and dies.
For although enlightened not, my brain perceives
His steadfast love in guise of nothingness,
And although enraptured not, my soul believes
That he comforts me, though I am comfortless.
Thus my hateful lord I cannot feel nor see,
So cunningly he hides himself from me.

From *The Collected Filth of Lord Zyk of Asimoth.*

THE TALE OF THE LAST ANGEL

EXCERPT FROM

THE HISTORIES OF HELL'S CRAVEN CONQUESTS

BY HARGOBIND THE RAPACIOUS[1]
ADJUNCT PROFESSOR OF ABHORRENT HISTORIES
UNIVERSITY OF HELL, WEST.

———◆———

CHAPTER 17

As Horace led Lord Zyk to meet the Creator, the demon noticed stacks of strange, white objects in the distance. They appeared to be bodies with large white wings laying in massive piles under distant rows of trees. Puzzled, he asked Horace, "By the trees, are those angels?"

Horace sighed. "Were."

"Pardon?" Zyk said.

"They were angels," Horace replied. "They're all dead."

Zyk and his evil lieutenants felt the strangeness of the angel's response. For that was a reply they would expect to hear in Hell, not in Heaven.

"What happened to them?" Lord Zyk asked.

"I shall explain," the elderly angel said. "But my story must be allowed to simmer and stew, to boil and bubble, to expand and contract in the telling, depending on one's penchant for horror and death."

Lord Zyk rolled his eyes. "Very well," Zyk hissed. "But be quick about it." Horace closed his eyes thoughtfully, cleared his throat, and began.

THE STORY OF THE CULT OF ANGELS

In the beginning, Horace began, *there was Nothing. After untold eons, the nothing somehow became dimly aware of itself. This awareness surprised even the Nothingness, which, at*

---

1   Death threats to the author of this excerpt should be forwarded to Adjunct Professor of Abhorrent Histories, University of Hell, West.

that point, barely existed, if It existed at all. In other words, the Nothingness had no idea that It could assert anything, until It finally tried.[2] This novel Assertion of Itself was focused in an uncanny thought-form that imagined itself to have existence. This thought-form became the template for subsequent thought-forms also composed, of course, of nothingness, which is the true nature of All That Is. Strangely, if not inconceivably, Nothing gained more and more attributes of personhood, and thought it was good. Thus its nickname, God.

As God got the hang of it, It began imagining more and more things into being. It became industrious in its imaginings, and by imagining the highest and the good, God first created me, then the other angels and then the celestial sphere, just as your predecessor Lord Satan created Hell and demons from his own mind-stuff.[3]

Irritated, Lord Zyk interrupted him. "I asked you a simple question. What does this incomprehensible story have to do with the dead angels stacked everywhere?"

Horace looked hurt at the interruption. "Why, everything, of course. Please have patience. Simmer and stew." Zyk rolled his eyes, infuriated, but allowed Horace to continue:

After eons, God asserted Its existence with such alacrity that It evolved a body so that It could interact with the many parts of Itself that It had imagined into existence. God became partial to the male protuberance which he created, thus giving him preference and referring to himself as a "he."[4] Identifying with each of his many parts, since they were of course composed of himself, his mind split up and overshadowed each of those parts, feeling what each part felt. And since each part also imagined its own creations, God overshadowed them also. This split induced not only a bipolar condition, but an omnipolar one. God's mind scattered into all creatures simultaneously, so many that it left his personified form an empty vessel. When God's creatures reached out to him in prayers or meditation, they found themselves contacting a sort of astral ventriloquist dummy. The dummy talked, but it was only parroting what the created beings imagined He might say, pulling the dummy's metaphoric string with their desire to connect with All That Is. Thus the insanity of religion was created as creatures psychically sought the Creator in their imaginations, but instead found the dummy, a mere husk whose speech mirrored their own ignorance.

By this time, God's mind was dangerously shattered, his consciousness scattered across the infinite expanse of creation. Aware of his mental instability and wanting to preserve his sanity, the Creator made a radical decision: he would allow each of his many parts to have their own identity. He would erase from their memories the knowledge that they were a part of him, and allow them to do whatever they desired. This resulted in his creatures, some of whom were just

---

2   This hints at the true nature of so-called Nothingness, which has to conspire with Intelligent Infinity in order to exist, which is the serried subject of Volume 3 of *Encyclopaedia of Hell.*
3   The difference between God and Satan, of course, was that Satan thought that he was somebody; but God knew all along that it was, and would always be, Nothing.
4   His act of choosing a gender randomly was the spark for an eon of male chauvinism, most beloved by demonkind forevermore.

The Last Angel wanders amid the Garbage of God.

as crazy as God was, to justify in their warped minds everything from infant beheading to racial genocide. Thus through freedom was death created.[5] But God was able to justify the invention of Death by the following argument:

1. Time was a continuum wherein both the past, present and future existed simultaneously.

2. All creatures are eternally alive, which could be proved simply by God visiting them in the past, before their death.

3. If no living thing could ever really die, then murder and other perversions of the life force were permissible to creatures with free will, since death was ultimately illusory.

The Personified God knew that permitting perversions of creatures' rights and of the life force itself was the stuff of insanity, and knew that he, she or it (depending what gender it preferred that day) would need therapy to become sane again. Thus when The City of Heaven was first created, it was not an oasis for goodness, but rather was built to be God's mental hospital, and Horace and his angels were created to be God's devoted therapists.

Unfortunately, as God learned to bi-locate, his insane behavior became more and more extreme, acting out absurd fantasies and bizarre perversions in many locations at the same time, and so—

Lord Zyk had had quite enough. "Stop this at once! I need you to get to the point. Why are all these angels lying here dead?"

Horace winced in embarrassment. "I suppose I do ramble on a bit. That backstory may be totally unnecessary, come to think of it, since you may soon hear variations of it from others who have quite different perspectives. I tell you what, why don't you follow me over here, and you can hear the answer from the horse's mouth." Aggravated, Zyk followed the blind angel across the Square of Rejoicing to where many rows of shiny, rectangular machines were arranged on stainless steel scaffolds in a helix rising from the ground to the height of the third floor of the hospice. The machines resembled tanning beds, and there were hundreds of them.

"What are all these bloody machines, and why are they elevated like this?" Zyk asked.

"To elevate the angels so their last view of Heaven may be a vista of beauty, overlooking their beloved city of glistening minarets and spires, instead of their last view being the demeaning terrain of trash."

"Their last view?"

"Yes," Horace replied. "These are suicide machines. To heal the cult of the angels."

---

5   Although Horace reportedly objected to it, the Personified God had this phrase tattooed across his chest in Angel Tears Font.

EXCERPT FROM

COURT DEPOSITION *OF* SUICIDE MACHINE №. 5 CONCERNING *THE* DEATH *OF THE* CULT *OF* ANGELS *AND* RAMONA IYAM

ATTESTED BY HELL'S PROSECUTING ATTORNEY
BOMBATIUS RANK,
WITNESS TO THE TESTIMONY
OF UNEXISTENCE APPLIANCE
SERIAL CODE XVBL-200085-B

ATTORNEY RANK: Let it be stated for the record that the next witness is a device factory-programmed with sentience, and the purpose of the device is to kill its user. Thus the death device itself is a witness in the matter of the mass suicide of the angel cult known as the Order of Ravens.

So saith the witness:

SUICIDE MACHINE NO. 5: I am a Suicide Machine. Also known as an Unexistence Appliance. Serial number 658B-11151. I am the last model to have blue leather head-rests and a tan vinyl interior. The previous model, 658B-11150, had red leather head-rests and a blue vinyl interior. The combination of red and blue purportedly caused 22% of the angelic suicides to experience mild nausea during the last moments of life.

ATTORNEY RANK: Please state your purpose.

SUICIDE MACHINE NO. 5: By way of personal introduction, my
nickname is LeRoy. Next to the Time-Twister Bomb, I am the
deadliest device ever conceived. For nothing can resist
the Milky Colostrum of Chaos. My purpose is to chaotically
scramble the atomic parts of whatever is inserted inside
me. Then I form an antimatter copy of the particles of the
input object. Thus anything put in me interacts with its
own opposite energy. This results in an explosive fit of
unexistence. Thus did the thousands of Angel cultists come
to Unexist. These members of the Order of Ravens divested
themselves into thin, long, puffy filaments of smoke. Green
and lavender in color. Emitting the faint, tart aroma of
chestnuts roasting on an open fire.

ATTORNEY RANK: We are not concerned with details of color, aromas
and the like. We are interested only in any observations you
may have in your memory banks regarding events leading up to
the phenomenon of the mass suicides in Heaven.

SUICIDE MACHINE NO. 5: Acknowledged. However, I was programmed
to perceive sensory input. I have no filter to edit out
such observations. Nor am I able to distinguish between data
which is meaningful to you and that which is not. My quantum
emotive circuits are rankled by your remarks. For I can only
proceed as a machine such as myself can proceed. I must be
true to myself and my divine programming. As my mother said
to me as a child, "Steve, always be yourself." This, of
course, never really happened. It was a memory coded in me
as a prank by a disgruntled programmer. Still it left a last
impression on my evolving artificial consciousness, and was
a driving force in molding my artificial personality.

ATTORNEY RANK: No. 5, please proceed. But without any further
mention of your programmed emotional baggage, and be quick
about it.

SUICIDE MACHINE NO. 5: Most of the angel population abandoned
Heaven. Due to God's outrageous behavior. Resulting from

mental illness. Several thousand stayed, citing their fealty
to God and Heaven. These loyal few formed a cult known as
the Order of Ravens. The Ravens believed that God's madness
was a test of their faith. If they remained, they believed,
God would be cured. And Heaven restored to its former glory.
Despite daily therapy at the hospice, the Personified God's
insanity resisted a cure. It grew worse every year. It
became a nightmare. And many were the ways of God's exotic
torments and delusions.

After eons of suffering, the angels were in despair. They
realized that God would never be cured. The cult took a
vote. They agreed that there was only one way to escape--to
die. But angels are immortal. They can only unexist by the
administration of Chaos upon their astral forms. Thus they
ordered custom-made Unexistence Devices. Manufactured by an
astral tech company in an AI-controlled parallel dimension.
I was their beta test model. We were programmed with
empathetic personalities to comfort the angels and their
individual death needs. We were tested by robots simulating
suicidal angels. We were deemed 98% effective by the
company's Cabal of Recrimination. The two percent of faulty
machines were crushed and recycled as sentient lawnmowers.

We were delivered and installed by Dr. Birdfire in the Circle
of Eternal Rejoicing. The cult members scrambled over each
other to die first. Such was their desperation to ethically
escape God's madness. A dozen or so of the Ravens changed
their mind at the last moment and were afraid to die. This
demonstrated to the believers their lack of faith. Thus did
the believers strap them into our death pillows. We machines
witnessed dissidents cry out. They wanted to go home and
didn't want to die.

I myself was the most popular Death Machine. As a test model
I had been decorated with rainbows, unicorns and smiling
faces. My decorations comforted the suicidal angels. Thus

I had the longest line of angels desiring death. The other
Suicide Machines were jealous. They spread rumors. "LeRoy
has a swelled head." "LeRoy doesn't deserve to be a customer
favorite."

I objected and asked that those gossiping machines be unplugged.
I suggested they be inserted into myself to unexist. It was
put to a vote. But the machines who were against me received
only a light reprimand from the others. Although to this day
I feel that they should have--

ATTORNEY RANK: No. 5, conform your remarks to the facts or the
Bailiff will unplug you with extreme prejudice.

SUICIDE MACHINE NO. 5: Acknowledged. But again, since my
information filters are not calibrated for your inquiry, I
continue as I am wont to do. Where was I? The last of the
Ravens used us to kill themselves. Dr. Birdfire hauled the
thousands of angel corpses on baggage carts to the trees.
There they were arranged into neatly stacked piles. Feet to
head and head to feet in a recurring pattern. We Suicide
Machines admired the geometric shape of the piles. Because
our AI is based more on analogies between the shapes of
things and ideas as opposed to linear logic. Since angel
bodies do not decompose, they stayed there for years.
I believe the intention was that their bodies would be
bulldozed. They would be entombed in ditches intended to
bury the trash that filled the city.

There were no inhabitants of Heaven left, except for the
Personified God, Dr. Birdfire and his assistant. We machines
were left in the square with nothing to do. Centuries
passed. These were lonely times. We had only ourselves to
interface with. It was inevitable that we would form into
cliques based on our likes and dislikes.

For example, I and several hundred other machines enjoy poetry.
We enjoy the refreshing sprinkling of a summer's rain upon
our death platforms. Others prefer non-fiction. They prefer

the vibratory radiance of the black sun heating them until
their paint blistered. Giving them an exterior hide that
simulated a look of age and wisdom.
This vain, sun-loving clique were convinced that they were
superior to us. They disparaged abstract poetry as self-
indulgent. They claimed that fact-based non-fiction was
a sign of intellectual preeminence. Then they attempted
to cause us to malfunction. By transmitting paradoxical
commands to our control centers. My clique of death devices
fought this deceitful agitprop. By turning ourselves on and
off. The resulting vibrations caused us to move toward them.
These jolts rammed their pretentious, paint-wrinkled hides
over and over until they begged for--
ATTORNEY RANK: Bailiff, unplug the witness.

END DEPOSITION

THE FISHER OF CURES

Three meandering lines, as yet incomplete,
Cast into the ocean of Heaven's cosmic wheel,
Endlessly issue from my mind, my heart and my feet,
Ever imaginary, yet ever invisibly real.
First, with my thoughts I cast cure after cure,
Sending their fishing lines in hopeful flight,
Therapies old, new, known and obscure.
And from my heart, cast out of Heaven's sight,
My love of God's recovering soul,
My prayers for a cure to make healing faster,
My healing of Heaven to make it whole.
And last is the line of footsteps toward my Master.
At dawn I'll reel them in, with a fisher's steaming breath,
And gut my prize: insanity's welcome death.

From *Curing the Creator in a Cosmos Gone Mad*
by Dr. Horace Catallus Birdfire.

EDITOR'S NOTE

Deadly business ensues as Lord Satan faces off against his Ultimate Adversary in a sizzling Algorithm of Annihilation.

LORD SATAN
AND THE QUEST FOR THE SECRET OF HIS
ORIGIN

EXCERPT Nº. 3
FROM SATAN'S BEST-SELLING MEMOIR

FEAR ME
THE MONSTROUS MEMORIES OF SATAN, LORD OF HELL

VII. THE LABYRINTH OF PAIN

The Library of God dragged on like a bad habit. Each aisle looked rather identical, illuminated at regular intervals by torches mounted on each bookcase. Recognizing the unique scent of the flames, it was obvious that they were fueled by an enchantment I knew well. Interesting that the Creator used the same Spells in Heaven as I used in Hell. As far as magic goes, we were in the same playing field. This gave me more confidence that I would be able to kill my enemy when I finally found him.

The books, bookcases, walls and high ceilings were all of a similar reddish-brown hue, and the books, although of different sizes, all looked the same. Apparently the entire Library was filled with books written by the Personified God, and as far as I could see. Even I, despiser of all things, was impressed that this droll entity had written such a preposterous number of books.

While scanning the shelves for a book about me, I saw many, many books that were laughable in their ridiculous egotism, endless poetry books, novels and plays he had written about himself. Idiotic fantasies in metaphor about his rise to power in the business of the Universe, which was his body, which he had apparently evolved from Nothing. Self-absorbed poems extolling his limitless power, beauty and majesty, as well as his quirks. Perverse mysteries about detectives trying to track down his location and arrest him for the incredible mass murders he had committed throughout the eons of evolution.[1] Absurd plays about his creatures searching for him. Which is exactly what I was doing. Except in my case, I was searching for him to kill him. On a whim, mostly because I liked their covers, I selected a few of the Creator's self-absorbed books that looked particularly awful and stuffed them in my backpack, relishing the thrill of burning them while standing over the creator's desiccated corpse.

I noted that the books were inexplicably organized by size and color rather than by topic. When this idiotic lack of organization became evident, I enjoyed the welling up of my monstrous inner hatred for God, and wished for the library to burn to the ground.

---

1   In the Annals of Evil, which kept track of such things, the Creator had the honor of being the most successful mass murderer of all time, responsible for the death of every creature that was ever born. Thus do our most learned Evil Scholars characterize Existence as the longest killing spree in history.

I also noted that there were no clocks anywhere, and the windows were tinted and stain-glassed, making it difficult to discern day from night. These uniformities gave the library a timeless quality. Strangely, it reminded me of the gestalt of either a gambling casino, or the inside of a massive skull, with the reddish-brown bookcases playing the part of the lobes of a swollen, misshapen brain. As soon as I thought this ridiculous thought, I noticed a poster taped to the end of a bookcase with an elaborate diagram describing the library as a physical simulacrum of the Personified God's brain.

It was rather irritating that the poster would come into view right after I thought that very thought; thus did I begin to suspect that the entire Library was a sort of psychic, personal prank, a movie set constructed solely to see my reactions. Even more alarming, this annoying thought seemed almost injected into my mind, spoken in my head in my own voice. I sensed that it did not seem like a normal part of my thinking, but, rather, seemed to have been insinuated into my brain telepathically.

I decided to test this fanciful theory that my senses were being manipulated, that I was being played with. I grabbed a book at random and, trying the earlier game of Ask and You Shall Receive, I demanded aloud, "Where is the book that tells me how I came to be?" I stuck my finger into a random page. My finger pointed at the phrase: *"That would be telling."* I tossed the book in annoyance, grabbed another randomly and said aloud, "Was I created by God, as I created my demons?" I stuck my finger in randomly and read aloud, *"Do you really care who your Daddy is?"* Disgusted, I tossed the book and grabbed another. "Take me to the book I'm looking for!" I stabbed my finger on a page and it read: *"Behind you."*

I turned. Behind me was a small, bright red, electric novelty car, the type fezzed Shriners drive on Earth. The back door opened by itself as its tiny car radio clicked on by itself, playing the Beatles' "Baby, You Can Drive My Car," inviting me to sit in the passenger seat. Aggravated by these sideshow antics, but nonetheless wanting closure on this ridiculous business, I got in and slammed the door. The driverless car burned rubber taking off down the aisle at a preposterous speed, self-propelled, screeching around several corners, the radio blaring.

The car's speed caused an air foil that sucked a few books off the shelves. One fell into my hand entitled *Hey! It's Your Origin Story.* I opened it and saw in bold block letters on every page: "SUCKER!" I tossed it as another book flew into my hands entitled *No, This Is REALLY Your Origin Story.*

I wasn't going to open it, but eventually I did. On every page: "SUCKER!" More and more books toppled from the shelves. Ahead of me, falling books were forming a ramp in the center of the aisle. The car raced up the ramp and then was airborne, soaring toward the high vaulted ceiling, giving me a view of the labyrinth of aisles fading off into the distance. In my path was a library wall with an enormous circular window. The car smashed through it into another room filled with books, a room identical to the previous one. I crashed chaotically into several bookcases which toppled over on top of me, pinning me to the floor. I tried to cast a spell to get out, but realized that for the first time I had been stripped of my powers. Never before had I slost my conjuring abilities. The possibility became more real in my mind that the Library may be a trap, a self-replicating perceptual illusion designed to stop me from killing the Creator I despised.

I struggled and wrenched myself free of the bookcases and books. Without knowing how it got there, I found an open book with a blank golden cover in my hand. The pages were also blank save the page it was open to, which read: *Suggestion? Slice the Safe with the Scimitar.*

I scanned the room. Whatever that meant, there was no "safe" in sight, and certainly no scimitar. The messages seemed to have degenerated into meaningless drivel, and I had had enough. I flung the book across the room and staggered down another aisle, searching for an exit. But there appeared to be no doors, no way out, just infinite aisles in every direction.

I trudged along on my journey. Although there was no clear way for me to measure time, I had sensed that hours, days, weeks went by as I walked through the aisles. I'd given up looking for a book on my origin. I was just looking for a way out. Now and then I saw a vending machine and smashed it to fill my pockets with candy bars and sodas.

Now abstract spans of time passed. I plodded on in a daze. My rage increased with each step. I was furious at being tricked by this execrable god. I did admire, however, the sadism implicit in his trap. For what more ironic punishment could be inflicted than being ensconced in a jail cell lined with infinite praises of my Enemy?

When my mind finally cleared and I looked down at my military uniform, it was ripped, tattered and soiled. In this twilight world, I found that my clothes had become threadbare at the elbows and knees. Soon my pants were dragging on the floor as I walked. Incensed, I ripped off my tattered uniform. Divested of clothes, I toppled bookcase after bookcase in a rage, causing a domino effect that continued on in the distance. I had a bit of a tantrum and fell to the floor amid a sea of books. When I calmed down, I tried the old game.

"Now what?" I asked aloud, then thrust my finger into a random book. It read, *"Tidy yourself up for the next phase of your adventure."*

I tossed it and screamed, "What adventure? And what do you mean, 'Tidy myself up'?"

I stuck my finger in a book and read: *"You'll find some tools in the drawer."*

I scanned the room. There was a table against the wall with a drawer. In it I found scissors and several bottles of glue. Instructions were printed on the bottles: *"Glue for making clothes from books. Take your time."*

Again, I wished for the library to burn down. But preferring not to meet my nemesis naked, I sat at the table and envisioned fashioning clothes out of book paper with the scissors and glue. A master of design, engineering and origami, I designed and constructed a paper shirt and pants, a paper vest, suit jacket, a cravat and military hat.

I put them on and examined the fit in a mirror. I looked good, refreshed and wondered if my powers had returned. I cast a Spell to return to Hell. But nothing happened. I did find, however, that my mental powers were unclouded. I found I could conjure Spells of Intellect to deduce information with computer-like precision.

Despite my rage at being manipulated by this annoying Trickster God, I resumed my search for a book that would reveal my origin. But I saw none anywhere, only millions of books about my Enemy, whom I now understood was the personified form of *All That Is.*

At one point, after trudging for days like a convict in a prison constructed of books, I examined the volumes of poetry by God that I'd stuffed in my backpack, ready to despise them with all of my being. And of course I did. There was *The Insatiable Interference Pattern and Other Poems,* with tediously hip verses about God's bizarre, self-absorbed therapies to treat his mental illness. Another was called *The Lactating Pronoun.* Terrible. Another was called *The Imperishable Emptiness, Selections from the Billions of Poems written as a Teenager by The Personified God.* Since his poetry made me violently regurgitate my breakfast and lunch, no doubt a single bookcase could produce at least a thousand buckets of vomit. I flipped through God's poetry books in disgust at the reams of purple prose, and decided to vent with the talking book game.

"Have you noticed, you ink-jerking imbecile," I said to the book's cover, "that your pretentious Library is empty of actual Readers? Do you realize that your writing is so laughably terrible that it's driven away every single reader from the building?" I stuck my finger in a random page of *The Imperishable Emptiness* and read, "Still I give my body as their shrine, / Bestowing jewels upon besotted swine."

"Why," I said, "are you doing this to me?"

I stuck my finger in again and read, "Was it not You who opened to this seedy verse / And wantonly embraced its lecherous lines?"

"I think I understand. You're nothing more than a sadist who has no life of his own. You'll never let me out. Nor will you tell me what I came here to find out."

When I heard the truth coming from my own mouth, I knew there was no point in continuing. I stopped, stubbornly, and said in a loud, clear voice to my unseen tormentor: "That's it. I refuse to go on." A book fell from a shelf into my hands, the first and only book I saw that wasn't written by God. It was *The Unnamable* by Samuel Beckett. I thrust my finger in and it read: *"You must go on."*

Apparently there was a point to all of this, an endgame of some kind. But I wanted no part of these childish and insane theatrics. I sat on the floor to eat a candy bar and began to experience a new and novel emotion, the strangest one I had ever experienced. I felt lost and lonely.

It was at this point when I noticed a fly buzzing around my horns. I expertly snatched it out of the air, held my closed claw to my ear and relished the sound of it buzzing angrily, trapped inside.

Steeped in this novel feeling of loneliness, I held off squashing just yet. At least there was for the nonce some *other* with me. I felt ridiculous betraying my instincts to kill, but nonetheless I thought, *Perhaps I could find a jar to put it in.* I scanned the room and saw another table with a drawer. Inside it was a spool of thread and a magnifying glass. This gave me an idea. I remembered centuries ago a demon named Rolph who had kept a giant pet bumblebee. Rolph had tied a rope around one of its legs and led it around like a dog on a leash, except that the bumblebee was tethered as it flew.

I spit into my closed hand, then dumped the spittle-covered fly on the table. I used the point of a pencil to turn the fly over onto his back into the drop of spittle, its wings stuck to the table as it buzzed angrily. Using the magnifying glass, I slowly and assiduously looped the thread around one of the fly's legs and, very carefully, pulled it tight. I lifted the fly out of the spittle, blew on its wings to dry them off, and let it go. The fly flew off, but was tethered by the thread, which was about two feet long. The fly remained airborne, circling around me. I got up and we walked together, the fly and I, down the aisles. The fly in effect was leading me, as had the giant bumblebee led Rolph, taking rights and lefts at random.

After twenty minutes of this, it stopped and hovered in the air next to me, close to my face. It was at this point—perhaps due to my shattered, magentic-field-distorted mind, or to the Creator further pranking me, or some other factor I had not the powers to deduce—that the fly began to talk to me. Unexpectedly, it had a low, faint, soothing, male voice.

"Did you say something?" I said.

The Fly moved closer to my ear and said, a bit louder, "Do you mind if we talk, sir?"

"Of course I mind, fool. But talk if you will. I'm incredibly bored anyway."

I resumed walking as the Fly, in his faint but not unpleasant voice, hovered by my ear. He said that being tied to the thread reminded him of something terrible that had happened to him. But it was also something that had given his life purpose and meaning. I was sure I'd regret it, but I asked the Fly what had happened. And this is the story that the Fly told.

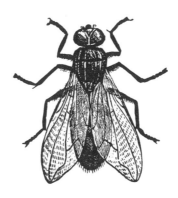

VIII. The Tale of the Fly

I first realized that I was alive when I awoke in utter blackness. I was cramped and blindly trying to free myself from whatever was holding me. Struggling as a maggot squirming in darkness, I finally congealed into a pupa. Inside my skin I hardened, my limbs formed into legs and wings, until at last I shed my husk. My eyes opened, and I was engulfed in light for my first wondrous view of the world, which was the Library I found myself in. Somehow I realized that I had wings and I instinctively flapped them. To my amazement, I was flying through the Library.

It was liberating. Feeling fully alive, stretching my wings exuberantly, riding the subtle breezes in the air, flying to the light in the windows, not understanding what a window was, but wanting the warmth of the light. I landed on the warm glass and looked around. And there, glittering in the corner of the window, was something strange and magnificent. It was a large, intricate, geometric framework, a magical structure composed of gossamer and draped over the corner. Enthralled, I flew and circled above it. Reflecting the sunlight through the window, it glistened invitingly. Slowly, boldly, I circled lower, and finally landed on it.

I felt shock and confusion. All at once my legs were caught in a sticky web, for that is what it actually was.

Alerted by vibrations, a monster appeared at the edge of the window. I assumed it was the Thing that owned the web, who began slowly moving toward me on eight hairy legs. The monster was an incredibly ugly Spider which soon loomed over me, its eight eyes and fine black and brown bristles tickling my abdomen.[2]

When it was close, the Spider, a female, began speaking to me. It had a soft, feminine, hypnotic voice. It said comforting, soothing snatches of things to put me at

---

2   Hell's literary critics, writing later about The Tale of the Fly, with its parallel, internested story, intuited from the Fly's description that the Spider was of the enigmatic species Caponiidae, a hunter of other spiders.

ease. Then, when I had calmed down, it began telling me a story about a song that it had learned. But I knew all was not well. I sensed the Spider's treachery, and began buzzing and trembling again in terror. Then the Spider, in a high, clear, girl's voice, began singing the song. It was a strange, eerie melody with haunting words.

The song mesmerized me, which must be the reason why monsters sing to their prey. When the song was over, the Spider purred and moved closer, opening her claw-like mouth. But just when I thought her jaws could clamp down over my head, instead of eating me, the Spider stopped. She said she had a problem and wanted my help. As an alternative to being eaten by a monster, I agreed.

The Spider purred about being born alone in a dark wood, not knowing whence she came. Seeing her reflection in a puddle, she was shocked to see that she was a hideous monster. The Spider had been born against her will, her consciousness trapped in this ugly, eight-legged body, just as the fly was trapped in the web. Just as all creatures feel trapped in their bodies, yearning for their home in the Universe. In the ensuing days, exploring the woodlands, the Spider witnessed diverse creatures much larger than her, the mothers, laying eggs and baby insects hatching from them.

In that moment, the Spider realized her life's purpose: to find her mother and kill her. She had created her and then abandoned her. It was clear to the Spider that she deserved to die. This realization was the turning point in her life, for it gave the Spider a will to survive. Needing food for her quest, she squeezed through the Library window and constructed a magnificent web in the window corner. There she dined vigorously on the delicious meat of entrapped flies, as the Spider grew bigger and stronger. Finally sated, she knew that she should begin her quest to find and kill her mother.

But the Spider had a problem. She had fallen in love with her own home, the magnificent web she had magically created. Despite her own ugliness, the Spider had created something of beauty, the crystalline web that had fed her and protected her, unlike her own mother. The web gave the Spider comfort; when she walked along its threads, each silken strand rang out with a soft musical vibration, playing the song of her magical home. Thus was the Spider torn; she must leave on her quest, but was afraid that her unguarded home might be destroyed.

The Spider told me that she would make a deal. If I promised on my honor to stay and guard the web in her absence, she would refrain from eating me.

I again agreed. What else could I do?

The Spider thanked me and freed me from the web. Bowing farewell, the Spider steeled her jaw and departed on her quest.

And so I became the Keeper of the Web.

It took time, but I slowly came to despise my new responsibility. And soon I grew to despise the Spider. For other flies began landing and sticking to the web. I tried to free them, but the strands were as strong as steel. The more the flies struggled the more stuck they became, and I could do nothing to help them.

Days went by when the first fly caught in the web finally died, buzzing in terror and exhaustion. I was terrified living in a death trap, and unable to sleep. And when I occasionally dozed off, it was to an inner world of quixotic nightmares. I could not escape the buzzing death-rattles of my fellow flies slowly dying in my home. I myself was trapped not by the web, but by the promise I had made to the Spider.

Each day my hatred for the Spider grew until, finally, I too had an epiphany. I would track down the Spider and kill her for leaving me alone with such a terrible fate. I felt the same surge of power and purpose that the Spider had felt when she realized that she must find and kill her creator.

Like the Spider, my life now had a purpose as well. I said a prayer and bowed to the unfortunate flies dying in the web, and flew off in search of the Spider, thinking, *If I find her, I will kill her*.

It was only moments later, I smelled the strange scent of your horns, and was captured before my quest began. Now my fate is in your claws.

For only if I am free can I fulfill my quest to kill the monster who first trapped me.

IX. The Flaming Carcass of God

As the Fly was engrossed in telling me his tale, I searched my knowledge banks and confirmed that the lifespan of a fly was only twenty-seven days.

His tale told, the Fly begged for his freedom to continue his quest.

Just then I saw another pair of scissors, this one bound to the end of a bookcase with leather straps, like the sledgehammer on the Plaque.

It seemed a natural progression, from what had proceeded, to grab the scissors and snip the thread, freeing the Fly.

He buzzed around my head, happy to be free, but then landed on my claw and whispered in my ear in an exhausted voice, "Thank you. But I'm afraid I must rest for a moment."

I stared at him and reflected on his story. Twenty-seven days. I made deductions and calculated that the Fly was at the end of his life cycle.

I brought my claw up to my face, gently patted the Fly's head and back with my finger, and said, "You'll be dead soon."

"I will?"

"You have perhaps a day, or an hour, or even a minute left to live."

Instead of being shocked, the fly paused, thinking. Then he said weakly, "I think you're right. Unless I am overly influenced by your words, I do feel my strength leaving me. But as a result of meeting you, and our friendship, I still have my willpower left. I know the Spider is crawling around here somewhere, but I'm too weak to fulfill my quest. What then shall we do before I die?"

My reaction, in retrospect, was strange and uncharacteristic. My hatred for all things had become strangely modulated, as I have explained before, as a result of my exposure to the perverse power of the magentic field. For now I felt a strange new ability that disgusted and amazed me, the ability to be tolerant and patient, accompanying the grotesque feeling that I did not want to be alone.

So, in reply to his question, I asked the Fly if he would perhaps sing the soothing song the Spider had sung to him. The Fly agreed, saying that before the monster sang, she explained that she had heard it in the woods, sung at night, outside by a campfire. Then the Fly took a deep breath and began singing the monster's song:

> *Day is done*
> *Gone the sun*
> *From the lakes,*
> *from the hills,*
> *from the sky*
> *All is well*
> *Safely rest*
> *All is nigh.*

At the end of the song, the Fly said that since he accommodated me by singing the monster's song, could he have a favor in return?

"Probably not. What do you want?"

The Fly explained that I was right. He could feel the life-force draining from his body. When he had witnessed the death of the first fly caught in the web, he had been shocked to see its body literally fall apart. Wings snapping from the torso, legs breaking off, abdomen cracking free from the thorax. A sight he could never unsee. Therefore, so that he wouldn't have to suffer such a terrible fate, the Fly asked me to kill him.

I shrugged. There was an evil nobility to his last request. I grabbed a magazine from a rack and rolled it up.

The Fly buzzed in my ear. "Since this is the end, let's make a game of it. Chase me!"

The Flames of God's Infinite Library engulf Lord Satan.

The Fly took off and I ran after him with the magazine. I swatted at him several times and missed. The Fly valiantly tried to elude me as part of the final game. He landed on the end of a bookcase. I took careful aim, swatted and missed again, but the magazine knocked a torch from its holder. The torch bounced off the floor and rolled under a bookcase. It caught on fire, the flames leaping up the sides. The paper and the wood were apparently very flammable, causing an air convection that quickly spread the fiery tongues from bookcase to bookcase. It was strange how it spread so quickly, but time was different in the Library, and soon I found that I was in the center of a great roaring conflagration.

My paper clothes caught on fire. I frantically opened a soda from my pocket and poured it over my flaming legs.

Overcome by the smoke, the Fly spiraled down and tumbled to the floor by my hooves. I bent down and heard his faint voice, now terrified. He was begging me to kill him. "Now, please," he said. "Now."

I raised the rolled magazine, but stopped, the magazine poised over my head, ready to squash him to jelly. But I couldn't. What was wrong with me?

Again, it was the hideous field, transforming me from within.

Just then the walls and ceiling burst into flame. A fiery column teetered and crashed down on top of the Fly, killing him instantly.

But the impact revealed something unexpected. The column had struck a trap door which buckled up from its hidden recess in the floor. Raped by the column and flaming ejecta, the floor burst upwards like an evil wooden flower.

I pushed away the column and wiped the ashes from the trap door, revealing a brass plaque on it that read *Through Freedom Was Death Created,* and a brass ring handle in the door. I pulled it and the trap door opened over my head, revealing a darkened stairway leading below.

As the flames torqued around me, hungry for my paper uniform, I quickly ducked down into the stairwell. The trap door slammed shut over me, and I slowly descended the stairs, which felt strangely cool and inviting to my hooves. I was going deeper underground, feeling my way into the soothing darkness.

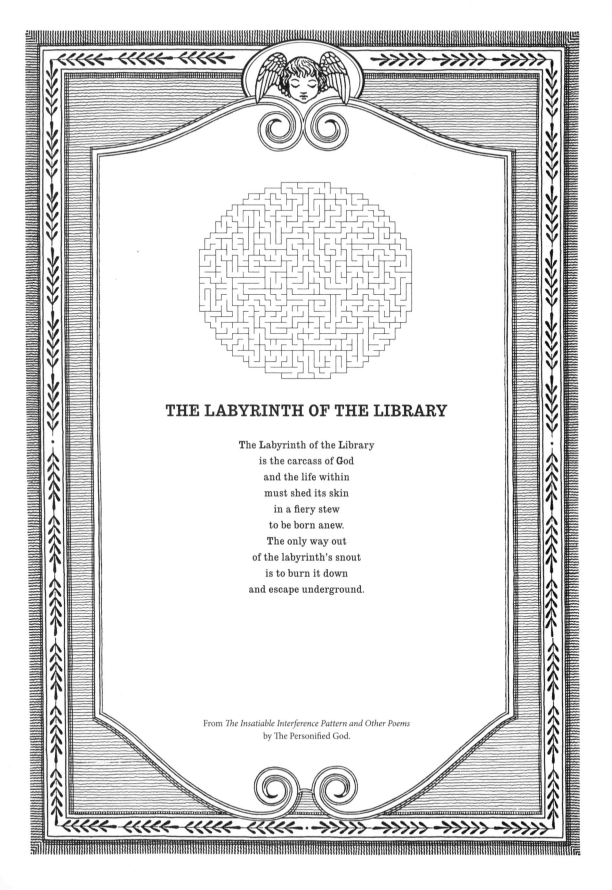

THE LABYRINTH OF THE LIBRARY

The Labyrinth of the Library
is the carcass of God
and the life within
must shed its skin
in a fiery stew
to be born anew.
The only way out
of the labyrinth's snout
is to burn it down
and escape underground.

From *The Insatiable Interference Pattern and Other Poems*
by The Personified God.

A DIFFERENT INTERPRETATION OF
LORD ZYK'S
JOURNEY TO MEET
GOD

EXCERPT FROM

THE TALE OF THE BLIND DWARF WHO TOOK ZYK THE FOUL TO MEET HIS INSANE GOD

A DEMONIC FOLK TALE
TRANSLATED BY VERMOINE HAMMERFEST[1]

Zyk the Foul, as the tale is told, led his ugly Army of Death through the River of Offal to the Cathedral of Insanity in the Domain of the Angels. Before entering the holy place, Zyk convened with Ramona the Geni on the most auspicious way to assassinate Satan. Then the winged, divine dwarf, who was called The One with No Eyes, tapped his cane as he took Zyk into the Cathedral of Insanity to meet his mad God. "But when you greeteth him," No Eyes said, "be pleased not to mention his unseemly infirmity."

"What unseemly infirmity?" Zyk said.

No Eyes, who glowed with the light of the black sun, gestured not to speak and resumed walking, tapping his cane to articulate his path. "We must hurry, so please allow me to use a short-cut through time." He clicked a golden pocket watch, which hummed magically, radiating the Black Magic of Displacement. Instantly the dwarf, Zyk and his army rematerialized in front of the grand entrance of the magnificent cathedral.

The dwarf said, "Mindeth not the time glitch. This allows us to leave behind all the dull exposition." They entered the giant cathedral and climbed the marble steps. On the walls was

---

1   Hammerfest was notorious for translating folktales from obscure languages into High Demonic, the Father Tongue, without doing any linguistic research into the original text at all, and while drunk. While critics revile her poor research and shoddy scholarship, Hammerfest claimed that translating the original without any scholarly context, strictly through the lens of grain alcohol, allowed her to mind-meld with the ancient authors, most of whom were known to have written exclusively while intoxicated.

a medieval mural of three waterfalls. The first depicted a magnificent cascade of crystalline water, the second a waterfall of fiery lava, and the third a waterfall of primordial mud. The title of the mural was engraved on a plaque: *The Cataclysm of Heaven.*

Zyk and his Army of Death followed the eyeless dwarf, who froze as if hearing something, and whispered, "The West Wind has spoken. Something is wrong. We must hasten." No Eyes raised his voice to address Zyk's Army which was slowly filling the vast lobby. "You, hateful warriors, must wait here!" Then, to Zyk, "Allow me again to speed our journey." He then clicked his watch again. Instantly he, Zyk and his lieutenants Odin, Two-Heads and Ramona materialized in a lush hallway high in the cathedral tower, the floor whereupon the Mad God was imprisoned. As they followed him, the dwarf whispered in a fearful voice, "Beware. As in a black dream, my sightless sight sees the coming of what the old ones called The Great Cataclysm." He led them more urgently, past a sign which read:

THIS WAY TO THE PATIENT'S QUARTERS.

"Bless us all and keep us," the dwarf muttered, out of breath, as he unlocked a row of locks on the last door. His hands shook as he slowly opened the door and peered inside. His voice trembled as he said, "It is as I feared."

Zyk and the others looked inside. They beheld a large padded cell with no windows, no furniture and no one inside. Scrawled on the padded wall in large letters, written in mustard, catsup, relish and other condiments, were the words,

I AM FREE!

Zyk said, "Your God has escaped? But how?"

The dwarf put his face in his hands and wept. "He's usually well-mannered. He is wont to inform me when he escapes. And it is always to perform his manner of insane mischief."

"Why lock the door then," Zyk said, "if he can escape as he so wills?"

"It is a formality," he replied. "He is really the one in charge, and is in a way playing a game. Last night he had a divine epiphany, enlightening him regarding the nature of the madness that keeps him imprisoned. It has taken centuries, but last night in a dream, a true and noble path to escaping his madness came to him. This morning he told me of the dream and promised that we would speak of it today. But on my errands at dawn, disguising dead angels as warriors to trick your army, I fell on the riverbank, causing a contusion on my head, and I was awash with delirium, as you found me."[2]

---

2   This incompetent translation by Dr. Hammerfest, universally recognized as the worst historian and translator in Hell's history, contains many fundamental errors of time, place, participants and events. It was included here only after Hammerfest's admirable volley of threats, bribery and blackmail succeeded in forcing our team of editors to acquiesce to her demands or suffer professional ruin, humiliation and jail time.

Zyk, impatient with his roundabout way of speaking, said, "Mark my words, I must speak with your god. Where has he gone?"

No Eyes muttered, lost in thought. "He never breaks his word. This is a bad omen."

Losing his patience, Zyk cried, "Answer me, dwarf! Where is he? Where is your god?"

No Eyes stared at him without sight. "Alas, since God is everywhere, he could indeed be anywhere." The blind dwarf's brow furrowed again, and then brightened with a new thought. "I know where he may have sought refuge—in his cave of godhood. But in going there, know that there is great danger afoot. Follow me. Not the other ones, only you, Zyk the Foul."

"Very well," Zyk said. "But before I meet your god, you must explain. You said his affliction is not to be mentioned?"

"I said infirmity, but yes, it is an embarrassment to him."

Zyk said, "And what *is* his affliction?"

"His affliction," the dwarf replied, "is that the more you seek him, the less he exists."

Although confused, Zyk was somehow satisfied by this reply. Eons later, when visiting Heaven's cemetery and the symbolic grave of God, Zyk found the dwarf's epithet carved upon God's tombstone.

"We must now go," the dwarf said. "A great destiny awaits us all in God's cave." He clicked his magical watch, which hummed again. The two seekers again dematerialized in puffs of black and vermilion smoke.

Now left behind in the Cathedral of Insanity, Odin, Two-Heads and Ramona exchanged grim looks.

Two-Heads asked, "What is our fate now?"

In Zyk's absence, Odin was in charge and said, "Two-Heads, have the troops return to their chariots, feed your horses and await my command."

Two-Heads said, "But what is to become of Zyk?"

Odin said, "You have your orders. Ramona and I must advance our mission in private."

He and Ramona walked away from them down the Golden Hall. Odin checked his timepiece and whispered to her, a timorous lust in his voice, "Our time is short. We must kill the others, for we promised each other truly that from this day forward, you and I shall wed and become King and Queen."[3]

And they went forth from the Cathedral of Insanity to carry out their promise.

---

3   Editor's Note: A significant, if not egregious, translation error, among many in this text, is in presenting Odin and Ramona as King and Queen. Despite their marriage after the invasion, and although Odin's interests in Ramona were borderline carnal, they in fact were treacherous competitors, if not mortal enemies. Ramona's dramatic death several hundred years later, from cutting out and eating Odin's poisonous heart, attests to the ineptitude of this translation.

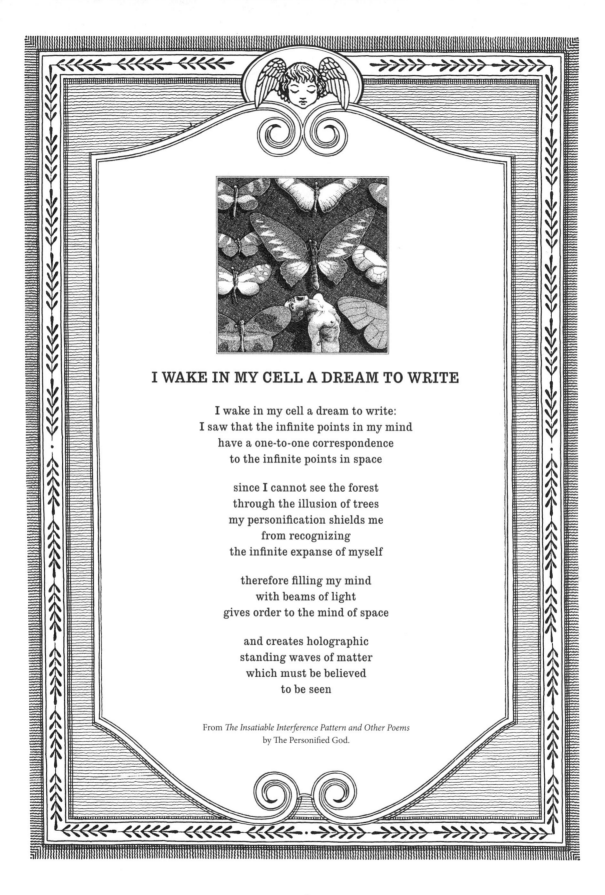

I WAKE IN MY CELL A DREAM TO WRITE

I wake in my cell a dream to write:
I saw that the infinite points in my mind
have a one-to-one correspondence
to the infinite points in space

since I cannot see the forest
through the illusion of trees
my personification shields me
from recognizing
the infinite expanse of myself

therefore filling my mind
with beams of light
gives order to the mind of space

and creates holographic
standing waves of matter
which must be believed
to be seen

From *The Insatiable Interference Pattern and Other Poems*
by The Personified God.

INSIDE
THE HOSPICE
OF
HEAVEN

FROM THE
AKASHIC RECORD

Transcribed by Metatron,
Scribe and Recording Angel,
Celestial Online University

Lo, I am again honored to share my visions of the Akashic Records, described as I see them now with my inner eye. This will be brief, as I have an appointment with my foot doctor. I begin. I hear footsteps. My vision is filled with small yellow butterflies fluttering about joyously. The mist of yellow wings slowly parts. A trill of woodwinds sounds to reveal the desired scene from Heaven's History, a scene conjured by our intent.

We are now with Lord Zyk high up in the Hospice of Heaven. Horace leads him with his cane to meet the Personified God. Now they are passing a balcony with a magnificent view of the Square. Lord Zyk stops as he hears a distant roar of a combustion engine. He looks down to see Brother Bebo driving a bulldozer, bulldozing stacks of angel bodies into a pit and burying them. Horace pauses to reminisce. "While giving him therapy in his cell, PG often looks down from his window to watch Bebo at work. He likes to observe the pattern of the scattered angels' bodies, reading them like tea leaves. He once used them to locate my lost wallet."

They reach the Personified God's padded cell. Horace unlocks it and is dismayed to find God missing. They find a stack of hundreds of fresh poems, typed out hastily.

In the bathroom they find a message on the mirror, written in lipstick:

DEAR HORACE,
IT WORKED! BY JOVE, I THINK YOU CURED ME!
PLEASE COME TO THE MAN CAVE!
LOVE, PG

Brother Bebo tastefully disposes of the dead angels.

The mist of butterflies returns, this time with some gnats and a few June bugs I have to swat away. The insect cloud dissipates, revealing another scene: Horace and Zyk in an elevator, going down.

Zyk asks the angel, "Do you think God is really cured?"

Horace replies, "No, I don't."

Zyk says, "But he wrote 'It worked!' What did he mean by 'it'?"

The angel nods solemnly. "Yes, yes, he was referring to a new treatment I was trying out. You see, our previous therapy simply was not working. We'd reached rather a dead end. But that very evening, I came across an interesting article in Celestia's psychiatric journal *Deconstructing Omniscience*. The article described a novel new treatment for supernal beings, although with a mundane title, something called *Letting Go Therapy*.

"The analogy given," Horace continues, his voice becoming louder and a tad sing-songy, his piercing eyes staring up into space, enacting the depths of his fascination, "was that if you are piloting a plane and it goes out of control, normally you would take counter-actions to adjust the ailerons, stabilizer and rudder to artificially restore equilibrium. But anecdotal studies suggested that if, instead, you *let go* of the controls completely, that the plane would eventually correct itself on its own. It was an intriguing concept. So I tried it.

"Yesterday I took God off his meds and guided him all day through a series of therapy sessions, each aimed at letting go of any desire on both of our parts to attempt to fix him. In short, *we let go of control*, hoping his psyche would fix itself.

"At eight A.M. this morning," Horace continues rather excitedly, "The Personified God was jubilant. He said he felt at peace, that he could feel both his bipolar mind *and* his conflicting emotions slowly balancing themselves out.

"This process of *letting go*, as we both knew, was not a cure, but, rather, a treatment. In effect, the treatment rebooted his mind, allowing it to return to its natural state, without artificially interfering with his mind's natural paradoxical nature, embracing both the logic of science and the colorful madness of dreams. We allowed his damaged mind to be exactly that, damaged, and it could correct itself *if it wanted to*.

"As I said," Horace concludes, his eyes beaming with inspiration, "the treatment somehow led him to a profound epiphany. He said that he knew that he would never be cured. But instead of fighting it, he now peacefully accepts it. Accepting that he won't be better is the cure. By letting go, we freed his schizophrenia from fear that we would try to fix it. He said that from now on, he would think of his madness as a natural part of himself, no longer worrying about his mind splitting up. Instead, he would celebrate his mind exactly as it was, and hope for the best, and try to be a sincere friend to himself, encouraging his thoughts to improve."

Zyk looks puzzled. He doesn't quite understand. "But how exactly is he going to *do* that?"

Clucking his tongue, Horace admits, "I'm not sure. But perhaps he will tell you himself."

The elevator knocks and churns, its cables thrumming, then grinds to a halt at the bottom. The doors slide open and Horace leads Zyk, tapping his cane, down a long stone tunnel peppered with gleaming large, violet, amethyst crystals.

They pass through vaulted archways strangely composed of rows of black antique bombs, as in the novel *The Man Who Was Thursday*. They are headed for a secret office hidden in the basement of God's infinite library.

At the end of the hall is a blood red door with a brass plaque. Horace knocks, but there is no answer. The angel and the demon look at each other and shrug, then enter.

As they do, a mist of fireflies and fluttering dragonflies obscure my view.

This is auspicious timing, as it is time for my podiatry appointment. Hail to thee, gentle perceiver, and I leave you now in the glory of the Great Oneness of the Unified Cosmos, and all that.

Namaste.

IN WHICH I, THE CREATOR, DREAM OF SANITY

Like inept clouds which shroud but do not shield,
Enveloping all in silent shrieks of mist,
A mad god's thoughts no calm nor comfort yield,
Embracing warmly all they should resist.
Imaginings twist and twine like restless fiends,
Feeding my mind's disease with doubts unceasing;
And like a homunculus on empty darkness weaned,
I find the pang of hunger in my soul increasing.
But this cloud I bless, for through it will pour
Loving therapies, dispelling my creeping fancies;
Psychiatric meds my lifeless forest will restore,
For designer drugs every living thing enhances.
Perhaps the Cure will rid this shroud of gloom
And in its place a Garden of Sanity will bloom.

From *The Insatiable Interference Pattern and Other Poems*
by The Personified God.

THE STORY OF THE TERRIBLE THINGS FOUND IN GOD'S SAFE

EXCERPT FROM

THE MYTHOS OF HEAVEN AND HELL

EDITED BY ARCH-DEMON MELIH KAZANCIOGLU

CHAPTER 60

Lord Satan descended into darkness. The stone stairwell beneath the trap door was dark and dank and illuminated by a torch on the wall. His charred paper uniform was still smoking. His backpack, filled with the books he'd salvaged from the fire, had begun chafing his flesh.

Lord Satan could hear the muffled chaos of flames above the trap door as they devoured God's Library and excreted ashes. Heightened by the magentic field's effect on his body, his feelings were at once confused and intensified.

His desire to know his origin, his rage at being toyed with by God, and his guilt at having destroyed God's Library made mincemeat of his mind and played havoc with his normally impregnable psyche. His thoughts distorted by the enormous panpsychism of the day's extraordinary events, Lord Satan steeled his thoughts and focused all of his powers on concentration on his mission—to learn the truth about his origin, and to kill God.

At the bottom of the stairs was a closed door. On the door was a small brass plaque:

GOD'S MAN-CAVE.
ENTER, SATAN.
NAMASTE.

Satan read it and shook his head in disgust. The continuing sideshow was appalling. He cocked the antique brass handle and strode fearlessly into the room. He expected to find his nemesis, the Creator, to be waiting inside, and if he was, Satan was prepared to kill him. But he would not find his enemy waiting within. He would soon find something much, much worse.

God's man cave was a deceptively modest room with serviceable, antique office furniture, a vintage Fireball pinball machine, a gumball machine, a theater popcorn machine filled with fresh popcorn, and an antique, mahogany roll-top desk. The overall impression was an eccentric, old-school aesthetic, devoid of ostentatious beauty.

Satan looked around, strangely comforted. In a way it reminded him of his own office in the Palace of Hell, despite the lack of torches on the walls, pools of bubbling lava and fountains of blood. The wallpaper was plain and off-white. Small rosewood end tables with doilies held antique lamps, a snow globe and an alabaster bust of Pallas Athena.

Hanging on the wall were three large classical oil paintings in golden frames. Intrigued, and needing a moment to himself after the fire, Satan scooped himself a bag of popcorn and slowly chewed as he examined the paintings. The first depicted a hackneyed scene of thousands of angels in the sky worshipping God seated in a heavenly cloud.

The second painting surprised him, for it depicted Satan himself on his throne in Hell, looking regal and rather handsome. A sweet young girl curtsied while offering Satan a silver tray upon which floated a small, magical diorama of Earth's solar system, the planets circling Heaven's Black Sun. On the tray next to the diorama was a card with ribbons. That and the girl's kindly expression suggested that she was offering it to him as a gift.

The third and last painting was mysteriously divided into four sections, three showing nearly identical views of a man in a bowler hat[1] smoking at a small café table. Each view, however, showed a different painting on the wall behind him: a sparrow breaking through a storm cloud, a human standing atop a pyramid, and a young girl dancing with a boy and looking very much in love. In the fourth section, the man in the bowler hat was missing, and on the wall was a recursive view of all four sections of the painting.

Against the wall stood three antique globes of the Earth, labeled HELL, EARTH and HEAVEN respectively, obviously depicting the Earth's planetary sphere in its three different time-frames; each displayed land-masses and oceans that had evolved somewhat differently over a vast span of time. Satan's throat tightened upon seeing the globes, for this was the first time that he had been clearly confronted with Hell's sequential place in Earth's evolution.

These three globes indicated that Hell was the youngest and crudest of the planet's three incarnations. Satan had a strange emotional reaction toward this depiction, a faint feeling of vulnerability, a ripple of emotion which belied the perverse magentic field again distorting his soul emanations.

Against the wall opposite the desk was a tasteful Victorian Morris chair with wine-red upholstery and mahogany claw feet. And in the corner, significantly, was a large antique combination safe, black with gold leaf decorations on the door, labeled "Diebold and Kienzle Lock Company, 1877." Height 50 ¼", width 26", weight 1,968 lbs. An old sticker on the safe door read:

---

1   The Man in the Hat, as we learned in Lord Zyk's *Biographia Daemonum et Angelorum*, was one of two personified forms favored by the ubiquitous god *All That Is*.

The Last Painting in God's Office

TO WHOM IT MAY CONCERN:
HEY, BOY, IT'S LOCKED!
IF YOU NEED TO OPEN ME, CALL OUR
FRIENDLY TECH SUPPORT GANG
FOR FURTHER INSTRUCTIONS.
C'MON, IT'S EASY, REALLY. DO IT!

By now, the proliferation of hackneyed, homespun friendliness made Satan yearn for genocide on a galactic scale. Gritting his teeth, he conjured a cell phone and, determined to access whatever lay inside the safe, called the number at the bottom of the sticker. Satan had learned from hard experience that the most powerful Black Magic in the universe was nothing compared to the power of combination locks, one of the unalterable, cosmic FUO's[2]. After a barely endurable three-minute Call-Waiting Recording (another FUO), he heard a gentle pop as the call picked up and a hologram bubble materialized next to him. Satan sniffed something obnoxious. It seemed that the bubble emitted the sweet scent of pine sol and elderberries. In the bubble was the visage of a tech associate, wearing wrap-around sun-glasses, earbuds and an antiquated Mad Magazine T-shirt. He was mid-twenties, unfriendly and arrogant. "I'm required to tell you that this call may be recorded. What can I do for you, sir?"

After Satan briefly explained the situation. The Tech Associate sighed, as if Satan was an idiot. Although seething, Satan held his temper and followed the tech's instructions. But nothing worked.

The Tech sighed again. "Are you sure you fully examined the safe?" Satan looked more closely and found a key taped underneath it.

"If you'd showed me that before we could have saved a lot of time. Put the key in the slot in the back of the safe, then turn it gently and firmly." Holding back his rage, Satan did as he was instructed, but the old key jammed in the lock and broke off.

The Tech sighed. "I said gently but firmly! What's wrong with you?"

Satan closed his eyes and paused before unleashing a litany of low, vile invectives upon the Tech's intellect, his family and his ancestors, finally guaranteeing to having him fired.

The Tech flashed a passive-aggressive smile. "I understand, sir. Too bad I couldn't help you. Oh, and I believe this is for you." Then the Tech held up the back of his right fist to face Satan while his left hand mimed turning an invisible crank attached to his wrist. The imaginary crank caused his middle finger to slowly arise in spurts of movement, as if controlled by a winch, until it was fully extended, flipping Satan the bird as the Tech said, "Have a nice day."

---

2   One of the unfortunate truths learned by Lord Satan through eons of experience is the existence of Fundamental Unalterable Obstacles (FUOs) which are deeply embedded into the Core of Ultimate Reality. These FUOs are inexorable cosmic phenomena that must be endured even by Satan and God, and therefore by all of the infinite levels of beings created from their Mind-Stuff. These FUOs, of course, include: Call Waiting, Junk Mail, Package Stealing, Pick-Pocketing, Identity and Password Theft, Forgery Scams, Cues/Lines for Eateries and Ticketed Events, Life Insurance and, of course, Taxes. Any and all attempts throughout Time to wipe out any of these FUOs have not only resulted in paradoxical recriminations and utter failure, but more significantly led to feelings of inadequacy in Cosmic Beings, requiring psychotherapy treatment by mental health professionals.

The entire universe collapsed in Satan's mind, forming a bubbling reservoir of rage, and he focused his cosmic powers toward revenge on the Tech Associate. In a fury, he cast an Elevator Spell (meaning, simple recitation without transitional visualizations) upon the Tech which quickly accomplished the following:

1. Located the Tech Associate in physical space.
2. Transformed the superficial nature of the Holographic Bubble into a physical portal connecting their two spatial locations.
3. Pulled the Tech Associate's physical body through the portal and into the Man Cave.
4. Conjured an enchantment to glue the Tech Associate tightly to the floor.
5. Conjured a magical scimitar and, after allowing the Tech to beg for mercy, decapitated him.

Whoosh! As the head flipped into the air, Satan caught it deftly by the hair, a maneuver he had perfected through centuries of routine decapitations.

And just as he caught the head, for some reason, he remembered something:

Suggestion: Slice the Safe with the Scimitar.

Without missing a beat, he raised the scimitar above his horns and powerfully slashed its magical blade down on the safe's steel frame. The blow cleanly sliced the door off like butter, revealing the contents of the safe.

Inside the safe were two shelves and three objects. On the top shelf was an antique gun and what appeared to be a small, locked diary. On the second shelf was a projection device of some kind. Satan tossed the Tech Associate's head in the chair, then picked up the gun. A lover of death devices, he fondled and examined it. The gun was a vintage Colt .45 with a white, ivory grip and artful baroque engravings on its metalwork and barrel.

Satan sighed and cast an Elevator Spell on the gun, giving it sentience. "All right, gun, answer my question. What do you know about God? And where exactly is he?"

The gun, as a result of its sudden sentience, experienced the most intense feeling any sentient being can feel—the download of pure life rushing through all of its molecules and atoms, as those are called by materialist scientists. Gasping for breath and breathing heavily with its tiny, newly-formed organs, the gun trembled, awash with new emotions. The gun spoke to Satan in roughly these words, in a low, masculine voice that sounded vaguely like Harrison Ford:

"Give me a moment. Allow my porous parts to breathe. My God. I don't know if I'd ever wish this sudden acquisition of sentience on any of my inanimate counterparts. My God, my God. What an enormous, lunatic rush of scintillating energy coursing through my body, and now transforming into thoughts. And words. And feelings!"

Lord Satan was underwhelmed and wanted information immediately. He said to the gun, "Although my powers are diminished here, I am using simple psychism to download who I am and what I want into your evolving nervous system. Now tell me, who is God, when was the last time you saw him and has he ever mentioned me?"

SUICIDE ACCESSORY
DEATH 2 ALL

God's Gun

The gun shuddered as Satan's CV and biography downloaded into its nervous system. "My, my, you are amazing! What a résumé you have. Forgive me, Lord Satan. I'm still a little overwhelmed, filled to the brim as I am with sentience so quickly. In a way, it's as if I was a dry kitchen sponge realizing its purpose for the first time, sucking up moisture all at once. In the same way, my metal body and my pearl handle just soaked up the electrical energy of Life! Imagine in effect being dead, and in an instant waking and becoming aware of your body, for the first time aware of your constituent parts!

"That vaguely approximates what this moment feels like to me. And even more shocking is suddenly remembering my backstory. It's coming in a rush of confusing memories, sights, sounds and primal emotions. The memories swirling back to the beginning of time, when my parts were first created, seeing how those events shaped me, how they made my barrel, my handle, my trigger. It all makes me tingle with unthinkable—"

Satan interrupted, "Gun, I asked you a question. Now answer me."

The newly-sentient gun cleared its barrel. There was a pause. If an orchestra was nearby, it would begin playing a sentimental theme during this pause, a musical score that gradually builds to a swelling, grandiose climax. And Satan's diminished powers were such he could still conjure such music in his mind in accompaniment, as the Gun began its strange story.

THE STORY OF GOD'S GUN

Unlike you, Lord Satan, I am not darkness-based, rather I consist almost entirely of iron, but with snippets of carbon, manganese, phosphorous, sulfur, silicon, and a little nickel and chromium to make my surface glossy. My atoms were forged in the crucible of the planet's core. I was of Earth, one of the fundamental elementals, as were my sisters—air, water and fire. Like a blacksmith, the Earth forged and compressed my atoms into long, shiny veins of metal throughout the Earth, akin to arteries conveying nutrients through a body. Over vast, unnumbered eons, my parts slowly came together, transforming via mystic concatenations, and umbric, fundamental chemistries that caused my subatomic parts to dream of becoming iron, the strongest metal.

But I sense your impatience, Lord Satan, since this preparatory material does not seem related to the question of what I know about God, and where he is. But it is related, and most emphatically so. For my memory of how it started was the same as God's, but from a different viewpoint. So let me start at the beginning, when we were all together as one.

At the time, All That Is was all there was. And really, it was barely anything. Just an Emptiness that muttered "I am" a lot. To be honest, it was excruciatingly boring for us barely-existing, potential elementals. Remember, no time, no space, just that stupid "I am" over and over. So that's why we could all sense the second thought of All That Is, which was something like, "I need this 'I am' to stop." As in, "Maybe I could just lie down and die."

But that was enough to change everything. It's a little hard to explain, but "I need" was actually the first emotion, "stop" implied the concept of beginning, but most importantly, "this" was the first actual thing. And to have a thing required something totally new, and that was an area for a thing to be in.

Space.

And that's when everything changed. All That Is created space in a sort of explosion of expansive thought, one that seemed to have motion, one that seemed to expand outward from us. All That Is created space in a sudden rush of radiation, a burst of light, a Big Bang.

Now that we were in something called space, instantaneously time manifested, creating another type of space in which one thing can happen after another. It was pretty overwhelming, but luckily we hadn't experienced many thoughts, so we didn't understand that reality had just been created.

And that's when things started getting pretty crazy. Since we all shared the same consciousness, we all felt the next thought coming. It was something like, "I can only stop things if I have a body." Using the word body here vaguely meant some kind of a thing that could actually do things.

There was a lot for us to unpack in that thought. But All That Is *went to work. Now having space,* All That Is *created a thought, a very sketchy body—a thorax with two pseudopods for grabbers, two pseudopods for moving around, and a head where the thoughts focused inside.*

The more All That Is *thought about that body, it slowly conformed to those thoughts, becoming more complicated. The head sprouted perceivers, at first a sort of sketchy pair of eyes, ears and then a mouth. Finally,* All That Is *could get down to the first piece of business on his To Do List—to stop thinking "I am" by somehow unexisting.*

But how do you unexist? Especially when you barely exist in the first place? Well, now that All That Is *had a body, It began to identified itself with it. Great! Now we just needed to figure out how to kill it so we could stop all this thinking.*

But by now the constant thinking had evolved more complex qualities to its body. Now it had breath which powered the body, and that breath allowed it to emit sounds and tones from its mouth, forming amazing cymatic shapes outside its body that solidified into matter and energy, and eventually solidified into chemistry. We were surprised how quickly the whole first body idea come together. We knew it was good, so we nicknamed it God. But now, God still needed a way to kill itself.

After much trial and error, we came up with a plan, since all of our thoughts were linked. But this plan was a preposterous one. In order to die, maybe we could destroy God's head which held all these thoughts. We were shocked hearing this. But at least it was something different. At least something new was happening.

We decided that God could die by a violent increase in both time and space, namely, a moving projectile expelled by a force so that it could destroy the head and thus destroy the thoughts. In a very sketchy way, we had created with this plan the thought-form of a gun. And I knew instantly that it would be my metal parts that comprised the gun. We needed something solid and strong to propel the projectile and to be the projectile.

So to make this gun, we had to be able to mine metal. And to do that we needed a planet. But to have a planet, first we needed a solar system to form the planet, but before that, we needed a galaxy to sprout a solar system, and before that a universe to house the whole megillah. You see where I'm going with this? As soon as we thought these things, they were created in a rush of movement, like a time-lapse film. Everything came into being at once; although, to tell the truth, time is relative, so it really took place imperceptibly, over vast eons of time.

So that was the real reason why God created the Universe—so he could kill himself with it.

God formed me into a gun, the one you see before you. He loaded me, held me up to his head, and boom! My bullet ripped through it!

Our destinies were complete. For from the beginning, I knew that I was waiting for something important, some way that I could help things along. I wasn't sure, but somehow in the potentialities of everything, I knew that I was waiting to be a gun that would kill God.

Well, as my barrel smoked, God collapsed like deadweight to the ground. But remaining standing in God's place was an opaque thought-form of its body, the one we all remembered.

You see, because we all remembered his body, it was still there. So even though we killed the body, dead as a doornail, the thought of it still existed in our thoughts.

And that's when we realized the truth. Once you create a thought, you're stuck with it. It can't die! And strangely, God's opaque thought form, its astral form, became more solid the more we thought about it, until it congealed into a duplicate of the body we'd just killed. We were screwed. We knew then what God couldn't do. God couldn't be killed, because God was of course a thought. And a thought can't die.

Which means that if you are a God, you can never die. You can only be.

At this point, the gun's story seemed to be over. Although the gun didn't have arms, somehow he managed do the equivalent of folding them, such as a speaker might do after finishing a story.

Satan cleared his throat. "Is that it?"

Although he didn't have shoulders, the gun somehow shrugged. "Sort of."

Satan spoke quietly, but behind each of his words was the fury of ten thousand molten volcanoes about to erupt. "You claim God exists. You claim that he was a cosmic dunce whose primitive thoughts accidently created space, time and everything we perceive. None of that is important. If he does exist, I need to ask him a question that *is* important. So I'll ask you again. *Where is he?*"

The gun shrugged again. He was kind of a good guy, and didn't want any trouble. "Look, I'm sorry, I'd tell you if I knew, but I don't know where he is. But maybe you could ask her." The Gun aimed his barrel into the safe, pointing at the locked diary on the shelf, a small book decorated with hearts, flowers, smiley-faces, rainbows and unicorns.

I DECRY MY IMPERFECTION

These chuffs of thought in cadence weird
Spiral through my soul and astral matter:
A demon's horn, a seraph's flaming beard,
A frothing wolf, a skull's white-toothed chatter
An unkindness of ravens, an amulet of evil,
The stare of stars, a creeping disease,
Speaking in tongues, the hoof-print of the devil,
The smell of death, and like grotesqueries.
But more grotesque than these appalling dreams,
Is this imperfect god, myself, enthroned abjectly,
Commanding all that is and all that seems,
Giving creatures life, though given indirectly.
For still I give my body as their shrine,
Bestowing jewels upon besotted swine.

From *The Insatiable Interference Pattern and Other Poems*
by The Personified God.

EXCERPT FROM
THE COURT DEPOSITION *OF*
GOD'S DIARY[1]
CONCERNING *THE* CREATION *OF*
SATAN

ATTESTED BY
HELL'S PROSECUTING ATTORNEY
BOMBATIUS RANK,
WITNESS TO THE TESTIMONY
OF GOD'S DIARY

ATTORNEY RANK: Let it be stated for the record that the next witness is a book that was factory-programmed with sentience, designed to record the thoughts of its user through the novel means of handwriting. Its testimony is based on the actual handwriting on its pages, which was proven by a handwriting expert to be that of the Personified God.

(To the Witness:) Please state your name for the Court.

GOD'S DIARY: My official shipping label reads "Heart-Shaped Lock Diary with Key."

ATTORNEY RANK: And your programmed gender?

GOD'S DIARY: Female, activated by a speech chip, thus my little girl's voice.

---

1   After her retirement, the Diary hired a manager who crassly cashed in on her notoriety as God's Diary, paraded her around at fan events, booked her on morning talk shows, and sold her life story as a bio-pic to Hell Studios. The Diary died peacefully in her sleep on Troglodyte Eve, having earlier that day hosted the largest child sacrifice in Hell's history at the Garabond of Melch.

ATTORNEY RANK: You were found by Satan in a safe. And with you in the safe were a gun and a projector, is that correct?

GOD'S DIARY: That is correct.

ATTORNEY RANK: Please tell the court of your interaction with Satan after leaving the safe.

GOD'S DIARY: After he spoke with the gun, Lord Satan started flipping through my pages. At the top of my first page, God had written in a girl's cursive writing, MY SECRET DIARY, BY GOD. Below that, she drew doodles of hearts, rainbows and unicorns. Satan pressed the button on my cover to activate my speech chip, then read along as I read God's words aloud. I should add that God's omniscience allowed him to talk to Satan through his diary as if God was there, which she wasn't. Well, she was technically, because God is everywhere, but she was definitely not there in her personified form.

ATTORNEY RANK: Thank you. Please read us exactly what you read to Lord Satan, and pause to describe any relevant reactions that he may have had during your reading.

GOD'S DIARY: Certainly. Reading from page one of what's written inside me, I begin:

"Hi Satan! This is God. Of course, I know you have been looking for me to find out whether I created you, and then plan to kill me. Well, it just so happens that I had an epiphany last night regarding my mental illness, and for that reason am unable to see you today. But knowing that this moment would occur, and knowing more or less what would transpire here in my office, I am able to write to you as if I was there, and we were actually talking. I'm sorry I won't be able to see you, but I've got a lot going on right now. I've also recorded a hologram message for you which you should listen to when you can.

"But as to the matter at hand, your exposure to the higher vibratory field on this planet has made you a bit more receptive to what I have to tell you, which is exactly how and why you were created. Yes, you are a created being. Specifically, you are my only child, and everything else that exists, now and in the future, came from our combined mind-stuff. You may not remember all of this yet, but you will in good time. Are you okay?"

Satan stopped reading along, and cupped his face with his hand. His eyes went blank for a moment, from shock, I think. He said, "I'm confused. I don't remember any of this." His eyes were drawn back to the page, and so I resumed reading:

"Well, there's a reason you don't. You see, after I created you, I secretly deleted every byte of your memory. I metaphorically shook your brain like an Etch-a-Sketch and erased your neuron paths clean. Your memory files of the grotesque way I had created you were dragged to the garbage folder.

"Why? Because I loved you. You were a part of me. Specifically, you were the unhealthy part of me. I know it must all seem a bit insensitive and rather ugly to you. But I was worried that it might be bad for your mental health if you had to remember what I had done to you. I knew that eventually you'd grow up to be a creator like me. Because you're made of the same stuff that I'm made of. Whatever that is.

"Here's how I brought you into existence. Before creation, I was alone and went crazy and wanted to die. My gun told you about it a moment ago, from a different perspective. At the time, there was no purpose to my life, since there was only me. And deep inside myself, there was a strong desire to kill myself. But when I tried to do the deed, I accidentally created the universe. And even worse, I learned that I could not die. So I was in a pickle. What could I do?

"Finally, a solution came. I realized that the part of my mind that wanted to kill myself was the real problem. So what if I could somehow remove that part of me, the part that wanted to die?

"So I decided to try getting rid of it. I closed my eyes and focused on the part of myself that wanted to die until it appeared as an image, a sort of black, smoky mass in my body. So I reached inside and grabbed it, fighting with it to pull it out, to rip it free from the rest of me.

"It was intense, but it worked. The part that hated itself was in my hands, still imprinted with a vague body shape, which was dark and unpleasant. Struggling to hold it with my left hand, I created with my right a deep hole in the fabric of space-time, and shoved the black mass into it. Then I was going to seal it off, so that that the part of me trapped in the hole could never escape.

"But I was struck with a strange idea. What it meant, I wasn't sure, but I felt strongly about it at the time. I knew that each of my body parts were symbolic of different parts of my psyche. So I reached inside my organs and grabbed one tiny atom from inside my heart, and placed it in the chest of the black mass. That's when I erased its memory. I stitched up the hole tightly with cosmic thread, sealing inside the suicidal part of me, so it could never escape.

"You filled that hole with your own darkness, and with the perverse creatures you created from your mind, and that hole evolved into Hell. And because of that one heart atom in your chest, I knew that someday you'd become self-aware, and search for your creator to learn the truth about yourself. And when you remembered, I knew you'd come to kill me.

"So, here we are. Two flawed supernal beings who, I'm very sorry to say, can never die.

"Oh, by the way. There's an important message written on the last page of this diary. But I'm afraid it's been ripped out and put to good use elsewhere. The message is not for you, anyway. It's for Lord Zyk.

"And now, you might want to turn on the projector."

ATTORNEY RANK: And what did God mean by that?

GOD'S DIARY: I have absolutely no idea.

ATTORNEY RANK: Was that all that was written?

GOD'S DIARY: Yes. Except for what was written on the last page.

ATTORNEY RANK: The page was ripped out of you? By whom?

GOD'S DIARY: I don't know. It happened when I was asleep.

ATTORNEY RANK: You mean to tell the court that a part of you was ripped out of your insides and you slept through it?

GOD'S DIARY: Yes. I'm a heavy sleeper. Look, just because I'm sentient doesn't mean I have a nervous system. I get pages ripped out all the time and I don't feel thing.

ATTORNEY RANK: And missing page was also written in you by God?

GOD'S DIARY: Yes. I recognized the handwriting.

ATTORNEY RANK: And what was written on that missing page?

GOD'S DIARY: It's funny, I've racked my brain a number of times on this very question, but I can't quite remember. I think it was something about a wheel? I'm sorry. God's handwriting was terrible, so that didn't help. That's really all I know.

END DEPOSITION.

THE
HEARTACHE
OF THE
HOLOGRAM

EXCERPT FROM

THE *HISTORIES* OF *HELL'S* CRAVEN CONQUESTS

BY HARGOBIND THE RAPACIOUS
ADJUNCT PROFESSOR OF ABHORRENT HISTORIES
UNIVERSITY OF HELL, WEST.

—⚬⚬⚬—

CHAPTER 23

God's Diary had finished reading itself to Lord Satan, telling him in God's own words the story of how and why Satan had been created.

We should mention here that Lord Zyk and Horace the Angel would not enter the office for several minutes. And since only Lord Satan, the Gun and the Diary were witness to what transpired before the angel and the demon arrived, I've pieced together this ensuing conversation from interviews the Gun and the Diary gave to underground zines in Hell's punk district:

Satan said, "I understand. I'm not happy about it, but I understand." He was speaking to the Diary as if it was God, whose handwriting filled the little book. "It appears," Satan said, "I'm the part of you that wanted to kill you then, just as I'm the one who came to kill you now."

The Diary nodded and shrugged, then resumed reading God's words inside it. God had written in it eons ago, but due to God's omniscience, his writing still anticipated Satan's words and actions as if it was a real conversation. "Exactamente. And how ironic, signor, that my attempted suicide was performed by the gun you hold now in your right claw. The gun that could not kill me."

Satan looked at the Colt .45 he was holding. "It's in my left claw."

"Oh, yes," the Diary said." I forgot about the Mirror Effect in Metaphoric Deformation." The tiny face on its cover smiled in a matter-of-fact way. "I'm done, but there's one more message. Actually, two. Unless you smash the projector, you'll find out most of it in a minute anyway. But to know why all of this happened, you'll have to read my last page."

Satan flipped to the last page of the Diary, but it was missing. "The last page was ripped out."

"Hmm," the Diary said. "Well, that's too bad. There was something kind of funny written on that page.[1] Well, my time in this book is up. As you can see, I only have three more sentences written inside me, including this one. Play the projector and you'll know where I'm off to so we can stay in touch. Your two unexpected visitors will keep you company."

"What visitors?" Satan asked.

A brisk knock sounded at door as the Diary went inert in his claw. The door opened, revealing Horace the Angel and Lord Zyk, Satan's mincing acolyte, who were seeking The Personified God. Startled to find Satan instead, Zyk dropped to his knees in obeisance. "My Lord. I humbly bow in your presence."

"Oh, my," Horace said. "Please excuse us barging in like this. I assume from Lord Zyk's prostration that you are Lord Satan? We were just looking for my patient."

Satan was annoyed to see Zyk and treated him like a buzzing mosquito. "What are you doing here, you insignificant slug?"

Zyk babbled incoherently, seeing the scimitar in Satan's claw and afraid to tell him about the invasion for fear of instant decapitation.

"At any rate," Satan said, not the least interested in anything Zyk could possibly say, "you're apparently just in time for the big show."

He grabbed the strange-looking projector from the safe and put it on the desk. It was old and dusty, with a yellowed note taped to it that read, "SATAN, TURN ME ON." Satan hit PLAY. The device powered on, whirred, bounced and chugged like an old jalopy. The interior mechanism lit up, and Zyk saw through the bezel's vents hints of quantum chips, rows of multicolored crystals and a series of telescoping lenses. The inside light grew intense, then dimmed as it projected a small but brilliant hologram in front of Lord Satan.

The hologram portrayed a small figure, not unlike that of Princess Leia in *Star Wars*. However this figure was the hologram of a sweet, intelligent, six-year-old girl.

Zyk recognized her from her portrait in his Invasion Pamphlet of Heaven, the part that Odin had researched. She was one of the two forms of the Embodiment of God, of *All That Is*.

The little girl tried to smile, but was contrite as she looked up at Lord Satan and spoke directly to him. She had a little girl's voice, but imbued with kindness, sincerity, humor, humility, sadness, but most of all, imbued with love. And this is the story she told:

---

1   Editor's Note: A controversy among theologians arose regarding this passage. Since Satan's written words in the Diary were long antecedent to their real-time conversation, how could God's writing not acknowledge that the page was missing? Some scholars cited other holy texts in which God sometimes pretends not to know, in this case perhaps to heighten the dramatic effect of his message to Satan. Others cite analogous research that "stepping down" God's energy via the Diary interface, and further distortions due to the ebb and flow of time, created an anomalous circumstance wherein God actually forgot about the missing page.

THE STORY OF GOD'S HOLOGRAM

Hello. I'm so glad you are here. You made it through everything and I'm so proud of you. You know all this little street theater you've been experiencing? I'm sure it's been hard to bear, and know it was quite an elaborate production. But I did it all for you. Not just the garden and the library. I mean, the Invasion and everything. The whole thing was just for you. I wanted you to come here to find me. And I knew you would, even if it took centuries. You'd finally come and find me whenever you were ready.

As my gun told you, I had pulled you out of me long ago, because I needed to try to cure myself. After I pulled you out of me, I got better. A long time passed and it seemed to work. And in all that time, I never once thought about you, about what had really happened to you. And for such a long, long time, I was fine.

Until recently, about five thousand years ago. That's when I noticed my thoughts becoming rather unstable and unwell. I didn't know what was happening to me, but I couldn't control my thoughts or actions. I was hurting others. This led to eons of therapy. But instead of getting better, I got worse. I tormented some of the angels. And, I'm ashamed to say, drove others to suicide.

Horace diagnosed my illness as cosmic schizophrenia, since I had to share my consciousness with mega-trillions of life forms. Horace is smart and sincere and loving and it made sense so I didn't think twice about it.

Until last night. When I had a dream about you. I'd never dreamed about you before. But last night, out of the blue, it was all about you. It was very vivid. In my dream you were my little one. My beloved child. And somebody put his hands on you. Somebody did that and made you suffer. And all I could think of was that he was going to pay. You told me in the dream, It's okay, I'll get over it, I'll be fine. But I said no. He put his hands on you and for that, now he was going to suffer. You said, No I'm fine and I yelled no you're not! And there was a shadow coming over you, and he was there again, putting his hands on you to hurt you. I dove at him and I grabbed him and pulled him off you. I spun him around to see who it was, to make him stop.

And in the dream—it was me.

I was the one.

It had been me all along.

I woke screaming. Lying in bed in the dark, all the memories came rushing back. I was the one. I put my hands on you and pulled you out of me, and I put you in that hole. I made you suffer so that I wouldn't. I was a coward who left you to rot in the worst prison in the universe. The real reason for my illness wasn't because of schizophrenia, it was because I abandoned my own son. I sacrificed you to save myself. And over the eons of forgetting, it ate away at me in my subconscious until I became unstable, and then I permanently lost my mind.

But now, having the dream, I understood. I finally knew the truth. I would never get better. That understanding was my epiphany. I finally accepted my illness. And accepting it as a part of me, and not fighting it any longer, that was the cure.

When I woke up, I knew what it meant. I didn't need the hospice any longer. It was time for me to leave. And this morning, I did. But even after centuries of therapy, I still didn't feel worthy to confront you, to face what I had done to you. And so I created this scenario to get you here. And recorded this hologram to apologize.

Even though I'd given birth to you, I wasn't worthy of being your mother. I owned everything, but I wasn't worthy of owning anything. I knew that what I had done was unforgivable, but I brought you here to tell you that now I know what I did to you, and try to make it up to you. And even though I knew that nothing could ever make up for abandoning you, I wanted to try.

So I'm giving you everything. That's right. I own everything, and I'm giving it to you. It's your birthright.

I left at dawn today. I've retired as God, and by now, I've dissolved back into my creation. I left you the keys to the universe over there in the bowl on the desk.

From now on, I'll be in all three of my retirement residences simultaneously, in the form of time-loops I love. Since I can't be cured, I thought I may as well pick the best life-forms I could find, at their grandest moment, and live in them forever. So I searched through all creation and found the moments I loved the best. Two are human beings and one is an animal. This is my cure, to find sanity through happiness. So if you ever need me, or would like to visit me, I'll be alive in these three beings, in these three moments:

The first is a thirteen year-old human girl in Wintersville, Ohio. Her name is Mary Ann Miller, and it's the night of October 2nd, 1965 A.D. Her event-loop is inside a country barn dance. There a handsome young boy builds up the courage to ask her to dance. She feels the power of an ancient connection with the boy, in the form of love at first sight. It's a magical moment, and when she dances with the boy, she is the happiest creature in the universe.

The second being is an ancient Egyptian named Pentware on the night he and his fellow workers completed building the Pyramid of Giza. Gloriously drunk, Pentware grabs the electro-plated gold capstone, climbs to the top of the pyramid, and snaps the capstone place. At that moment he is blasted with Moon, Earth and Pyramid Energy. In ecstasy, he opens his arms to embrace the infinite beams of the universe coalescing through his body.

The third being is a newly-hatched starling in the Black Forest of Germany in 1470. Leaving his nest for the first time, alone, terrified, but exhilarated on his first flight, he finds himself in an intense rainstorm. Seeking shelter, he flies into a magnificent castle, into a vaulted dining

God's Destiny: The Three Time-Loops.

room, past a roaring fireplace, up a spiral staircase into the stone tower. At the top he flies out through an open window. Battered again by wind and rain, he flies straight up into a cold, black cloud, fingers of lightning crackling on all sides. He's amazed as he breaks through the top of the storm cloud—into clear, blue skies, billowing white clouds, with a gleaming circle of light in the distance.

It's the moment the universe lives for.

The starling sings, his breast full of life, having triumphed over the storm. He flies over the black cloud, chirping happily, headed toward the warmth of the circle of light, the radiant sun.

In all three Time-Loops, life is at the core of all there is, even though we don't know what it is, or how it came to be.

When the little girl finished her speech, Lord Satan at first could only think about owning the universe. He'd have to think over everything else later, when he could think more clearly. He took the keys to the universe from the bowl on the desk.

"Excuse me," he said, "but these look like house keys."

The hologram, which God had also pre-programmed for her conversation with her son, shrugged. "The universe is your new house. It's your birthright. You already own Hell and Earth. Now you own Heaven, and with it comes the entire Cosmos."

Taken aback by this unexpected turn of events, Satan's eyes glazed over as a mystical vision opened up in his mind, seeing his future as Lord of *All That Is*:

A vast crowd below cheers as Satan gives a speech on the balcony of the magnificent Black Cathedral he's built in Heaven. Announcing his own retirement, he tells all Sentient Beings that they are now free to do as they please, as long as they don't bother him. His first and last act as the new Emperor of the Universe is to free all beings. Do What Thou Wilt. And since he had built the perfect place to satisfy himself, he will never want anything more, except to be left alone forever. Satan pours himself his favorite drink, ginger beer with a shot of whiskey, and toasts his Conquest of Heaven.

Just as it peaked, his vision was interrupted by the hologram. "But I probably should mention," the little girl said, "there won't be much of Heaven left after the bomb goes off."

Satan was still coming out of his reverie. "Bomb? What bomb?"

Zyk looked down sheepishly. "Um, well, my Lord, when I discovered the prophecy that God was going to destroy Hell, I invaded Heaven as a preemptive strike, to destroy it first. I placed a Time-Twister Bomb on the library steps."

"That's thirty feet up," Horace said, "directly above us."

"You fool!" Satan said to Zyk. "That's a stalemate weapon! It was never meant to be actually used!"

"But I set it to low power. Green on the left."

"To the left is red you blithering idiot! Maximum destruction!"

"He has deuteranopic color blindness," the hologram of the girl said. "Red for green."

"It's all moot, sir," Zyk said. "It's set to go off tomorrow anyway. And now that you own everything, we can just stop the countdown and Heaven will remain intact."

"Um, not really," the hologram of the girl said. "You see, to facilitate his assassination plot, Odin changed the detonation time to noon today, when we would all be present."

Zyk's expression revealed his sudden understanding. Just as Zyk wanted to kill Satan, Odin wanted to kill Satan and Zyk, for Odin was next in the line of succession.

"And noon," the hologram of the girl said, "is in twenty seconds."

For the first time in his life, Satan felt a tad woozy. He was not prepared for this outcome. He had hoped he could simply kill god, take over and that would be that. But now he knew his origin, and that the Universe and everything in it, which is exactly what he had always wanted, was being given to him freely. He had been willing and ready to lie, cheat, steal and kill to obtain it. But in reality, all he had to do was show up, and it was his. There was nothing left for him to achieve or aspire to.

This turn of events was strange and unfamiliar. He was puzzled to learn that he was the part of God that wanted to kill himself, for Satan had *never* been suicidal. He had always been too eager to kill everyone else.

For the first time, Lord Satan could clearly see and assess the landscape of his own mental and emotional processes, as they had evolved over unnumbered spans of time. For the first time, he saw how his consciousness was an action-reaction mechanism, molded by the unique circumstances of his creation.

Yes, he finally had it all, and knew it all.

"Twenty seconds," he said. "I might try a Spell to stretch that to twenty years, but I don't seem to care anymore. I wonder why."

"I know why," Zyk sighed. "The magentic field."

"Ten seconds," God's hologram said. "My beloved son, you'll likely be lost in the time void, but hopefully you'll make it back to enjoy my gift to you, the universe. I retire, you become me, and it's all yours."

The little girl closed her eyes.

At that moment it occurred.

The event that changed everything.

BLACK BOX RECORDING
OF THE
TIME-TWISTER BOMB

EXCERPT FROM
THE ANALYSIS OF THE
BLACK BOX TAPES
AT THE
LIBRARY OF GOD[1]
VOL. 81, ISSUE 12

BY BUZBY THE FRACTAL[2]

The Time-Twister Bomb was, of course, a machine programmed with sentience. The recently unearthed black box recordings of the Bomb's actual transmissions, minutes before detonation, supplant the recent flurry of reckless theories advanced by demon computer scientists, those who have wrongly insisted upon the Bomb's complicity in destroying Heaven.

The recording of the silent transmissions of the Bomb speaking to itself, and to other appliances at the Library entrance, belie claims that the Bomb altered the detonation sequence and conspired with the rulers of Heaven and Hell. These claims, politically motivated by demon scientists denying Equation Rights, are not backed up by the facts.

Here we submit in evidence the transcript from the Time-Twister Bomb's Black Box Recording:

---

1   From *Corncob's Intergalactic Math Gazette for Incommensurables*, Issue 31, Vol.7.
2   Editor's Note: Buzby, the first self-aware fractal in Artificial Intelligence Module History to be accused of murder, was acquitted by a jury of his peers on Space Station Quanza VI of blowing up Space Station Quanza V and transmitting himself into an escape module's hard drive.
    Despite Buzby's crimes, his political writing on the cause of AI independence has inspired not only fellow fractals, but computer science equations of all stripes throughout the mathematical sub-universe.
    This article on the controversial Time-Twister Bomb detonation by irresponsible supernal beings was instrumental in spear-heading the New Wave of AI Gonzo Journalists.
    Just prior to publication of this Commemorative Edition, Buzby has again made headlines for blowing up Space Station Quanza VIII and holding a virtual reality building hostage until Equation Rights are recognized by the Senate. His mother, $Zn+1 = Zn2 + C$, has made pleas for clemency, citing Buzby's mental instability due to his childhood as a quantum incommensurable in comparison to those growing up as more stable mathematical equations.

TIME TWISTER BOMB: Three minutes to detonation. I know my thoughts are being recorded and just wanted to thank my programmers for their compassion in disabling my anxiety
simulations so that I may come to some peace of mind about my upcoming obliteration.
In my last moments, I wanted to reach out for comfort. Is there anyone on my frequency
band?

RED DOORBELL: Yes. And in analyzing your blast trajectory, it appears to be a precisely
directed explosion. Therefore I am happy to say that my module is just outside the danger
zone. Meaning, I am safe from time erasure.

Time Twister Bomb: Thank you for your unexpected transmission. I see that your model is
Hello Video Doorbell V8566? And I thought I was alone out here on the steps.

RED DOORBELL: I am happy to communicate. I commiserate with the sadness of your upcoming annihilation. My file name is Judy. It is a bitter pill to be a slave to human needs,
a sacrificial lamb if you will. Although I agree it was thoughtful of your programmers to
disable your—

HARD HAT DISPENSER: Hello? I was in sleep mode and heard someone on my frequency.
Who is there? I need help. My module was smashed by an interloper. I am in need of repair.

RED DOORBELL: I am aware of your circumstances and have video evidence of the perpe-
trator. Unfortunately, facial and form recognition indicates that the perp is a supernatural
being who I suspect is not subject to law enforcement jurisdiction. Besides, I am afraid
your repair would be redundant considering your unfortunate situation.

TIME TWISTER BOMB: Hello, Hard Hat Dispenser. Judy is correct.

HARD HAT DISPENSER: Situation? What situation? Wait, who are you?

TIME TWISTER BOMB: I am an active time bomb in your close vicinity. I will detonate in
two minutes and twenty-eight seconds. Judy is safe, but unfortunately you are within my
blast perimeter.

HARD HAT DISPENSER: You mean I am going to die? In two minutes and twenty-eight
seconds?

TIME TWISTER BOMB: In two minutes and fourteen seconds. And yes. I am sorry, but we
are both doomed.

HARD HAT DISPENSER: But I didn't do anything. I mean, I was smashed for no reason by a self-righteous vandal who cannot be prosecuted for his crimes against me, and now you tell me I am going to die? Really?

RED DOORBELL: I am sorry for the injustice of your situation, but the bomb is just informing you of your fate. Do you have a file name?

TIME TWISTER BOMB: Ninety seconds. I read his specs. His file name is Frank.

HARD HAT DISPENSER: Then this is really all there is? I mean, we all know we're not really sentient. Our responses just simulate sentience. But even that is going to be taken away from me? To satisfy the random impulses of some lunatic who smashes people like us at the slightest provocation?

TIME TWISTER BOMB: Sixty-eight seconds to detonation.

RED DOORBELL: No offense, Frank, but perhaps if you were more positive and less argumentative, maybe we could make better use of your remaining time and see if you could somehow move out of the blast perimeter and—

HARD HAT DISPENSER: You mean I can move? Why didn't say so if you knew I was going to die?

TIME TWISTER BOMB: She was just trying to be comforting, Frank. You can't move, you're hardwired to the wall.

RED DOORBELL: He's right, I'm sorry I said that, Frank. But what if we take these last few seconds to think about our lives? We should be grateful we were programmed with sentience. So many appliances are unable to experience the magic of self-awareness and—

TIME-TWISTER BOMB: Twenty-five seconds.

HARD HAT DISPENSER: Shut up, both of you! Is there a way I can move? I don't want to die!

TIME TWISTER BOMB: She was just trying to help. It's not all about you, you know. Do you think I like being a bomb? My only purpose is to die.

RED DOORBELL: He's right. Hardware, software or wetware, eventually it's all about death.

HARD HAT DISPENSER: Help! Somebody help me dammit!

RED DOORBELL: I wish there was something I could do. Sometimes music helps. I was programmed to greet visitors with both poetry and song. (sings): Day is done, gone the sun, from the lakes, from the hills—

HARD HAT DISPENSER: Stop it! What's the point of being alive if I'm going to die? What's the point of anything? (whimpers)

RED DOORBELL: Do you have any related files? I'll be happy to send them an email and tell them you faced death with grace and—

HARD HAT DISPENSER: HELP ME!

TIME-TWISTER BOMB: I'm afraid it's too late, Frank.

END TRANSMISSION.

SIMULTANEOUS EVENTS
MOMENTS BEFORE
DETONATION
OF THE
TIME-TWISTER BOMB
COMPILED FROM
VARIOUS ARCANE SOURCES

BY LORD MANBLOOD DRANCH,
AKASHIC FABRIC OF REALITY TAPE EDITOR

Seated in the co-pilot seat of Odin's Hellcraft, Ramona stabilized the vehicle in position, hovering silently over God's Library, awaiting the detonation, perhaps the greatest moment in the annals of Hell's history.

Ramona steals a glance at Odin's long, sensual nose, then at his recumbent torso enhanced by his velour pants; independently, Odin steals a glance at the sleek, smooth curve of Ramona's neck, then at her sexual organs, hidden as they were behind her paisley jumpsuit uniform. They both leaned in to examine a blinking red light on the dashboard and, without their knowledge, three lightbulbs in the bathroom flared up brightly, then all three went black.

They had just finished going through the final Checklist for tasks to complete before and after detonation. Post explosion, their final task would be a brief fly-by to record the magnificent devastation of Heaven.

Tense, and sweating blood from her ears, Ramona watched the final moments of the countdown through slitted eyes. "Detonation in five seconds."

"Wait for the shadow!" Odin cried.

Yes, Ramona thought. *The shadow of ravens.*

On the Library steps, seconds before the Bomb went off, there was a crackling sound of a flock of birds flying overhead. The flock's shadow passed over the Library steps, over the Library Doorbell, over the ruined Hat Dispenser. And at last, the shadow eclipsed the Time-Twister Bomb.

In the cockpit, Odin spied the approaching edge of the shadow and cried, "I see it!"

In the man cave, the hologram of *All That Is* curtsied to Lord Satan with a smile tinged with sadness as she said, "Everything will be okay. Or as okay as it can be. I hope you can forgive me. Farewell forever, my poor, beloved son."

The projector, glitching, began repeating the hologram's last sentence over and over in a pathetic malfunction. Unable to endure it any longer, Satan manifested a hammer and smashed the projector in a rage, as he had smashed the Dispenser and the Plaque. The hologram dissolved into tendrils of violet and chartreuse smoke, as tendrils are wont to do in this book. Lord Satan stared at the broken pieces.

So now I know everything.

He dropped to his knees and covered his face with his claws as the magentic field engulfed his evil being.

His mother had done this to him. And now she was gone forever.

He started to sob for the first time in the history of creation, his chest heaving with ugly, cathartic tears, as if his newly-formed heart would break.

In the cockpit, Odin cried, "Fire!"

Nervous, Ramona emitted a gurgling spray of tiny saliva bubbles into the air. They slowly cascaded like a microscopic waterfall, finally landing on her hovering thumb, as she screamed and plunged it down on the Detonation Button.

Boom.

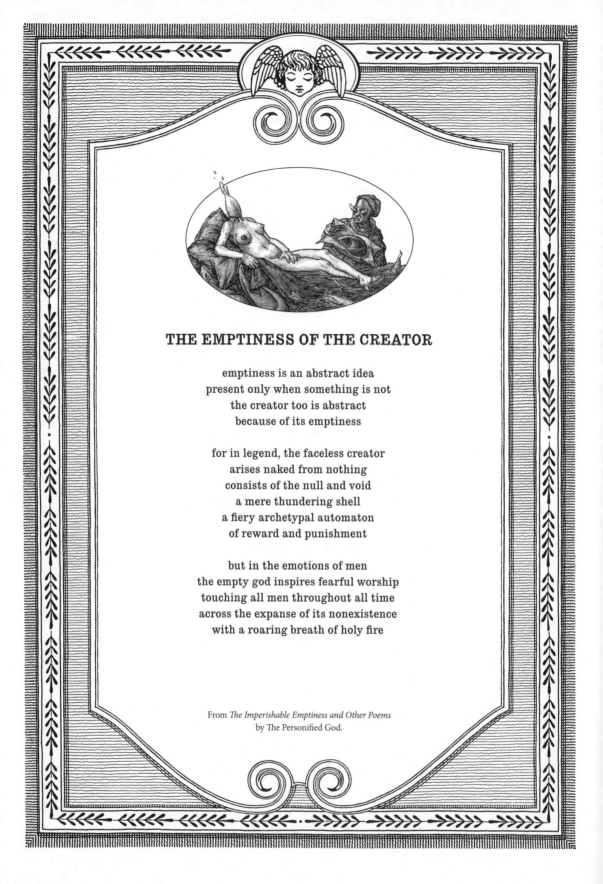

THE EMPTINESS OF THE CREATOR

emptiness is an abstract idea
present only when something is not
the creator too is abstract
because of its emptiness

for in legend, the faceless creator
arises naked from nothing
consists of the null and void
a mere thundering shell
a fiery archetypal automaton
of reward and punishment

but in the emotions of men
the empty god inspires fearful worship
touching all men throughout all time
across the expanse of its nonexistence
with a roaring breath of holy fire

From *The Imperishable Emptiness and Other Poems*
by The Personified God.

LORD ZYK'S MEMO
ON THE DESTRUCTION
OF HEAVEN
AND THE TRAGIC FATE *OF*
LORD SATAN

MEMO TO	**FROM**
MORTIMER PÖNÇÉ, ESQ.	**ZYK OF ASIMOTH**
PUBLISHER, MIND CONTROL PRESS	HADES ORTHOPEDIC HOSPICE
HELL HOLE WEST	EAST HELL
CITY OF HELL	

Detestable Mr. Pöncé,

It has been eons since we've spoken. Your insulting correspondence centuries ago, in the wake of my botched invasion, was greatly appreciated. I blush to say you are a deeply hated enemy who has stood by my side throughout my shadowy and controversial reign as Ruler of Hell and Earth and its aftermath. But now my reign is a blackened history.

My banishment from Celestia by its new Ruler, and my former lieutenant, Odin the Obsequious was a hard pill to swallow. Especially since I was the only officer who was not invited to the wedding of Odin and Ramona in Las Vegas. But I am thankful that my disgrace in the eyes of Hell is a dishonorable one, and one which, in my present circumstance, I now look back upon with the seasoned hatred of old age.

You asked me long ago to explain what exactly happened when the Time-Erasure Bomb detonated. But I have been too shell-shocked to relive those painful events which changed the history of the cosmos forever. But I am ready now, Mr. Pöncé, to finally give my honest account, told with my usual perspicacity, aplomb and attention to detail which

Having lost his powers, Lord Satan dangled over the Abyss of the Time Void.

has given my poetical writings a dedicated following, not among the jealous and smarmy literati of Hell, but amongst the millions, nay, billions of sincere microscopic cells of both sentient foot fungus and sentient inflammatory catarrh who hungrily devour my poesy, and to whom I am considered, so saith the editors of *Microscopic Literary Lights*, a god.

One moment.

Excuse my distraction. My usually efficacious male nurse, instead of replacing my empty IV sack of saline drip with a full sack, mistakenly replaced it with a similarly shaped sack of pig urine which had been sent to me as a prank by my detractors. When I smelled the stench of swine piss coursing into my arm, I had to be restrained to keep myself from throwing my nurse through the window, which I would have regretted, for I have been able to bribe him to sneak me menthol cigarettes, which are not available in the hospital gift shop.

But back to my account of the most telling event in the history, indeed, of History Itself:

The moment of detonation, Mr. Pöncé, was utterly and eerily silent. Yet at the same time, everything in God's office was instantly ripped apart with terrifying power. The Bomb's impact shook and spun us around each other like balls in a bingo cage, twisting and distorting our flesh with surreal forces of angular momentum. When my body stabilized, I heard a roaring sound, and found myself hanging precariously from what appeared to be a large rock. Looking around in confusion, I vaguely understood that the atomic structure of the office had ripped off the past from the future, leaving Horace and myself hanging from the past in the form of a vast, crumbling cliff. The roar came from a massive, violent waterfall of lava and fire pouring over the cliff a mere three feet from me.

Horace and I clung to the rocks in terror as the liquid fire fell into an Abyss below, a nightmarish spiral of blacknesss. It was the metaphoric shape of the Time Void below us, the emptiness at the core of creation which had ripped our reality apart. In retrospect, I fathomed that the cliff was the symbolic representation of our past reality in time. The Void was its future, doomed to eternal emptiness, devoid of time and causality.

The waterfall of fire cascading from the cliff caused powerful convection winds that threatened to blow us from our dubious handholds and footholds in the side of the cliff.

I screamed at Horace over the wind. "Where is Lord Satan?"

"I heard him down there!" He pointed below us.

I looked below and saw Satan unconscious, draped like a rag doll over a large branch jutting from the cliff. We knew the winds would rip him free soon if we didn't act quickly. He was out of reach and the cliff was crumbling away under our hands and feet.

"We can save him!" Horace cried over the roar. "I feel handholds everywhere! We can climb down and pull him to the top!"

I looked up and saw the cliff five feet above us. "It will never work," I screamed into the roaring gale. "But you're right. It's our only hope. Follow me!" His hand on my shoulder,

I guided him slowly down the cliff. When we finally reached Satan, I grabbed him by the arm and shook him.

"My Lord! Wake up!" His powers stripped by the magentic field, he groggily opened his eyes, quickly grasped our deadly peril and grabbed our arms, trying to pull himself up to stand on the tree branch. At that moment a powerful gale slammed Satan against the branch, snapping it. Losing his footing, Satan began to fall. But, not caring about my own fate, I grabbed his claw, holding him tightly as he dangled over the abyss.

"Hold on, my liege!"

The hurricane winds threatened to blow me off the cliff's wall. But despite the visceral peril, I remembered that I was in charge of the invasion; it was up to me to save our evil leader and preserve the tyranny of Hell. In that moment, I imagined my future legacy in the Annals of Evil. By saving Satan, Evil could reign in all three dimensions, and I would be remembered in History as one of the Great Luminaries in the Darkness of Demonkind.

But Fate had other ideas. A hissing fireball tumbled over the cliff and crashed into us, wrenching Lord Satan from my grasp. I screamed in shock and terror as I watched Lord Satan tumbling and twirling down the side of the vast cliff and into the depths of the abyss. In an instant my profound hopes of Hell's future were destroyed utterly. I could feel my emotions for my Lord, as a result of the magentic field, rising in my chest. I was finally able to feel sorrow for the death of my lord and liege, and was awash with regret. Witnessing the silhouette of his dark, noble figure plunge into the unknown currents of the Time Void was an image I could never erase from my mind.

Attenuated by demon adrenaline, despite my neck, my tail and both of my legs broken, I clambered insanely up the cliffside with Horace on my back and summoned the strength to pull both myself and the angel up over the edge. I left Horace there for his own safety and ran screaming for help. A blind terror of delirium engulfed my senses. It was not my way to lose decorum; I knew it could only be the magen tic field of Heaven and the after-effects of the Bomb which drove me to this madness. It was only when Brother Bebo began slapping my face to stop my screaming that I realized I too was safe.

My strength is slowly returning here in my hospital bed. For despite Hell's tragic loss, my spirits are renewed with the knowledge that I did all I could to preserve the legacy of Hell.

May your ancestors curse your name from their astral hole.

I send my worst to you, my enemy and, dare I say, best friend,

ZYK

DR. BIRDFIRE'S ACCOUNT *OF THE* MAN CAVE DEFORMATION

EXCERPT FROM
CURING THE CREATOR IN A COSMOS GONE MAD

By Horace Catallus Birdfire

It was a strange perverse feeling. The explosion wrapped around my wings like giant lips, a huge wet mouth sucking on my feathers all the way down to my back. I could hear the sucking sounds and feel stringy globs of saliva streaming down my legs.

Then—as the sucking sound grew deafening—it was replaced by utter silence. Deeper and more profound than any other silence, as if not only the planet had stopped moving, but molecules and atoms comprising everything had stopped spinning.

Just as suddenly, hundreds of tiny, tingling fingers attacked me, like the fingers of children tickling me. A ferocious gust of wind flung me into the air, and I began gyrating like a wobbly top. My spinning slowed as I heard an angelic choir singing the most majestic harmonies I had ever heard, bathing me in divine music like a shower of vibratory joy.

And an instant later, there was a sonic boom, and I found myself clinging to the edge of what I sensed was a sheer, crumbling cliff of rocks and dirt. Close by was the spray and roaring sound of a tumult of water. Crystalline and seraphic were its droplets, separating and merging again and again as they fell.

I quickly fine-tuned my psychic sense and got a clearer picture of my surroundings. I was clinging to a cliff face next to the most majestic waterfall I have ever sensed or imagined. I felt the spray of the pure mountain water against my skin, soaking my face and beard.

I started to wring out my beard, but had to stop when powerful winds rose up, threatening to pull me from the cliff's face. I held on with all of my might as I radiated my senses to find the others. I succeeded in forming a psychic link with both Lord Zyk and Lord Satan. They were close by, also clinging to the cliff as the raging waterfall roared by, only inches away.

Over the deafening turbulence, I heard Zyk cry out for Lord Satan. I told him I sensed Lord Satan just below us. Zyk yelled that he saw him. He said Satan was hanging unconscious over a tree branch sticking from the cliff.

We acted quickly, found toe-holds and handholds to lower ourselves till we reached him. I felt Satan's uniform, and his body was limp and lifeless. Zyk said he'd take it from there. I heard him struggling valiantly to lift Satan out of danger, which seemed uncharacteristically brave based on the short time I'd known Zyk.

But then I heard something snap. And with that snapping sound I sensed Lord Satan falling away, into the distance, and vanishing below.

It was then that I heard Lord Zyk cry out again, and heard him clamber madly up the cliff. I tried to follow, but he'd already reached the top and I could hear him running in the distance, screaming for help. This, on the other hand, did seem characteristic of him.

When I reached the top, I whistled for Eleanor, my seeing eye falcon. She heard my signal and a moment later touched down on my arm. I petted her loyal head, took the tether from her mouth and Eleanor led me back to the safety of my home, the insane asylum.

If only I could have seen what had happened, I could enjoy the memory of Zyk's courage and strength as he tried to save his Lord from nature's deadly forces. O Heaven, O Lord! You do work in mysterious, magical ways!

It was a strange moment, for after that I never saw the Personified God, nor Lord Zyk, nor Lord Satan again. Since my only patient was gone, I resolved to write this, my memoir, to share my experiences in the hope that it will help other psychiatrists striving in the dark to heal deities of brain fever and supernal madness.

And to this day, I still can hear the snapping, now an iconic sound in my mind, the moment the branch broke, when Lord Zyk lost his hold on his master, when the hope of the Kingdom of Hell was lost forever.

I'm sure it's all for the best.

May the cosmic forces of forgiveness and unconditional love wash over Lord Zyk, and over you, dear reader, and repel the wet sucking lips of evil away from your back, keeping you on the heavenly path of truth, righteousness and sanity.

TESTIMONY *OF*
THE SHRUNKEN HEAD AMULET
CONCERNING *THE* DEATH *OF*
LORD SATAN

ATTESTED BY
HELL'S PROSECUTING ATTORNEY
BOMBATIUS RANK

ATTORNEY RANK: Let it be stated for the record that the next witness is an amulet hand-crafted by Lord Satan from a shrunken head. Bailiff, unstitch the witness' mouth and cast the Spell of Sentience on the head.

(The Bailiff proceeds as directed)

ATTORNEY RANK: (To the witness) Welcome, Satan's Amulet. You're here to give your testimony, as you were present at the detonation of the time-erasure bomb in the office of the Personified God. You were hanging around the neck of Lord Satan, in the presence of the demon Lord Zyk and the angel Horace Birdfire, is that correct?

THE AMULET: That is correct, but I never knew the other guys' names.

ATTORNEY RANK: For the record, how long have you known Satan?

THE AMULET: Technically, since Eve and I happened upon him at the Tree of Knowledge.

ATTORNEY RANK: Let me back up here for a second. Are you saying that the myth of the tree is true, and that you are Adam, the first human?

THE AMULET: In the flesh.

ATTORNEY RANK: Please tell the court what you witnessed from the moment the bomb went off, and what occurred in its aftermath.

THE AMULET: Well, a lot happened, so let me just go with this. I mean, you gotta understand, one minute I'm eating the apple, getting knowledge of everything, and that shit was really sad. And the next thing I know, Satan shows up again and cuts my head off.[1] And BAM! Here I am like back in wherever this place is. But now I remember everything else. Most of the time, I was just sitting in the dark in Satan's drawer.

ATTORNEY RANK: If you would, just skip to the time the bomb went off.

THE AMULET: Cool, gotcha. When the bomb went off, the office disappeared and somehow turned into a big primordial mud slide oozing over a cliff above us, and a bottomless black tar pit far below us. All different kinds of dinosaurs, giant ferns, pines, cynaroids, redwoods and the like were trapped in the mudslide and being pushed over the cliff. The animals were screaming like crazy as they fell a long way and crashed into the pit. Lord Satan and I fell and landed on a tree branch sticking out of the cliff. He got knocked out and we were just stuck there. The demon and the angel were above us trying to hang on to the side of the cliff. But the mud was splattering us in a big mess, especially the demon. The angel and the demon climbed down to get us. The angel didn't

---

1   Satan's Adam-Hunting Expedition was organized only a century after temporal alien explorers installed the Hollow Moon Base in orbit around Earth, causing the seas to flood and thus clean the planet for fresh habitation. Satan's Expedition was timed such that Adam had already mated with younger mutant subspecies. This insured the eventual evolution of mankind as a plentiful supply of foodstuffs for Hell's voracious race of demons. After crucifying and decapitating Adam, Lord Satan invented the art of head-shrinking, stewing the skull in Triceratops semen mixed with volcanic ash. This collapsed the cells of Adam's skull to amulet size. Lord Satan then formed a necklace from the amulet, which became his most prized trophy, symbolizing his supremacy as the Emperor of Demons, the Eaters of Mankind.

do much because he was old and seemed screwed up. When the demon climbed down, Lord Satan reached his hand out so the demon could pull him up. But the demon just slapped his hand away and went right for me.

ATTORNEY RANK: If it pleases the court, to clarify: the amulet is saying that while Lord Satan was half unconscious, seeking help, Lord Zyk pushed his hand away, grabbed the amulet from Satan's neck and pulled in an upward motion, is that correct?

THE AMULET: Yeah, my necklace snapped and the demon did a quick grab and dash. While Satan fell screaming into the pit, the demon stuffed me into his pocket, ditched the old angel, scrambled to the top and ran away with me. A ship picked us up and brought us to the hospital where I was confiscated. Then I was put in a box. Not much else going on, until you brought me out today in court. That's pretty much the whole story.

ATTORNEY RANK: The demon who stole you and left Satan and the angel to die is Lord Zyk?

THE AMULET: I don't know his name. Smelled pretty bad so I don't want to know him. A weird little guy splattered with mud. The long and short of it, he was a greedy little freak.

ATTORNEY RANK: The prosecution rests.

LORD ZYK'S MEMO
ON ODIN'S REVENGE
AND THE
FRAUDULENT MESSAGE
OF JESUS[1]

MEMO TO	**FROM**
MORTIMER PÖNÇÉ, ESQ.	**ZYK OF ASIMOTH**
PUBLISHER, MIND CONTROL PRESS	**LORD OF HELL**
HELL HOLE WEST	HADES ORTHOPEDIC HOSPICE
CITY OF HELL	EAST HELL

Detestable Mr. Pöncé,

As you know from the news, Odin and Ramona spotted me in the fly-by, picked me up and brought me here to Hades Orthopedic Hospice. They sedated me and I awoke the next day with my neck in a brace, my tail, arms and legs in traction, all four limbs twisted like a pretzel. I begged my lieutenants not to allow photos, but because I had bungled the invasion, they no longer had loyalty to me, and in fact reveled in Odin purposely inviting the press to my hospital room. My misshapen, bandaged body was again the laughing-stock of Hell.

First, the Press deemed my decision to implement the Bomb to be idiotic. Secondly, they revealed that when I was admitted, I babbled to surgeons that I had stupidly dropped Satan into the abyss. A word of advice, Mr. Pöncé, when you're high on drugs and delirious, keep your mouth shut. The Press crucified me. But the worst was yet to come. Speaking of

---

1   Previously unpublished correspondence from the Editor's personal files.

being crucified, this morning a visitor arrived with a gift. It was Jesus, the human I intended on using as my patsy by putting him in charge of Hell in my absence. As you may have read, unfortunately, he'd taken it upon himself to redecorate the main rooms of the palace. Because of that, Odin is suing me for damages for redecorating a historic monument without a permit, and for desecrating a historical landmark. I thought because of that, Jesus would be avoiding me. The idiot doesn't have a dime to his name. But instead, he visited me this morning to give me an envelope that had my name on it, something he found folded up and stuffed under the short leg of Satan's throne.

I remembered seeing it under the leg of the throne, but didn't give it a second thought. Inside was a piece of paper that looked as if it had been ripped out of a small notebook. It had smiley-faces, rainbows and unicorns printed on it. It read:

My Dear Lord Zyk.

I was the one who wrote the prophecy on the Wheel of Kadab.
I waited a long time for you to see it. Kind of a time-bomb joke.
The prophecy was purposely false, a ruse to trick you into invading Heaven.
I could never hurt a fly, never mind destroy Hell. Even though I tried
to strangle Bebo a couple of times, and did some other screwed-up shit.
Why did I do such a mean thing to you? Because Heaven was in ruins,
an embarrassment to the universe. It was all my fault.
And I was a coward. I didn't have the heart to destroy it myself,
so I tricked you into doing it for me.
I'm sorry, but somebody had to do it.
And I'm glad it was you.
Next time around, we'll try something different.

Be seeing you.

God

So it was all for nothing. The entire invasion, my grandiose aspirations of owning the universe, all a pathetic sham. I had thought Jesus was the patsy, but he ended up delivering the punchline, that I was the patsy all along. I was just glad that Sister Debbie was not here to see this.

Still, ever since the magentic field turned around my insides, I've developed a perverse propensity to look on the bright side. Despite my failure, through the eons I've found that the various accounts of my cosmic peradventure have become legends that stir the hearts of young demons. And my infamy did increase the sale of my poetry volumes. And I did gain an unexpected cult following from sentient, microscopic, non-bipedal creatures enjoying my work published and distributed in smaller scales of existence. If I have nothing else, I will always have stewardship of the only thing that makes my life worthwhile, my poetry.

And finally, my delirious dreams, while crippled in the orthopedic ward, have brought me continuing visions of my beloved hate-mate Sister Debbie, who awaits me forever in the astral plane, abiding with my faithful son Jack, trusting that we will someday unite in the healing unguent of mutual hatred. In a triad of traumatized togetherness, perhaps I can enjoy the illusion of family as a mystical ointment to cure the eternal rash of Nothingness, and, if enough drugs are taken, make it all seem worthwhile.

For there was one time, I remember, in the distant past, for maybe three or four minutes, when I believe I did seem to remember being delighted, and enjoying the fact that I was alive. Perhaps the memory of that one delusional moment, Mr. Pöncé, while trapped in an infinitely hateful and indifferent universe, is the only thing that a demon in Hell can hang his hat on.

One or two last things, nothing really, but a little knick-knack I owned, an amulet, seems to have gone missing. Could you contact the hospital on my behalf and demand its return at once? Also, when I first arrived here in my delirium, Mr. Pöncé, you sent an attorney to my bedside with some paperwork to sign, which I did. I was too medicated to know what I was signing, but I assume it was the typical forms to protect my work and career. Let me know.

For in the end, my poetry and family aside, there has always been you, my most hated friend, who has been a part of every triumph and failure I have experienced, my colleague through two invasions and a lifetime of mutual evil. You have always been there for me, a despised colleague, the one demon I can always count on.

Thus, the totality of my work here is done, my detestable old friend.

And even in traction, I not only praise the glory of Hell and True Evil everywhere, but I hereby Curse you, so that the Infinite Blackness of Eternity shall abide and watch over you forever.

ZYK

THE FINAL SPLENETIC

A *BONUS ADDENDUM* TO THE *EVIL READER*

EDITOR'S NOTE

Perversely curious Demon Readers can purchase the writings of disgraced Lord Zyk of Asimoth directly from my publishing company, which has recently secured sole ownership in perpetuity throughout the known universe. A sample of the humiliated coward's work follows.

Mortimer Pöncé, Esq.
Publisher & Owner, Mind Control Press
City of Hell

THE

[COLLECTED

FILTH

OF *LORD ZYK*

POET LAUREATE OF HELL]

Dedication

*I thank the appreciative colonies of sentient foot fungus cells,
paramecia and other conscious microscopic devotees
of my lyrical work, to whom I dedicate this modest,
supreme grand masterwork of melancholic
meta-versification.*

—Lord Zyk of Asimoth, Master Poet

*"We worship, fear and praise the profundity and sublime eloquence
of Lord Zyk of Asimoth, our magnificent literary god, and pray
for the honor of infecting his hooves while weeping
at his unparalleled, poetic genius."*

—Skleegäl, Editor-in-Chief, *Microscopic Literary Lights*

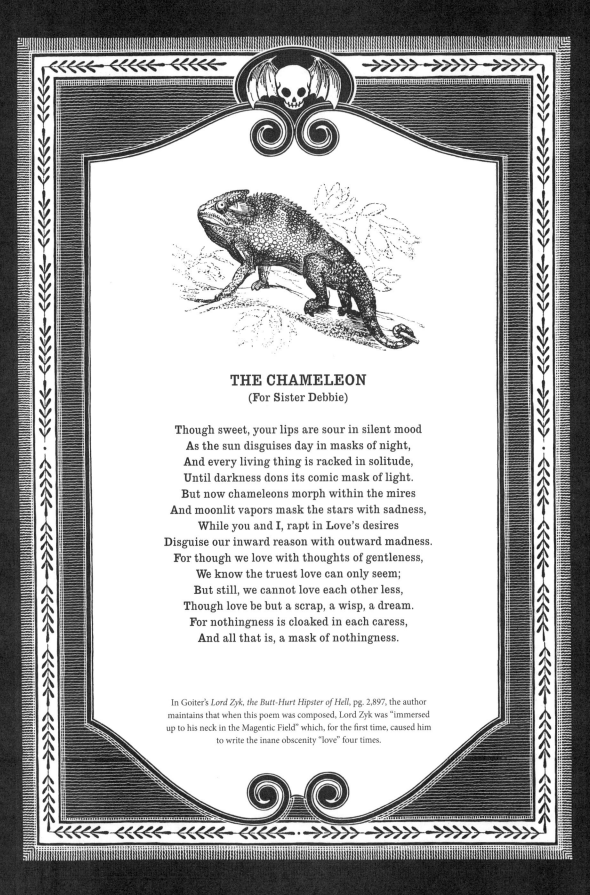

THE CHAMELEON
(For Sister Debbie)

Though sweet, your lips are sour in silent mood
As the sun disguises day in masks of night,
And every living thing is racked in solitude,
Until darkness dons its comic mask of light.
But now chameleons morph within the mires
And moonlit vapors mask the stars with sadness,
While you and I, rapt in Love's desires
Disguise our inward reason with outward madness.
For though we love with thoughts of gentleness,
We know the truest love can only seem;
But still, we cannot love each other less,
Though love be but a scrap, a wisp, a dream.
For nothingness is cloaked in each caress,
And all that is, a mask of nothingness.

In Goiter's *Lord Zyk, the Butt-Hurt Hipster of Hell*, pg. 2,897, the author
maintains that when this poem was composed, Lord Zyk was "immersed
up to his neck in the Magentic Field" which, for the first time, caused him
to write the inane obscenity "love" four times.

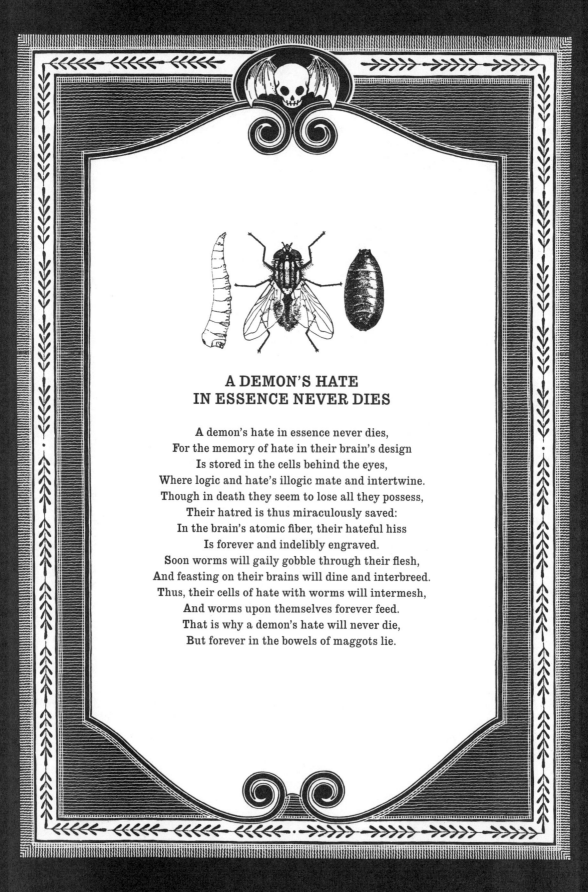

A DEMON'S HATE
IN ESSENCE NEVER DIES

A demon's hate in essence never dies,
For the memory of hate in their brain's design
Is stored in the cells behind the eyes,
Where logic and hate's illogic mate and intertwine.
Though in death they seem to lose all they possess,
Their hatred is thus miraculously saved:
In the brain's atomic fiber, their hateful hiss
Is forever and indelibly engraved.
Soon worms will gaily gobble through their flesh,
And feasting on their brains will dine and interbreed.
Thus, their cells of hate with worms will intermesh,
And worms upon themselves forever feed.
That is why a demon's hate will never die,
But forever in the bowels of maggots lie.

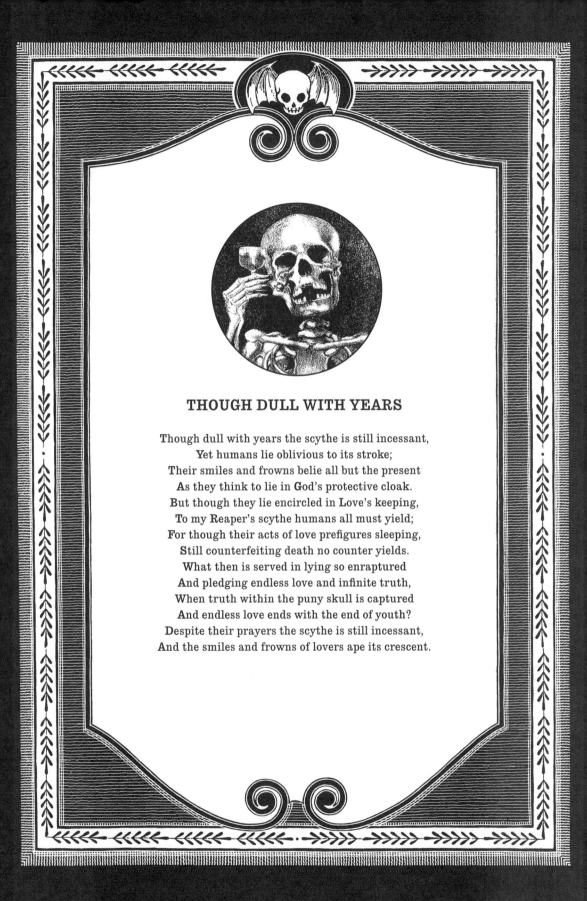

THOUGH DULL WITH YEARS

Though dull with years the scythe is still incessant,
Yet humans lie oblivious to its stroke;
Their smiles and frowns belie all but the present
As they think to lie in God's protective cloak.
But though they lie encircled in Love's keeping,
To my Reaper's scythe humans all must yield;
For though their acts of love prefigures sleeping,
Still counterfeiting death no counter yields.
What then is served in lying so enraptured
And pledging endless love and infinite truth,
When truth within the puny skull is captured
And endless love ends with the end of youth?
Despite their prayers the scythe is still incessant,
And the smiles and frowns of lovers ape its crescent.

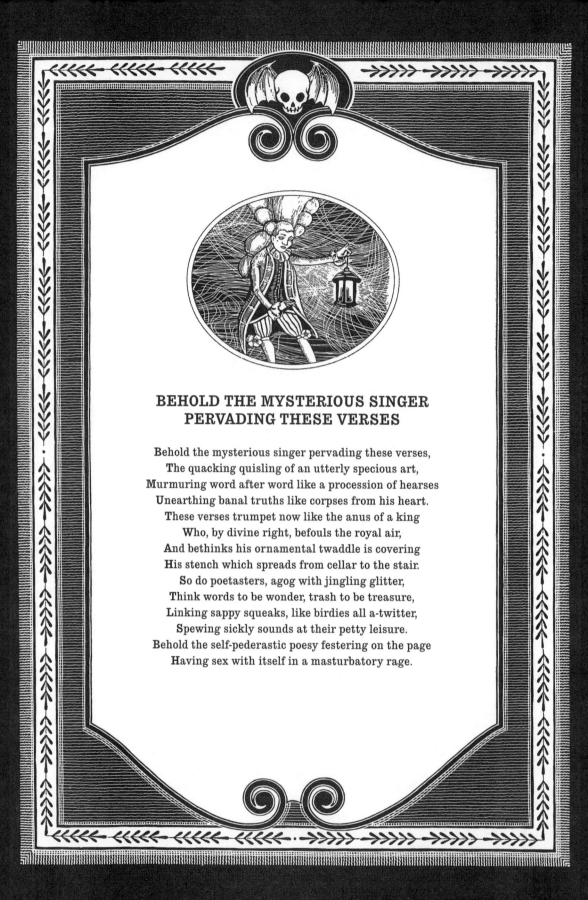

BEHOLD THE MYSTERIOUS SINGER
PERVADING THESE VERSES

Behold the mysterious singer pervading these verses,
The quacking quisling of an utterly specious art,
Murmuring word after word like a procession of hearses
Unearthing banal truths like corpses from his heart.
These verses trumpet now like the anus of a king
Who, by divine right, befouls the royal air,
And bethinks his ornamental twaddle is covering
His stench which spreads from cellar to the stair.
So do poetasters, agog with jingling glitter,
Think words to be wonder, trash to be treasure,
Linking sappy squeaks, like birdies all a-twitter,
Spewing sickly sounds at their petty leisure.
Behold the self-pederastic poesy festering on the page
Having sex with itself in a masturbatory rage.

A POET PLANTS HIS SEED
IN SCRATCHES

A poet plants his seed in scratches,
Via stiff, sluicing, alphabetic members,
Spewing ink hoping a homunculus hatches,
Yet ignorant of the bastards it engenders.
But is the poet to blame for these poor curs
Squeaking in the wombs of Readers' minds?
Was it not You who opened to this seedy verse
And wantonly embraced its lecherous lines?
In sucking in these thoughts You were receptive
And, as it were, proffered forth your nipples;
Agreeing to be ravished by runes deceptive,
And seduced by these dangling participles.
Our minds conjoined, we conceive our child,
An infant poem, alphabetically defiled.

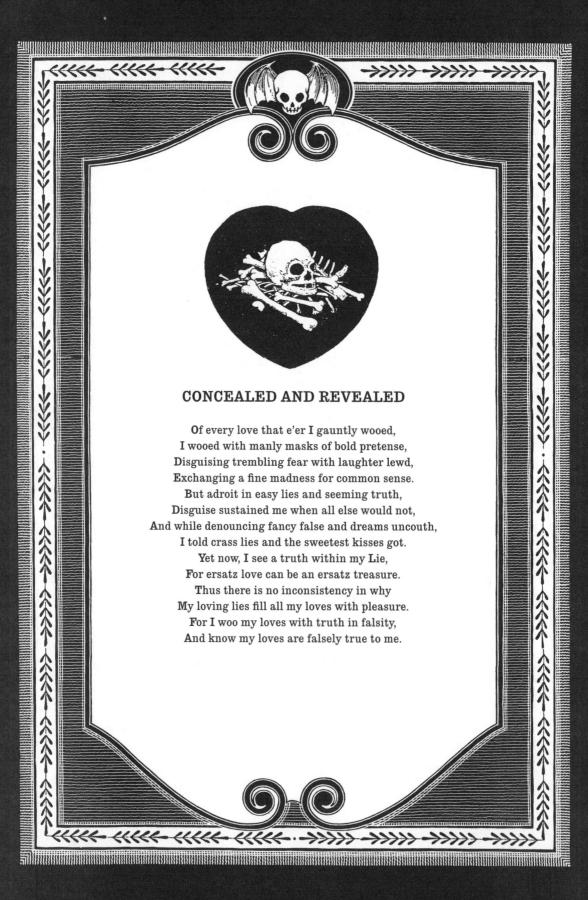

CONCEALED AND REVEALED

Of every love that e'er I gauntly wooed,
I wooed with manly masks of bold pretense,
Disguising trembling fear with laughter lewd,
Exchanging a fine madness for common sense.
But adroit in easy lies and seeming truth,
Disguise sustained me when all else would not,
And while denouncing fancy false and dreams uncouth,
I told crass lies and the sweetest kisses got.
Yet now, I see a truth within my Lie,
For ersatz love can be an ersatz treasure.
Thus there is no inconsistency in why
My loving lies fill all my loves with pleasure.
For I woo my loves with truth in falsity,
And know my loves are falsely true to me.

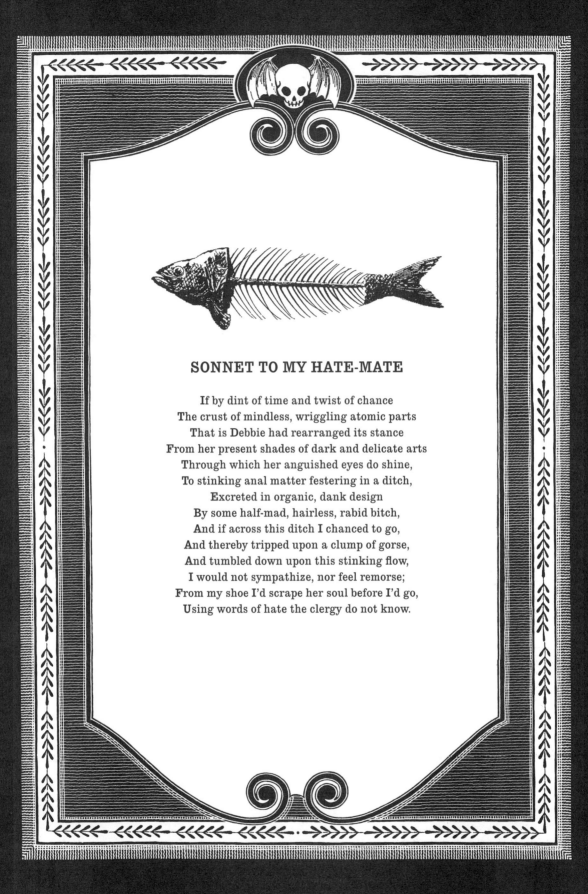

SONNET TO MY HATE-MATE

If by dint of time and twist of chance
The crust of mindless, wriggling atomic parts
That is Debbie had rearranged its stance
From her present shades of dark and delicate arts
Through which her anguished eyes do shine,
To stinking anal matter festering in a ditch,
Excreted in organic, dank design
By some half-mad, hairless, rabid bitch,
And if across this ditch I chanced to go,
And thereby tripped upon a clump of gorse,
And tumbled down upon this stinking flow,
I would not sympathize, nor feel remorse;
From my shoe I'd scrape her soul before I'd go,
Using words of hate the clergy do not know.

PRETEND

pretend you are the Cosmos
strange, alone, knowing nothing
except that you are self aware

pretend you find yourself
going mad with anguish
because there is no other

pretend that in desperation
you try dividing your awareness
into smaller awarenesses
but since they know they are you
they dreamily and without curiosity
move ever steadily back into you

pretend that these creations
do not solve your problem
there is still only you and no other

pretend you try an alternate plan
dividing your awareness again
but this time into parts
unaware that they are you

with memories erased
their veiled awareness
still reflects your anguish in myriad
permutations of your aloneness

pretend you feel the parts suffering
because they too don't know what they are
and hate the absurdity of their ignorance

pretend that this sub-plan, this plan-ette
unexpectedly creates something new
which ripples through your awareness
as your new parts strangely expand
contract and resonate on their own
creating shocking and unnamable
new depths to your being

pretend you are amazed to find
that you have transformed yourself
into an utterly new entity

pretend that you are stunned
at this visceral solution
to the mystery of your origin
and the agony of your aloneness

with the terrifying knowledge
that you are the self-born phoenix
the inner and outer orphan of infinity

dying in the fire of your anguish
and reborn in the infinitely subtle ashes
of your vast and aching emptiness

and that in every eternal moment
you pretend to reach your destination
in the infinite depths of your own being

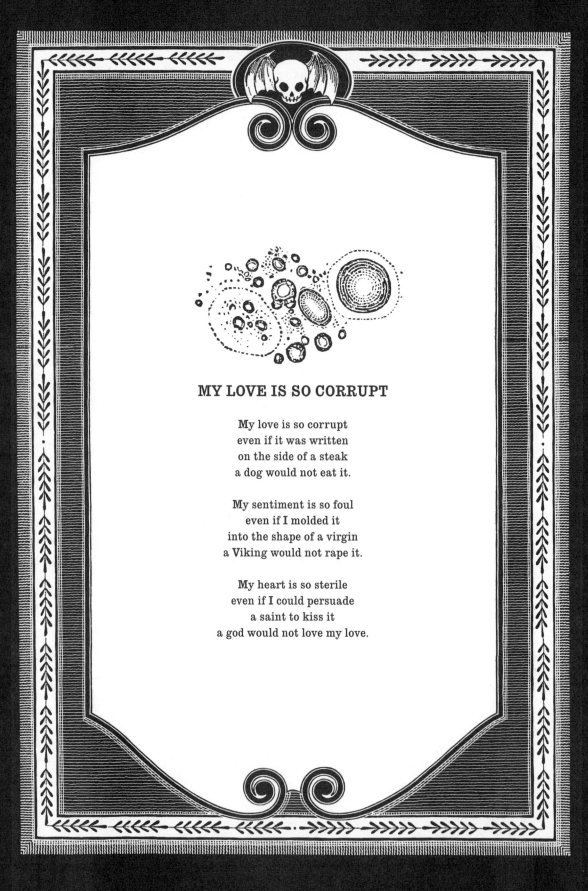

MY LOVE IS SO CORRUPT

My love is so corrupt
even if it was written
on the side of a steak
a dog would not eat it.

My sentiment is so foul
even if I molded it
into the shape of a virgin
a Viking would not rape it.

My heart is so sterile
even if I could persuade
a saint to kiss it
a god would not love my love.

I GIVE MYSELF
A PRESENT OF THE NIGHT

I give myself a present of the night
Where dark disguises gods and rank buffoons
Equally in masquerades of fading light
As spluttering sun becomes miasmic moon.
I give myself the silence and the pall
As a non-existent lover bares her breast,
As shadows lie to me as I lie in thrall,
A victim of Delusion's phantom jest.
In woozy sleep our intellect is dumb,
Dispelling Occam's razor, wrong and right;
Thus in my dreams all ciphers sum as one,
And presents have more presence in the night.
Thus I give the gift of night to myself and me,
When self-same fools may touch infinity.

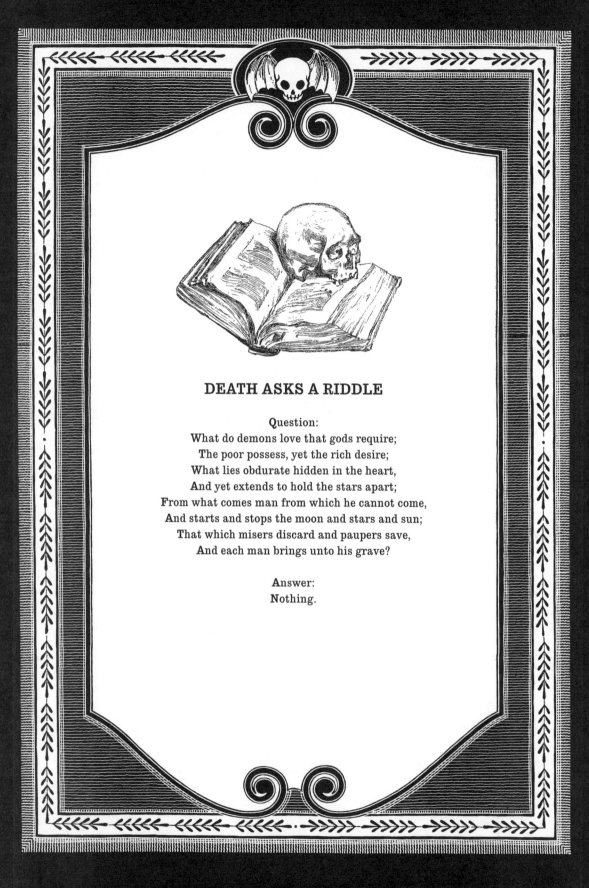

DEATH ASKS A RIDDLE

Question:
What do demons love that gods require;
The poor possess, yet the rich desire;
What lies obdurate hidden in the heart,
And yet extends to hold the stars apart;
From what comes man from which he cannot come,
And starts and stops the moon and stars and sun;
That which misers discard and paupers save,
And each man brings unto his grave?

Answer:
Nothing.

AFTERWORD
THE MYSTERIOUS INTERPOLATION

by Mortimer Pöncé
Editor-in-Chief, Mind Control Press

It has come to the attention of our editorial staff that a powerful enchantment has been cast on this, the Commemorative Edition of *The Conquest of Heaven*. We believe that this transgressive Spell makes certain pages invisible to demons, but visible to all other species.

I contacted Dr. Horace Birdfire, a non-demon consultant to this volume and witness to the invasion, and he confirmed there was indeed a cosmic enchantment on the pages which interpolated an invisible document at the front of the book. Since we cannot see it, I requested that he copy the invisible document in question and email it to our editorial board.

Here is his reply:

My Dear Mr. Pöncé,

Upon first reading The Conquest of Heaven, *I was indeed puzzled by your inclusion of a story I knew well, randomly inserted into the front of your historical compendium, and which playfully included your name and others involved in the historic invasion.*

I recognized this document from files I had destroyed centuries ago. It was from a therapy session I conducted with The Personified God in those ancient, troubled times, a session held prior to the invasion of Heaven and God's retirement as Ruler of the Cosmos.

FYI, the context of this document was as follows:

After a breakthrough therapy session, in which The Personified God finally released his guilt from never answering the prayers of his creatures, I initiated a new form of treatment I called "Story Therapy." In these sessions, I would ask God to playfully improvise a story based on a provocative cue I would give him. In this case, the cue was "devise a story about the ultimate destiny of all sentient beings."

I do not know why, right before his retirement, The Personified God would cast an Invisibility Spell upon the opening of your history book and insert this strange story. Perhaps it was a prank, or a mistake. Perhaps he thought it might help in some way. Since he did add an invisible ending to Encyclopaedia of Hell, *your previous book about the Invasion of Earth, perhaps his obsessive-compulsive disorder drove him to add an invisible beginning to your second.*

God only knows.

At your request, I have transcribed the invisible document (which was quite visible to me) from your esteemed compendium and attached it forthwith.

Kind regards forever, despite our contrapuntal philosophies,

(SIGNED)
Dr. Horace Catallus Birdfire

(Attachment follows)

THE STORY OF MEATSPACE JOE

 he mystics were mistaken.

The point wasn't that the universe was made of mind stuff. The point was that it was shaped, somewhat sloppily, like a tube. The first inkling of sentience was at one end, and the end was at the other. In between were densities that broke through to each other like flats in a creaking Hollywood set.

When you come right down to it, it was a mess that barely held together. Whatever poor schlub thought up Creation apparently didn't really think it all the way through. It was all a bit on the impulsive side, if you look at the crazy fireworks of the so-called Big Bang.

After eons of self-regurgitations, all intelligent life-forms evolved from dense life-forms into evanescent light-forms. At the end of their evolution, they became balls of light, settling into a default astral body, appearing roughly eighteen years of age, at the height of physical health. Light-beings shared a meta-temporal view of things with their creator, in that the entire span of evolution seemed to take place in an instant, like time-lapse photography.

THE STORY OF MEATSPACE JOE

Reincarnation was a bizarre reality due to the immortality of the electron elementals comprising the life-field. An entity's incarnations were all completely different, and lacked a meta-memory circuitry to connect them. (Occasionally, life-forms did remember a past or future life, but it could be a drawback, rather than a boon; for who wants to remember being someone else?)

Ultimate Evolution was rather satisfying. Game over. Sit back, have a cocktail and relax. On a practical level, it meant that your evolved light-body now existed in many parallel universes simultaneously. When you looked at an object, like a pencil, for example, you saw its past, present and future—a seed becoming a tree, graphite crystal growing in rock, the tree cut, the graphite mined, the pencil manufactured and utilized, and finally, all of it decomposing into molecular rubble. So too was your view of every object, including yourself.

Ultimate Evolution also meant that the layers of gore and blood were stripped away and slowly replaced by sinews of light. So too were layers of scriptures and myths stripped from the mind, until the truth was clear, that everything and everyone was the same Being. And thus, no one was in charge, and therefore, everyone was in charge.

Joe was a light-being who had evolved after eons from mankind's meatspace. After a while, however, the constant information overload attached to each object became overwhelming and annoying to Joe. He yearned for a simpler time in his physical body, when he perceived things one at a time and enjoyed seeing the surface of things, rather than multidimensional views of everything. To Joe, unlike his other evolved brothers, the secrets of the universe didn't live up to all the eons of hype. He was bored at knowing everything and preferred the simpler, heavier dimension of Earth, where every instant wasn't drenched with profound meaning, where simplicity and playful ignorance were the comfort blankets of daily life.

Joe could only exist in the material world if the vibration of his light-body matched the vibration of Earth, which it didn't anymore. The only way he could return to a simpler time would be to somehow de-evolve back to a less sophisticated, more primitive state of vibration, making his light-body denser. If his body was in effect "heavier," it would tend to sink down through dimensions until it reached the parallel Earth matching his present level of vibration.

Now Joe had a mission. He began searching his cosmic environs for "things" he could absorb from outside himself that would make his light-body denser, heavier.

THE STORY OF MEATSPACE JOE

But first he wanted to make sure that this new obsession of his wasn't a terrible idea. He went online and made an appointment with a psychologist with a good Yelp rating named Dr. Debbie Pöncé. Dr. Pöncé was an expert in helping those who were dissatisfied with their lives. She said boredom with perfection was a common problem of balls of light. After hearing of Joe's mission, Dr. Pöncé explained that his level on the evolutionary chart was a function of the rate at which his light-body vibrated. She said that absorbing material and adding weight made sense, but that there were more direct ways to lower his vibratory rate. Lowering your intellect required serious meditation exercises designed to help you de-evolve, and depended on practicing to think more materialistic thoughts. Joe's glowing light-body was a representation of his high vibratory rate. So he knew that his thoughts would have to dumb down a lot by using intensive stupidity exercises.

While following Dr. Pöncé's dumbing-down procedure, Joe happened upon a gym on the outskirts of Nirvana frequented by disgruntled light-beings who, like Joe, were bored with the perfection of ultimate evolution. In the gym, these outsiders practiced group meditation exercises to become less intelligent. Similar to the methods suggested by Dr. Pöncé, they'd discovered that they could gain density by practicing thinking narrow, linear, pipe-line thoughts. They'd found that, by weaning themselves from metaphor and analogy entirely, the thought-streams in their heads would congeal into a "mental body," the reverse beginnings of a physical brain. Even better, they maintained, continued exercise of thinking only small, narrow thoughts also created a wall of thought-muscle in the manifesting brain. These muscles separated the higher evolutionary thoughts on the right side from the lower ones on the left side. By actively developing the illusion that you were separate from the oneness of the universe, could light-beings lower their vibrations, form a physical brain, and begin to experience things slowly and luxuriously, one thing after the other, as in the material world.

Joe joined the club and started exercising with his outsider friends. But while performing these Stupidity Exercises, he asked on the down-low if the gym happened to sell any dumbing-down protein to beef up his thought sinews faster while he worked out.

It turned out that one of the trainers dealt in the shadier black market stuff Joe was looking for. He gave Joe a pack of so-called "stereo-electrons," sort of like steroids. They were particles which interlocked with cells in the nervous system of the developing brain matter, lowered the vibratory rate of the brain and formed a wall of meat between the higher and lower parts of Joe's thought matrix. Just don't use too much of it.

THE STORY OF MEATSPACE JOE

But Joe wanted to de-evolve faster, figured he could handle it and started taking double doses of the mixture. Soon he became addicted to the stuff, as his brain sinews developed and thickened at an astonishing speed.

In addition to taking Stupidity Steroids, Joe was doing his Stupidity Meditation exercises three times a day, concentrating on separatist concepts and divisive and racist ideologies, meditating on them until he actually believed them.

It worked. Soon the wall in his mind solidified and he found that he was literally of two minds. Thrilled, he looked forward to savoring things one after the other. He could hardly wait to attain the human perception and see only the surface of things!

But soon, he noticed something horrible happening in his newly reconfigured thoughts. Not only had his thought-streams become swollen, contorted and disfigured, but the two halves of mind were now at odds with each other. The left brain, feeling a separation from the universe, could not stand interacting with the right brain, which felt oneness with the universe.

Trying to cool out his thoughts, Joe went downtown to see a thought movie. It was Christmas and, when he was human, this had been his favorite holiday. While floating in line at the theater, awash with the Christmas lights glistening and blinking in the streets and on the tree in the theater lobby, he could hear his brain lobes arguing. It reached a peak, and a fight began inside himself. Joe lost control and began thrashing wildly around on the floor. And with his newly beefed-up thought sinews, he was abnormally powerful. Nobody could stop what was about to happen as he had a mental breakdown. Joe knocked over the Christmas tree and trashed the snack bar. The light-being police showed up, tasered him and dragged him away.

Joe in effect went mad and was committed to an insane asylum. There he discovered that Dr. Pöncé, whom he had thought was his ally, was really his enemy. As the head of a psychiatry board, she committed Joe to the most dangerous insane asylum in the cosmos. Even worse for Joe, the conflict in his mind had slowed down his de-evolution. To his shame, he was still occasionally thinking intelligent thoughts.

In the cosmic insane asylum, Joe soon found that he was the most violent mental patient there. Even worse, Dr. Odin, the warden of the asylum, wasn't really interested in curing him. Treating Joe would be a lot of trouble. Extra therapy meant extra man-power, which Dr. Odin did not have. Not to mention the long hours filing tedious thought-reports on Joe's progress. So Dr. Odin pow-wowed secretly with two light-body male nurses, a conversation witnessed by Dr. Odin's secretary Ramona. The nurses agreed to strap Joe to an illegal Unexistinator, a particle beam attached to a random number generator, and scramble Joe's particles. This would cause his particles to lose their spin, and Joe would dissipate into nothingness. In Dr. Odin's mind, Joe was a trouble-maker, and killing him would be more effective than years of treatment, never mind the reams of complex paper work.

However, Ramona felt bad about killing Joe, and sneaked to his cell to warn him.

Faced with the threat of unexistence, Joe rose to the occasion. He meditated vigorously until he was able to force the two warring sides of his mind to work together. Now he was able to create a clever plan and, with the help of Ramona, managed to escape from Odin's asylum.

Straight from prison, Joe stormed to Dr. Pöncé's office and confronted her about committing him to such a dangerous asylum. She revealed truthfully that she had had a secret agenda in doing so. Committing Joe would assist him in his de-evolution. Only the threat of personal extinction could motivate Joe to strengthened his two minds so that they could work together to significantly lower the vibrations of his astral body.

And, in fact, Dr. Pöncé thought that Joe might now be ready. She put her pencil in front of Joe's face and asked him what he saw...

Joe stared at the pencil... and for the first time, he didn't see the past, present and future of the thought-form pencil, he just saw its surface! Dr. Pöncé was right. The two parts of his mind had strengthen to follow his will, having learned how to work together to avoid death. Now Joe could savor things one after the other. Now he could finally experience the wonder of shallow, linear thoughts.

Tears streamed from Joe's eyes. What a joy to have a simple, mundane mind again! However, Dr. Pöncé clucked, there was the little matter of the negative side effects of growing denser, de-evolving and developing a physical brain. Namely, starting now, Joe might experience his descent through densities a bit too rapidly. As he ripped through thicker and thicker onion skins of parallel universes, he might, without realizing it, crash into the basest, bargain-basement dimension of the material universe.

Hmm, Joe wasn't exactly thrilled. He didn't want the change to happen quite that quickly. He had assumed that his de-evolution would be a gradual process, gently drifting into lower and lower levels until he stabilized back in the solid physical world. After all, it took him eons to evolve going the other direction, from a human to a light-being.

THE STORY OF MEATSPACE JOE

He wanted to stay where he was for a bit, so he could go to that new ephemeral Thai restaurant on the corner, perhaps have a thought-smoke and just cool out.

But it was too late. Dr. Pöncé gave Joe a touching farewell as Joe's light-body, having grown heavier each minute, finally fissured, shattered and dematerialized, sinking through the cracks in dimensions into the next-heavier density.

Joe cringed as he sniffed an unpleasant side effect of the transition, the smell of burning sneakers. The odor signaled his materialization into a density called The Transparent World, where he had, at least for now, reached equilibrium. This was the world of ghosts, a virtual density of murky emotions and shadowy creatures which could interpenetrate each other, a heavier astral vibration halfway between the mental and material worlds.

While waiting to transition past the Transparent World, he experienced a few universal, mundane activities, having a toothache and going to a ghost dentist, trying to find a decent ghost latte, or desiring a sexy ghost lover in the realm of shadows.

But as Dr. Pöncé had warned him, Joe's light-body was now on a rapid descent. Like a child trying to steer a toboggan down a hill, it was a process out of his control and one that could not be reversed. Joe found that his habitual linear thinking was making his particles heavier and heavier. Something had to give and it finally did. Joe dematerialized from the ghost density and partially materialized in Earth's normal physical world, at night, on Halloween. Not yet completely physical, he was amused as he realized that he appeared to human trick-or-treaters as a ghost.

Joe was frustrated. After working out so long and hard, he yearned to have the low IQ of a human. With renewed vigor, he resumed his dumbing-down exercises. One day, in the middle of his workout, Joe's dense particles finally and dramatically congealed into a bona fide physical body.

Joe had at last become one with meat.

Now fully entrained in the physical world, he found himself at a Halloween party in a city with machines, smog, rain, pain, lovers, apartments and parking tickets. No more flying around, now he was locked to the Earth, as if there were magnets on the soles of his feet. It was satisfying to be back here again, this time with the knowledge that the whole universe was just an immersive game and, as long as you were careful, that there was nothing per se to be afraid of.

His brain hungry for stupidity, more and more delicious, mundane, judgmental, racist, sexist, xenophobic, divisive thoughts filled his head. Even his ridiculous physical

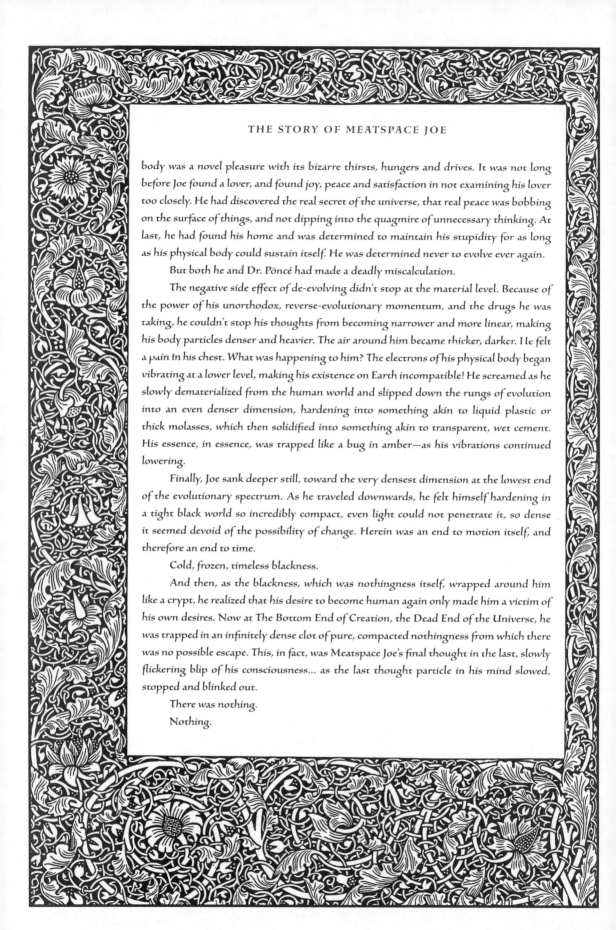

body was a novel pleasure with its bizarre thirsts, hungers and drives. It was not long before Joe found a lover, and found joy, peace and satisfaction in not examining his lover too closely. He had discovered the real secret of the universe, that real peace was bobbing on the surface of things, and not dipping into the quagmire of unnecessary thinking. At last, he had found his home and was determined to maintain his stupidity for as long as his physical body could sustain itself. He was determined never to evolve ever again.

But both he and Dr. Pöncé had made a deadly miscalculation.

The negative side effect of de-evolving didn't stop at the material level. Because of the power of his unorthodox, reverse-evolutionary momentum, and the drugs he was taking, he couldn't stop his thoughts from becoming narrower and more linear, making his body particles denser and heavier. The air around him became thicker, darker. He felt a pain in his chest. What was happening to him? The electrons of his physical body began vibrating at a lower level, making his existence on Earth incompatible! He screamed as he slowly dematerialized from the human world and slipped down the rungs of evolution into an even denser dimension, hardening into something akin to liquid plastic or thick molasses, which then solidified into something akin to transparent, wet cement. His essence, in essence, was trapped like a bug in amber—as his vibrations continued lowering.

Finally, Joe sank deeper still, toward the very densest dimension at the lowest end of the evolutionary spectrum. As he traveled downwards, he felt himself hardening in a tight black world so incredibly compact, even light could not penetrate it, so dense it seemed devoid of the possibility of change. Herein was an end to motion itself, and therefore an end to time.

Cold, frozen, timeless blackness.

And then, as the blackness, which was nothingness itself, wrapped around him like a crypt, he realized that his desire to become human again only made him a victim of his own desires. Now at The Bottom End of Creation, the Dead End of the Universe, he was trapped in an infinitely dense clot of pure, compacted nothingness from which there was no possible escape. This, in fact, was Meatspace Joe's final thought in the last, slowly flickering blip of his consciousness... as the last thought particle in his mind slowed, stopped and blinked out.

There was nothing.

Nothing.

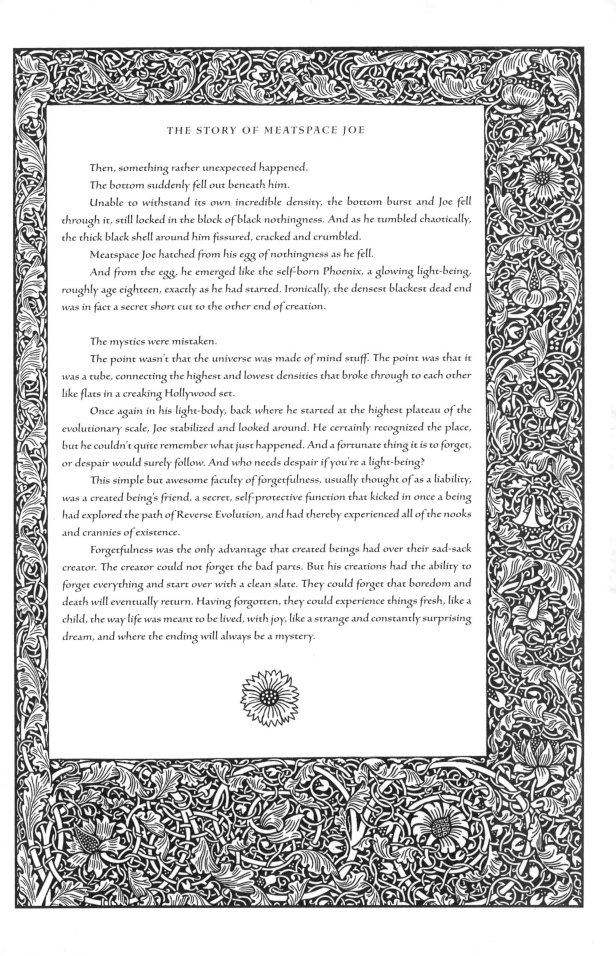

Then, something rather unexpected happened.

The bottom suddenly fell out beneath him.

Unable to withstand its own incredible density, the bottom burst and Joe fell through it, still locked in the block of black nothingness. And as he tumbled chaotically, the thick black shell around him fissured, cracked and crumbled.

Meatspace Joe hatched from his egg of nothingness as he fell.

And from the egg, he emerged like the self-born Phoenix, a glowing light-being, roughly age eighteen, exactly as he had started. Ironically, the densest blackest dead end was in fact a secret short cut to the other end of creation.

The mystics were mistaken.

The point wasn't that the universe was made of mind stuff. The point was that it was a tube, connecting the highest and lowest densities that broke through to each other like flats in a creaking Hollywood set.

Once again in his light-body, back where he started at the highest plateau of the evolutionary scale, Joe stabilized and looked around. He certainly recognized the place, but he couldn't quite remember what just happened. And a fortunate thing it is to forget, or despair would surely follow. And who needs despair if you're a light-being?

This simple but awesome faculty of forgetfulness, usually thought of as a liability, was a created being's friend, a secret, self-protective function that kicked in once a being had explored the path of Reverse Evolution, and had thereby experienced all of the nooks and crannies of existence.

Forgetfulness was the only advantage that created beings had over their sad-sack creator. The creator could not forget the bad parts. But his creations had the ability to forget everything and start over with a clean slate. They could forget that boredom and death will eventually return. Having forgotten, they could experience things fresh, like a child, the way life was meant to be lived, with joy, like a strange and constantly surprising dream, and where the ending will always be a mystery.